HOPE BLOOMS IN TUPPENNY BRIDGE

SHARON BOOTH

Storm
PUBLISHING

To request permissions, contact the publisher at rights@stormpublishing.co

Ebook ISBN: 978-1-80508-639-0
Paperback ISBN: 978-1-80508-640-6

Cover design: Debbie Clement
Cover images: Shutterstock

Published by Storm Publishing.
For further information, visit:
www.stormpublishing.co

A Merry Bramblewick Christmas

Summer at the Country Practice

Christmas at Cuckoo Nest Cottage

The Moorland Heroes Series

Resisting Mr Rochester

Saving Mr Scrooge

The Witches of Castle Clair Series

Belle, Book and Candle

My Favourite Witch

To Catch a Witch

Will of the Witch

His Lawful Wedded Witch

Destiny of the Witch

The Other Half Series

How the Other Half Lives

How the Other Half Lies

How the Other Half Loses

How the Other Half Loves

PROLOGUE

8 OCTOBER

There was a hushed silence as Zach Barrington climbed the steps to the pulpit. Just moments before, he'd heard the low hum of voices as the residents of Tuppenny Bridge shifted in their seats, murmuring to each other as they settled down and prepared for the service to start. Now as he stood and faced them, all he felt was a flutter of apprehension at the sight of so many expectant faces.

It was a good turnout. More than he'd expected. He gazed around the congregation, noting the familiar and not-so-familiar faces. He wondered if Jennifer had ever imagined so many people would turn up for Leon's memorial service. It must be gratifying, he thought, to know that fifteen years after her eldest son's untimely death so many people cared enough to be here with her today. He was glad for her. Glad that, despite his worries, recent events hadn't prevented people from attending.

He could hardly believe it had been fifteen years since Leon's accident. He remembered it as if it were only yesterday. He'd not been in Tuppenny Bridge long when it happened and was only just getting to know his parishioners.

The news, when it filtered through to the vicarage, had

shaken him to the core, and the events that followed in the days, weeks, and months afterwards had put demands on him that he'd never expected and hadn't been altogether sure he was capable of meeting.

It hadn't helped that Ava had been pregnant with their second child, Beatrix, and had been suffering from terrible morning sickness. She was also preoccupied with settling Dion into his new school, reassuring him that he would soon make friends. Not to mention getting used to the large, draughty old vicarage, and making it a warmer, more comfortable place for their little family. He freely admitted he relied on Ava. She gave him confidence, but back then she'd had more than enough to do without being burdened by his troubles and admissions of insecurity and doubt.

He remembered how he'd been thrown in at the deep end. Miss Eugenie Lavender hadn't been the strong, bossy, rather opinionated lady that he knew today. Well, that wasn't exactly true, he supposed, but that side of her had been buried under an avalanche of grief and fear at the time.

The Pennyfeather sisters, who he now knew well and loved for their eccentricity and sunny dispositions, had been shaken and sorrowful for months. Looking at them as they sat together, just behind Eugenie, he thought it was hard to believe how different they'd been fifteen years ago.

And they weren't the only ones whose lives had been shattered by Leon's accident.

He forced a reassuring smile, aware that his parishioners were waiting for him to begin. He could see the anxiety in their faces. They were still in shock, he knew. Not about Leon, but about recent events that had caused ripples of disbelief and anger, grief and guilt throughout the little market town.

They were looking to him, once again, to make sense of everything for them. To reassure them. To make everything all right again. Just as they'd looked to him fifteen years ago.

He warmly welcomed them to All Hallows Church and gently reminded them why they were here—as if they'd have forgotten.

Jennifer gave him a weak smile and he nodded kindly at her, aware that this anniversary was always a painful time for her and, despite the remarkable progress she'd made over the course of the past year, this wasn't going to be easy for her.

He cleared his throat and informed his flock that they were gathered here in the name of Jesus, and wished them grace and mercy, to which they solemnly replied in kind.

Birdie Pennyfeather sneezed and, for once, Miss Lavender didn't give her a warning look. Indeed, he didn't think she'd even noticed, which was unthinkable for Eugenie. Although, he realised, she had other things on her mind—wondering, no doubt, how she, of all people, had missed what was going on right under her nose in this town.

He'd asked himself the same question. He was the vicar of this parish and felt he should have seen the truth much sooner. Taken the warnings more seriously. He'd had a couple of sleepless nights recently, although Ava had reassured him repeatedly that he wasn't to blame.

His anxious gaze found his wife sitting a few rows from the front, flanked by Beatrix and Dion. Elegant and beautiful as always, with her dark hair and hazel eyes. His heart swelled with love for her as she nodded and smiled at him, silently sending her love and support the way she always did. But then, she didn't know the full story. No one did except him.

He thought he'd carried a heavy burden before, but now...

As he continued to speak to the congregation his gaze landed on all the key players. All the "Bridgers", as they called themselves, who had been involved in this drama directly or indirectly. Fifteen years...

Ben and Jamie, Leon's younger brothers, sat pale-faced and serious beside their mother, Jennifer, who was dressed head to toe in black. Next to Ben was Summer Fletcher, his fiancée, and stepdaughter of Zach's best friend, Rafferty Kingston.

A few rows behind them were Kat and Jonah Brewster. Kat had been Leon's girlfriend at the time of his death, and Jonah, the local blacksmith, had been his best friend. Now they were married with a baby of their own on the way.

Across the centre aisle sat vet Clive Browning, supported by Bethany Marshall, his partner. He noticed Clive kept giving Jennifer worried glances and understood all too well why. Jennifer had been through enough over the last fifteen years, and Clive had always been protective of her. Of the whole Callaghan family.

And there was Ross with his girlfriend Clemmie, sitting silently beside Eugenie Lavender. Ross—Eugenie's great-nephew—looked as if he hadn't slept in days. Zach's heart went out to him. He could only imagine how terrible Ross must be feeling.

Zach led the parishioners in prayer then invited Ben up to give a reading in place of Jennifer. That morning, she'd informed him she didn't feel able to do it, and that Ben had offered instead.

Ben was clearly nervous, but Zach nodded encouragingly at him and, slowly and hesitantly, Ben began to read from a sheet of paper in his trembling hand. Zach could almost feel Clive mentally willing him on.

Zach scanned the back rows of the nave, noticing Daisy sitting quietly by herself in the very last pew. She must have arrived later than the others. He thought it a shame that she was alone, but maybe she'd chosen to be.

He noticed how drawn she looked and sighed inwardly. A relative newcomer to Tuppenny Bridge, she'd certainly been through the mill lately. His heart went out to her. Still, at least she was here.

Two of his parishioners were missing, and he felt their loss keenly. They had, after all, been close to Leon back in the day. It seemed all wrong that they weren't here now but, given what had happened recently, it was hardly surprising.

Under normal circumstances, of course, they'd have been sitting with Miss Lavender. Isobel would have been preening at having provided the flowers for the service. Noah, meanwhile, would have been supporting his great aunt the way he always did, flashing sympathetic looks at Jennifer, Ben, and Jamie.

Noah and Isobel, however, weren't here.

Ben finished reading, and Zach smiled and nodded at him as he returned to his seat. Time now for Zach to do his job and give a reading from the New Testament. Then there'd be a short sermon and hymns, carefully chosen by Jennifer weeks ago.

And all the while the absence of Noah and Isobel hung over them; the events of the last few months almost overshadowing this long-planned service for Leon.

He glanced at the photograph of the smiling, dark-haired young man that Jennifer had given him to place in the church for this memorial, and he wondered what his parishioners would say if they each knew the truth. Not just bits of it, but all of it.

So many secrets and lies, so much pain and guilt.

He glanced down at the open pages of the New Testament, quickly scanning the passage from Ecclesiastes that he intended to read: "To everything there is a season…"

But it was a passage from Ephesians that flashed through his mind:

"And be ye kind one to another, tender-hearted, forgiving one another, even as God for Christ's sake hath forgiven you."

He thought, sometimes, forgiveness was a big ask.

ONE

SATURDAY 6 JULY

Three months earlier...

Daisy Jackson loved Saturday mornings. Not only was she guaranteed to be kept busy in The Crafty Cook Café—because there was nothing worse than hanging around all day, bored—but also because she loved the bustle of Tuppenny Bridge on market days.

Running her own café meant early starts for her, even though she only opened the doors to customers at 10am. The lights, till, and coffee machine needed to be switched on, tables set, and food prepared.

She liked to bake fresh every day, which took some planning, although she did keep a few cakes in the freezer for emergencies, which just needed decorating. The Crafty Cook Café menu wasn't particularly extensive, but it was good quality food that was right for the location of her premises and the sort of customer she attracted.

Her initial idea had been to open the café Tuesdays to Saturdays from early in the morning until around 5pm, but she'd quickly realised that it made more sense to leave the fried breakfasts to The Market Café on the opposite side of the market square, which dealt with heartier fare for a different type of customer.

With the focus on light lunches and snacks, afternoon tea (pre-booked only), a selection of cakes and scones, and various teas, coffees and hot chocolates, as well as soft drinks, Daisy seemed to be building a reputation in Tuppenny Bridge for quality. Her cakes were in such demand that she'd even taken orders specifically for birthdays and other special occasions, so the buyers could collect them from her. She certainly hadn't expected that to happen.

Almost immediately she'd decided to change her working hours, and now opened the café at ten in the morning and closed at four, seven days a week rather than five, and had taken on two assistants—college students who worked weekends, which enabled Daisy to take either the Saturday or Sunday off.

It didn't leave her much time for socialising, but then, that had never been Daisy's thing. As long as she could escape into the countryside to hike one day a week, it was enough.

She'd been used to working all her life. When she was a little girl, she'd helped her mother around the house, and worked with her father and brother, Tom, on their farm in Upper Skimmerdale. After her mother's death she'd taken care of the home and looked after the menfolk. It was what she was used to.

Crowscar Farm had been pretty isolated, so she hadn't made many friends. When she moved to Leeds to live with her brother, after their father went into a care home, she'd focused on working in pubs and cafés in the area, visiting her dad, and making sure Tom was fed and the house kept clean, as payment for living under his roof. He hadn't asked her to do that, but it wouldn't have occurred to Daisy not to.

Now she'd started over in Tuppenny Bridge in Lower Skimmerdale. She'd been here less than a year which, in Yorkshire

Dales terms, meant she was a complete newcomer, even though she was Dales born and bred. She'd rented a little flat over the Cutting it Fine hair salon in Market Square, made friends with many of the locals, including her landlady, Bluebell; Kat, who owned the craft shop below her café; and Bethany, who was even newer to the town than she was. Even so, her social life was almost non-existent and that was fine by Daisy. Work was her comfort zone. She felt blessed to have her own flat and business, and didn't expect anything else.

Even though the café didn't open until ten she liked to be there by seven so she could start baking. Crossing the market square she smiled, seeing the market traders already arriving and setting up their stalls. By the time she opened the doors to her first customers this area would be heaving with people. Many of them would, hopefully, pop into the café for something to eat. The market was good for her business and brought plenty of visitors to the town.

The sun was shining on Tuppenny Bridge this morning. She raised her face to the sky and closed her eyes, feeling the warmth on her skin despite the early hour. She loved the summer and hoped for plenty more sunshine and blue skies in the coming months.

She felt a pang suddenly, remembering July days on the farm. Remembering, too, the village of Beckthwaite where she'd grown up, and Ravensbridge where she'd gone to school. Remembering Crowscar with her sullen father and resentful brother. Remembering Wildflower Farm, where she'd sought refuge and escape in the company of her brother's best friend, Eliot Harland...

Making her way up the stairs to the café she tried to push all thoughts of Eliot from her mind. Still, the memory nagged away at her.

Even as she focused on getting the café presentable for the customers, making sure the craft areas were tidy and in order, switching on the till and coffee machine, and putting on her apron to start baking, her mind kept wandering back to those busy summers with the Harlands. She sometimes wondered if she'd ever been happier than she had been back then.

'Coffee cake,' she said aloud, determined not to dwell on the past. 'Orange and lemon cake. Oh, and the white chocolate and caramel cake,' she added, remembering that Noah had eaten the last slice yesterday. He loved it so much he'd be disappointed if he didn't get any today.

Then she remembered it was Saturday and Noah wouldn't be in today. He only ever popped in for half an hour during his lunch break. He was the headmaster of the local primary school, and seemed to have decided that The Crafty Cook Café was his place of refuge during the day.

'Isobel wouldn't approve,' he'd admitted to her just a couple of weeks ago. 'Still, what she doesn't know won't hurt her, will it?'

She'd been half tempted to push him on that subject. The state of Isobel and Noah Lavender's marriage had been the cause of much speculation in recent weeks. Daisy hadn't known them long, but apparently, they'd been together for years—since they were teenagers. The consensus had always been that Isobel was not a nice person and that she dominated Noah.

However, Isobel herself had recently told the guests at Kat's hen party that it was Noah who kept control of her eating habits, watching what she ate and monitoring her weight. Daisy wasn't convinced that was true. She didn't know Noah very well, but he just didn't seem the sort to her. But, as her new friend Bethany had pointed out, no one knew what went on between a husband and wife behind closed doors, so how could they judge? Daisy knew she was right, but part of her hoped Isobel had exaggerated. She didn't like to think of Noah as the controlling sort.

Then again, her judgement of men was notoriously bad.

Look how she'd convinced herself for years that Eliot secretly loved her!

She could feel her face burning with embarrassment at the thought, even all these years later.

'Plain scones, cheese scones, sultana scones,' she said firmly. 'That will do for today. Better get started before Tess and Rowan arrive.'

She'd baked some large quiches last night and stored them in the fridge so she wouldn't have to make them this morning. The salad needed washing and preparing but that wouldn't take long.

Daisy assembled her first set of ingredients, switched on the radio, and, humming along to one of her favourite songs, got to work.

'Do we have to have this racket on?'

Noah glanced up as Isobel entered the kitchen, her face already set in a scowl. She didn't wait for his reply as she wandered over to the radio and flicked it off.

He didn't protest. She would be leaving for work soon anyway. He could put the radio back on then.

'How can you listen to that at this time of the morning?' she demanded irritably. 'Have you never heard of easing your way into the day?'

'It's at low volume, and I only put it on while you were upstairs,' he said mildly. 'Anyway, your coffee's ready for you.' He folded the newspaper and lay it on the table. 'What would you like for breakfast? I wasn't sure so I didn't—'

She tutted and waved a hand at the paper. 'Why do you persist in getting one of those delivered? Honestly, no one reads physical newspapers any longer. It's all online. You're so old fashioned.'

It wasn't the first time he'd been called that, and not just by

Isobel. He knew he was viewed with some amusement by the staff and parents at his school, but he saw nothing wrong with good manners and politeness. He liked routine and familiarity, and knew he was a bit of a stick-in-the-mud. He found the presence of a newspaper on his doormat each morning comforting somehow. Reading it on his phone wouldn't have been anywhere near as pleasurable.

'Boiled egg?' he enquired mildly. 'Toast?'

She shook her head. 'I'm not hungry. And I don't want coffee today. I want tea.'

'I'll boil the kettle,' he said, half rising to his feet, but she waved a hand at him.

'I can do it myself. Stop fussing.'

Noah sat down again and took a sip of coffee, not entirely sure what to do or say next. He glanced at the clock and mentally calculated how long it would be before she left for work. She'd have been long gone if it was her turn to go to the flower market, but her assistant Kelly was going today. About half an hour he thought. Just thirty minutes...

He watched as she busied herself making a cup of tea, dressed as smartly as she always was in black trousers and a Wedgewood blue top, her baby blonde hair immaculately styled. Soon, he knew, she'd don her usual skyscraper heels before heading out, even though she'd be on her feet all day at the florist's. He had no idea how she managed it. Sheer willpower probably. Isobel was never short of that.

Cutting off that train of thought he allowed his mind to drift to the day ahead. He'd promised to visit his great aunt later this afternoon, and this morning he'd a list of jobs to do around the house. But tomorrow he'd take the opportunity to get away from Tuppenny Bridge. He'd expected to be at home with Isobel all Sunday, but she'd announced she was going to meet her grandmother in Leeds for shopping and afternoon tea, which was fine by him.

Noah had been daydreaming of an excursion for weeks and the unexpected freedom to carry out his plans felt quite intoxicating. He'd thought he'd missed his chance this year, and there was so little time left. Another week or so and it would be too late, so this was perfect timing. He could hardly believe his luck and even Isobel's deliberate banging and clattering as she opened the cupboard doors and drawer didn't unduly disturb him.

When she eventually sat down, mug of tea in hand, he gave her a polite smile.

'Will you be home for lunch?'

'I doubt it. It's Saturday and you know how busy the shop gets on Saturdays. Although...' She scowled again. 'Did you know a flower stall has opened on the market? I mean, how rude is that?'

Noah chose his words carefully. 'I shouldn't think they'll attract the same customers as you do. Your shop's been here years, and you have a loyal customer base. It will be mainly visitors to the market rather than locals who use the stall. I shouldn't worry.'

'Who says I'm worrying?'

He smiled. 'Well, that's good then.' He drained his coffee cup, aware that she was watching him thoughtfully.

'What are your plans for today?'

'I thought I'd put a wash load on,' he said. 'It's bright and warm with a good breeze—perfect drying weather.'

Isobel rolled her eyes. 'I've always said you'd make someone a lovely wife.'

He shrugged. 'Men are just as capable of doing housework as women, and you're busy today so why shouldn't I help?'

'Yeah, yeah. So, what else are you doing?'

'I'm not sure really.' He hesitated. 'I promised Aunt Eugenie I'd pop by and see her later.'

'Why?' she asked, immediately on guard. 'What does she want?'

'Nothing,' he assured her. 'Just a catch up. I haven't seen her for a couple of weeks, and you know how she likes to be kept in the loop.'

'Huh! Well, there's not a lot to tell her is there? Not like we ever do anything exciting, is it?' She sighed. 'Look at us, Noah. Thirty-seven years old and we live like crumblies. Your great aunt has more of a social life than we do and she's eighty! Did you ever think life would be this dull when you were at university?'

'Life,' he said slowly, 'never turns out exactly as you plan.'

'You can say that again,' she said bitterly.

He waited, wondering if she'd expand on that remark but to his relief she didn't. Instead, she surprised him by reaching out and squeezing his hand.

'It's all work, isn't it? Maybe we ought to think about taking a holiday somewhere.'

He raised his eyebrows, astonished. 'We *could,* but I think we may have left it a little late, don't you? School holidays start in just over a fortnight and I doubt we'd get anywhere decent with such short notice.'

'Oh, but Noah!' She looked downcast, her blue eyes clouded with disappointment. For a moment it seemed she was going to protest, but then she tucked a strand of hair behind her ear and sat up straight. 'Ah well, it can't be helped. It's such a shame because Kelly's gran offered to cover for me. You know, she was a florist, but she retired far too early and Kelly says she's itching to get back to it, even if it's only temporarily. It would have been so nice, don't you think?' she added wistfully.

He nodded. 'It would have been,' he told her gently. 'Perhaps we could think about a few days away at half term in October instead?'

'Hmm. Maybe.' She drained her tea and slammed the mug on the table. 'Well, I think I'll get off. No rest for the wicked.'

He didn't reply and she bent over and kissed the top of his head.

'Have a lovely day,' she told him brightly, before ruffling his tawny coloured hair with something akin to affection. 'See you tonight.'

'Was there anything you particularly wanted for dinner?' he asked her, keen to make this unexpected thaw in their relationship last a little longer.

'Oh, surprise me. I'm sure whatever you make will be delicious. You're a much better cook than I am, after all.'

Feeling ridiculously happy as she smiled at him, he smiled back. As she grabbed her bag and left Peony Cottage, he settled back in his chair for a moment and considered the unexpectedly bright start to the day. Maybe he'd pop to the travel agent on Station Road before visiting Aunt Eugenie. There might be some last-minute bargains to be had. You never knew.

Whistling softly, he strode over to the worktop and switched the radio back on.

TWO

As she'd predicted, Saturday was a busy day for Daisy. The market brought lots more visitors to Tuppenny Bridge, particularly in good weather, and today was a lovely sunny day in early July. She couldn't help wondering, as she hurriedly buttered bread and toasted paninis, how she'd managed so long without help.

Tess and Rowan were godsends. Both had waitressed before, and Tess had also worked in a pub kitchen at Lingham-on-Skimmer, so they were experienced. Helpful, efficient, and good with the customers, Daisy thought she was lucky to have found them. She'd already decided to hire one or both of them throughout the week during their holidays, as she had a feeling the café was going to be even busier once the summer season really got underway.

For now, though, just having them here at weekends was a blessing. The queue at the counter was already stretching as far as the top of the stairs. If she'd been on her own there'd have been customers waiting all the way down to Kat's craft shop on the ground floor.

The three of them took it in turns to snatch a fifteen-minute lunch break. Daisy tried to make the girls take longer but they both refused, insisting fifteen minutes was long enough, and laughingly waving away her protestations about employee rights and employer responsibilities.

By the time it got round to Daisy's turn she was almost too tired to eat, but on Rowan's insistence she grabbed herself a bowl of soup and a crusty roll and carried them over to a recently vacated table by the window, with a good view over the market square.

At least the lunchtime rush was over, and although there was still a steady stream of customers the frantic pace had slackened, allowing her time to eat her soup without feeling the need to gulp it down as fast as she could.

'Mind if I join you?'

Daisy glanced up and beamed in delight as she saw her friend, Bethany Marshall, smiling down at her.

'Of course! Pull up a seat.'

Bethany sat down and sniffed appreciatively. 'Oh my, that soup smells delicious. Wish I'd got that now, but I've ordered an egg mayonnaise sandwich so that will be here in a minute. How are things?' She glanced around. 'Doing well, I see.'

'I'm very lucky,' Daisy admitted. 'When I took this place on, I had no idea if I could make it work. Somehow, it's really taken off.'

'Not luck,' Bethany assured her. 'Hard work and talent. I reckon people come from miles around just for a slice of your heavenly cakes. And who could blame them?'

Daisy laughed, still unused to such glowing compliments. Eliot and his older kids, Liberty and Ophelia, had always said her baking was brilliant, while little George had shown his appreciation by eating everything she offered him. Deep down, though, she'd often thought they were just being kind, because they thought they owed her. Well, maybe not George, but he'd happily eat cat food if they'd let him so that was hardly a glowing recommendation. As for her dad and Tom—they'd never uttered a word of praise for anything she made them. She'd have thought there was something wrong with them if they had.

'What brings you here today?' she asked Bethany, thinking how lovely her friend looked. There was a glow about her that was quite noticeable. Bethany was an attractive woman anyway, with a honey blonde bob, dark blue eyes, and a fabulous complexion even in her mid-fifties. These days, though, there was an added something about her.

Love, Daisy thought suddenly. It's because she's in love.

Bethany had recently started a relationship with vet, Clive Browning, and the two of them were besotted with each other. It was quite sweet really. According to the Lavender Ladies—and if anyone in Tuppenny Bridge should know it would be those three —Clive had been a confirmed bachelor all his life, and everyone was over the moon to see him so loved up and happy at last.

Clive lived and worked at Stepping Stones, a large house and veterinary surgery overlooking the village green. Bethany, meanwhile, owned Whispering Willows, a rambling country house set in acres of land that was also home to rescued horses, ponies, and donkeys.

Bethany was in the process of not only renovating her house but also having a lot of building work done outside, as the firm she had hired had demolished the old outbuildings to make way for new state-of-the-art stabling facilities and an equine veterinary unit. She had a lot going on, so Daisy certainly hadn't expected to see her at the café any time soon.

'I needed a break,' Bethany admitted. 'Ben, Summer, and I have been erecting temporary wooden loose boxes in the near paddock for the few animals that need to be indoors at night.

Clive's on call this morning but he's coming round after lunch to help us finish. Ben and Summer are going to eat at my place, so I thought I'd pop here to have a catch-up with you. It seems ages since we talked properly.'

'I've only got fifteen minutes,' Daisy told her regretfully.

'I know.' Bethany smiled at Rowan as she placed her order on the table. 'Thank you.'

As Rowan nodded and headed away, Bethany eyed the sandwiches, crisps, coleslaw and salad with appreciation. 'I'm so ready for this.'

She crunched a few crisps and closed her eyes. 'I hadn't realised how hungry I was.'

Daisy took a spoonful of soup and realised she hadn't known how hungry *she* was either.

They ate in silence for a few minutes, then Bethany said, 'Are you going to Dolly's party?'

Daisy considered. 'I haven't responded to the invitation yet. Bit rude of me, isn't it? I'd forgotten to be honest. When is it again?'

'Twenty-seventh of July. It's a Saturday so you could take the next day off to recover, since you've got Rowan and Tess to hold the fort here.'

'I do prefer to take Sundays off, rather than Saturdays,' Daisy confessed. 'It gets so busy on market days. Mind you, Sundays have picked up massively recently, too. I'm starting to feel guilty about taking those off.'

'You have to have one day a week away from this place at least,' Bethany told her. She bit into her sandwich and chewed thoughtfully. 'So, are you going then?'

'To the party? I'm not sure. Are you going?'

'Oh yes. According to Clive Dolly's great fun. Besides, Clemmie was lovely to me when I first arrived here, and since she's the one organising this for her aunt I think it's only fair.'

'I can't think of anything worse than a surprise party,' Daisy admitted with a shudder.

Bethany laughed. 'Summer said it's not really a surprise at all. Apparently, Dolly's instructed Clemmie every step of the way, telling her what food she wants, where she wanted it to be held, even how she wants it decorating. Yet she's going to act all shocked when she turns up as if she knew nothing about it. She sounds a real character.'

Having encountered Dolly, the owner of The Corner Cottage Bookshop and best-selling saga writer, Daisy had already realised that, as short as the birthday girl was, she had a huge personality.

'It's at The White Hart Inn, right?'

'That's right. Oh, do go, Daisy! It will be fun, and you need a break from this place.'

'I'm getting a break tomorrow,' Daisy said, a warmth creeping through her at the thought. 'I'm having a day out.'

'Ooh!' Bethany's eyes widened. 'Who with?'

'By myself,' Daisy said firmly. 'I'm heading up to Upper Skimmerdale for a hike round the wildflower meadows. I'm really hoping they haven't been cut down yet. Haven't seen them for years and I'm looking forward to it.'

'Don't you mind going by yourself?' Bethany asked. She spooned some coleslaw into her mouth and shook her head. 'This is gorgeous!'

'Thank you. To answer your question, no I don't. In fact, I prefer it. I love walking the Dales and it's been way too long. I was stuck in Leeds for ages, and I felt as if I were slowly dying inside. I can't explain how trapped I felt. Being back here is a dream come true and now the business is properly up and running I'm going to take some time to get out and about in the countryside again. Besides, it helps me clear my head.'

'Do you need your head clearing?' Bethany asked, sounding concerned. 'Everything's okay, isn't it?'

'Everything's fine,' Daisy said quickly. 'It's just a figure of speech. We all need time to be alone and think, don't we?'

'To be honest,' Bethany said, 'I feel as if I've spent most of my life alone. I'm enjoying being around people again. It's so good to have Clive and Summer and Ben, and Maya and Lennox too. I feel like I've got my own little family at Whispering Willows.'

Daisy nodded, understanding. She'd felt like she had her own little family at Wildflower Farm once upon a time. Life with her father was so bleak up at Crowscar that the Harlands' home had been a blissful escape. She'd kidded herself for a long time that she, Eliot, and his children were a family. She'd been very wrong. Now she had accepted that this was her time to be alone.

It wasn't what she'd expected from her life, but she wasn't complaining. For the first time she wasn't dependent on anyone else. She wasn't seeking approval from anyone either. She was running her own life her way, and she loved it.

'So will you come to the party?' Bethany asked again, clearly determined that Daisy wasn't going to get out of it.

Daisy hesitated then shrugged. 'Why not?'

'Brilliant! It will be a lot of fun, I'm sure of it. Just about everyone's going as far as I can tell.' She finished eating a tomato then leaned towards Daisy, lowering her voice as she spoke. 'I hope Isobel doesn't go, though. She has a habit of making me feel like the lowest of the low.'

When Daisy didn't reply she added, 'Has he been in here recently? Noah, I mean. Still stuffing himself with cake while Isobel's calorie counting?'

'We don't know that's what happened,' Daisy reminded her.

'No, we don't. But why would Isobel say it if it wasn't true? It's such an odd thing to say, don't you think?'

'I think Isobel's an odd person,' Daisy said.

'Oh, she is, no two ways about it. Even so.' Bethany looked

uncomfortable. 'Kat told me that Isobel broke her fingers last autumn. They were all strapped up apparently.'

Daisy stared at her. 'Meaning what?'

Bethany shrugged. 'I don't know, but it's a bit worrying, isn't it? I don't like the woman and I can't pretend I do, but if he *is* bullying her—well, we don't know how far it's gone, do we?'

'Noah? He wouldn't hurt her!' The words tumbled out of Daisy's mouth before she had the chance to stop them.

'But how do you know?' Bethany persisted. 'It's like I told you before, you never know what's going on between a husband and wife behind closed doors.'

Daisy thought about Eliot and Jemima, his first wife, and the mother of his children. Everyone had thought they'd had a perfect marriage. When Jemima died people had assumed that Eliot's grief was for the woman he'd loved with all his heart. Not many people knew the truth, though Daisy was one of them. She'd seen behind the facade. Bethany was right. No one knew what really went on in a marriage except the two people concerned. Not unless one or both of them was broken and so full of despair that they finally confided the truth.

But this was Noah, the politest man she'd ever met.

'I just can't believe it of him,' she said. 'He's so gentle and quiet.'

'They say the quiet ones are the worst.' Bethany sighed. 'I just know how manipulative some people can be. And I also know what it's like to live in the shadow of a bully. I wouldn't wish it on anyone, even Isobel.'

Neither would Daisy. She was all too familiar with bullies herself. She had to admit Isobel had seemed genuinely anxious when she'd spotted Noah in the café that day of Kat's hen party. She'd been afraid he'd see her eating afternoon tea. And the fact that she'd had an injury in the autumn was worrying.

Could they really rule out the unthinkable?

'Well, if they're at the party we should keep an eye on

them,' Bethany said. 'I'm sure you're right and Noah wouldn't do such a thing, but just to be certain. Just to put our minds at rest.'

Daisy pushed her empty bowl away. Bethany was right, of course. She'd never forgive herself if Isobel was being bullied by her husband and Daisy had done nothing to help her.

Even so... Noah?

THREE

Noah was just reaching for the latch on the gate to Peony Cottage when he heard Isobel's voice. Her flower shop, Petalicious, was just a few doors away from their home. He glanced at his watch, surprised to see it was closing time. He hadn't realised he'd stayed so long at Aunt Eugenie's.

'Where have you been till this time?' she asked, frowning as he pushed open the gate and headed up the path.

'At Lavender House,' he said. 'I told you; Aunt Eugenie invited me round.'

'I thought you were going there after lunch?' She sounded suspicious. 'Are you sure that's where you've been? Nowhere else?'

Noah took a deep breath. Not this again, surely?

'Nowhere else. Oh!' He turned the key and pushed open the front door of Peony Cottage, standing aside to let her through first. 'I did call somewhere before I went to see her, though. I'll tell you about it when we get in.'

She headed straight into the kitchen, not saying a word, and his throat tightened. Had she had a bad day at work or something?

'Go on then,' she said, throwing her bag onto the island and turning to face him. 'Where did you go?'

'Shall I make us a cup of tea first?' he asked. He wanted to tell her when she was in a more receptive mood. He'd planned it very differently to this.

'Never mind the tea, just tell me. Where did you go?'

Noah pulled out a stool and sat at the island. He gave her a smile that he hoped would reassure her.

'To the travel agents. I got us some brochures and...'

His voice trailed off as he realised with dismay that he'd left them at Lavender House.

'Really? So where are they?' Her tone told him she didn't believe him.

'I've forgotten them,' he admitted bleakly. 'They'll be on Aunt Eugenie's coffee table. I was showing them to her.'

'Well, that's convenient,' she said. 'Who goes to a travel agent these days, anyway? Normal people book online.'

'But it's good to have the brochures in front of you, don't you think?'

When she didn't reply he said, 'Isobel, I'm sorry.' He shook his head, in despair at his own stupidity. 'I'll call at Lavender House tomorrow and get them back for you. The travel agent was really helpful, by the way. He reckons there are still a few last-minute bargains to be had, and we might be lucky depending on where we want to go.'

'I'm out tomorrow,' she said flatly, turning to fill the kettle. 'I suppose you'd forgotten that.'

'Let me make the drinks,' he said, jumping up from the stool. 'You've been at work all day.'

'Yes, I have, but I can make a cup of tea, thank you very much.'

She opened the cupboard door and took out a mug. 'I suppose you want one?'

'If it's not too much trouble?'

Her heavy sigh told him it was, actually, but that she was noble enough to make him one anyway. She took out a second mug and busied herself putting teabags into them. No sugar, of course. They didn't have sugar at Peony Cottage. Any visitors who took it in their beverages were out of luck, unless they'd accept a sweetener instead. Not that they had many visitors. Even his aunt and Ross rarely came here.

'So where were you thinking?' she asked at last.

Noah brightened. 'The travel agent suggested Turkey. He says it's very popular and—'

'No thanks.' She poured boiling water over the teabags and headed to the fridge for milk. 'Don't fancy Turkey.'

'Okay.' Noah frowned. Hadn't she said only last year that she'd always wanted to visit Turkey? 'What about Spain then? I'm sure—'

'We've been to Spain. Twice. You haven't got much imagination, have you?'

'Spain's a big country,' he pointed out carefully. 'You can't possibly see it all in two visits. We could go somewhere different. When I get the brochures—'

She slammed his mug on the island, spilling tea on the work surface. 'Don't bother. Anyway, I've sorted something out myself.'

Noah tore some kitchen paper from the roll and mopped up the tea. 'Oh? You've found us a holiday?'

Isobel leaned against the sink, cradling her own mug in her hands. There was a look on her face that made him uneasy. She was up to something.

'Actually, I didn't find it. Granny called. She's going to visit Daddy at his new house, and thought I might like to go with her, so I'm going over to Portugal at the end of July.'

'Portugal? Your dad's moved to Portugal?' It was the first he'd heard of it. 'When did that happen?'

'Last month apparently.' She shrugged, not meeting his gaze.

'And you didn't know?' His heart swelled with sympathy for her, but too late he realised he'd betrayed his feelings in his tone of voice.

She glared at him. 'He's a busy man! For goodness' sake, we're not joined at the hip. Daddy has so many business interests that you can't expect him to give me a running commentary on his every move. I expect you find that hard to understand, what with you being surgically attached to your aunt.'

He understood where her anger was coming from so didn't argue the point. Instead, he focused on something else she'd said.

'When you say *you're* going over...'

'Just me,' she confirmed, without a trace of awkwardness or embarrassment. 'Well, me and Granny obviously. Daddy and I see each other so rarely. We need some time together as a family. I suppose you're going to be difficult about it?'

'N-not at all.' His heart sank as it dawned on him that she'd never had any intention of going on holiday with him. She'd only brought up the subject as a way of easing him into the fact that she was going to Portugal to be with her dad. He knew how Isobel's mind worked. He should do after all these years. 'It will do you good to get away, and if you think Kelly can manage in the shop...'

'I already told you that, too. Kelly's gran's a retired florist. She's going to take the reins while I'm away. It's already arranged.'

She'd told him Kelly's gran had offered *if* Isobel decided to go on holiday, not that it was already arranged. He said nothing but sipped his tea.

'I hope I can trust you while I'm away,' she said pointedly.

He fought the urge to snap at her, sick to death of hearing her constant suspicions and accusations. He would never betray

Isobel, and had no interest in other women. He wished she would believe that instead of always expecting the worst of him.

'Of course you can trust me,' he said, not looking at her. He put the mug back on the island. 'When do you go?'

'The twenty-second. I'll be away a fortnight.'

The day before school term ended. He would spend the first two weeks of his summer holidays alone then.

'Is that all right with you?' she asked, a challenge in her tone.

'Of course. Whatever makes you happy.' He managed a smile.

'So what will you do with yourself while I'm away?' she asked. 'You won't have work to keep you occupied and even you can't spend a whole two weeks glued to Aunt Eugenie.'

'I expect I'll f-find something to do,' he said.

'Like what?' Her eyes narrowed and he wondered why he was being cross examined as if her going away and leaving him alone had been his idea.

'I'll catch up with Ross for one thing,' he said. 'We've hardly seen anything of each other since the art school opened. I'd l-like to see how it's going up there.'

'I'll bet you would,' she muttered. 'Running life classes, is he?'

Noah buried a sigh of impatience. 'I can do some work in the garden, too. And I might paint the bathroom. You said it could do with refreshing. Maybe you could choose the colour before you leave.'

'I'll be far too busy to worry about paint samples! Can't you decide anything for yourself?'

'Of course. A surprise then.'

'Hmm. Maybe not. Not with your taste. I'll look at some online tonight and leave you with a shortlist.'

'Fine,' he said wearily. 'Now, what would you like for dinner?'

'Oh, make what you like,' she told him, waving her hand dismissively. 'I'm too excited to worry about food. Besides, I want to look good in my bikini. Although,' she added, a gleam in her eyes, 'I'm going to treat myself to some new ones. A whole new holiday wardrobe, I think. Gran and I are going to shop till we drop tomorrow. We're going to Leeds, did I mention?'

'You did. I hope you have a wonderful time.'

Isobel viewed him suspiciously. 'What's that supposed to mean?'

'What I said. Nothing more.'

'And just what will you be doing while I'm in Leeds and out of the way?' she asked.

'Reading the Sunday p-papers,' he said quickly. 'And finishing off some odds and ends for work.'

She poured the remains of her tea down the sink and turned to face him. 'This is a small town,' she said slowly. 'You know how gossip spreads. Don't think I won't get to hear about it if you're doing something you shouldn't. I know how your mind works. While the cat's away and all that.'

It was on the tip of his tongue to say that if she was so worried about him misbehaving maybe she ought to stay in Tuppenny Bridge instead of heading off to Portugal without him.

But he didn't, and after a few minutes of silence she said, 'I'm going upstairs for a shower.'

As she flounced past him, she called over her shoulder, 'Salmon! I want salmon, new potatoes, and asparagus for dinner.'

'I don't think we've got—' he began, but she cut him off.

'Maister's is still open. Don't be long.'

Noah winced as the door slammed behind her.

FOUR

Daisy thanked the driver as she stepped off the bus, butterflies swooshing around in her stomach as she set foot in Camacker for the first time since leaving Upper Skimmerdale—what, five, six years ago?

She gazed around the pretty village nestled on the banks of the River Skimmer, at the familiar church of St Mary's with the old vicarage standing close by, The Shepherd's Crook pub, the village hall, the black-faced, horned Swaledale sheep wandering along the road past the general store and the teashop.

She knew this village almost as well as she knew Beckthwaite, the village closest to Crowscar Farm where she'd grown up, and where she'd worked at The King's Head for years as a way of escaping the oppressive atmosphere at home with her father, especially after Tom had left for Leeds.

Why had it taken her so long to return? Partly, she thought, as she hitched up her backpack and began to walk, because she'd been afraid of bumping into Eliot or, perhaps even worse, Eden, his girlfriend. Possibly, by now, his second wife.

The humiliation would have been too much to bear. And what if they had the kids with them? She swallowed down a lump in her throat at the thought of Liberty, Ophelia, and little George. She'd taken care of those children for years after their mother died, and had loved them like her own. She didn't know how she'd react if she saw them again.

But now, she thought determinedly, as she strode along the pavement towards the village post box, it was time to face up to the past. She had a new life. A home she loved in a little town she adored. She had her own business. Things were good and she could look Eliot in the eye if she saw him again and tell him so. Besides, it wasn't likely that he'd be around. After all, he didn't come into Camacker that often, unless things had changed since she'd been at Wildflower Farm.

It was July. There'd be a lot to do on the farm. On all the farms. She wondered if the haymaking had started and hoped not. It would be good to see the wildflowers, but they were usually cut down before mid-July, and it was the seventh today so...

Despite promising Tess and Rowan that she wouldn't, she took out her phone and called the café, knowing that a signal would be patchy once she left the village, and that the internet would be non-existent.

It took a few rings before Tess answered.

'Hello, The Crafty Cook Café, Tess speaking. How can I help?'

Very well done, Daisy thought, impressed. 'Hiya, Tess. It's me, Daisy.'

Tess laughed. 'What did we tell you? Didn't you promise you'd put us out of your mind and just enjoy yourself?'

'I know...' Daisy watched a couple of sheep grazing on the verge across the road and thought she should be more like them. They were so chilled with no thought for the future, just enjoying the moment. Although, being sheep, that was probably for the best. 'Is everything okay, though?'

'We haven't burned the place down if that's what you're worrying about.'

'Is it really busy? Do you think I've left you enough food?'

'Daisy! Look, it's half past ten. We've only been open for half an hour. You know what Sundays are like and you've left plenty of food, so stop worrying and go and enjoy yourself. Otherwise, what's the point?'

Tess was quite right.

'If you're sure...'

'I'm positive. Now hang up and have a great day off. Don't ring again. If we need help, we'll let you know.'

'But the signal—'

'Daisy!'

Daisy laughed. 'Okay, point taken. Thanks, Tess. Bye.'

She shoved her mobile phone into her jacket pocket and sighed. Tess and Rowan were perfectly capable of running the café for one day. She had to learn to switch off and relax.

She was deep in thought as she passed the small cottage that was now the tourist information centre. So deep in thought, in fact, that at first, she didn't register properly when a voice said, in obvious surprise, 'Miss Jackson?'

For a split second she froze. Eliot? But then she relaxed as she realised Eliot would never call her Miss Jackson. In fact, she could only think of one person who would and did, and she smiled as her gaze fell upon a slender, slightly freckle-faced man with tawny hair and blue eyes.

'Noah? What on earth are you doing here?'

He returned her smile. 'It *is* you! I couldn't believe it. I'm out for a hike.' He gave her a sheepish look. 'Hoping to see the wildflowers. I've just got a map of the Meadows Walking Trail from in there.' He jerked his thumb in the direction of the tourist information centre. 'What about you?'

She nodded. 'Same. Although I don't need a map. I know the trail like the back of my hand.'

'Lucky you. I didn't know you were into hiking.'

'Oh yes.' She nodded enthusiastically. 'It's the best cure I know for the blues. I used to walk this particular route a lot when I lived round here but it's the first time I've been back in ages.'

'Well...' He gave her an awkward look. 'I suppose...'

She hesitated. 'No Isobel?'

He shrugged. 'N-no. She's out shopping in Leeds with her gran.'

'Right.' Reluctantly she said, 'Look, we could always walk it together if you like?'

He beamed at her. 'Really? That would be great. I guess I can put this away then.'

He folded up the map and stuffed it, with some difficulty, into his jacket pocket. She realised she'd never seen him in jeans and walking boots before. He was usually so smartly dressed in a suit, shirt and tie, with being a headmaster. It made him look younger somehow.

'Where are you parked?' she enquired politely as they began to walk.

He glanced back at the bridge over the Skimmer.

'Car park just over the water,' he told her, much as she'd expected. 'Did you drive here? I wasn't sure if you had a car.'

'No,' she told him. 'I don't. I got the bus. Well, two buses actually.'

'I could give you a lift back later if you like?' he offered.

'That would be great,' she said. 'If you're sure.'

'Of course. No problem.'

Daisy couldn't help wishing that she hadn't bumped into him today. Noah had always been nice to her, but the thought of Isobel's broken fingers kept nagging away at her. Besides, he was very polite and a bit, well, quiet and shy. She wondered how on earth he'd ever become a headmaster and tried to imagine him in charge of an entire school. He just didn't seem the type.

It meant, of course, that she'd have to be quiet and polite, too. Not that she'd have been talking to herself as she walked—well, not much—but she often sang to herself, and besides, she liked to think. There was no better place to think than while out walking, especially somewhere so beautiful. Not much chance of thinking time now.

Having reached the post box, Daisy turned right and followed the flagged footpath, Noah just behind her.

'What's the terrain like?' he enquired after a few moments.

'Oh, it's quite a gentle walk really,' she assured him. 'There are a few uphill bits that might tax you a little, but mostly it's fairly level ground. It's not like some of the walks round here. Honestly, for those you need oxygen!'

He laughed. 'Not sure I'm ready for that, but I do like being out and about walking. It's good for the soul.'

She glanced at him, curious. Although he was clearly trying to sound light-hearted, she thought she detected something in his voice that she'd heard before. A note of sadness that she couldn't quite put her finger on. In fact, there was something about Noah that always made her feel protective, which was stupid really. He was a professional man with a lot more going for him than she had. He might just be a very good actor. How could she possibly tell?

'Before we go any further,' she said, as a thought struck her, 'have you put sun lotion on? You definitely don't want to be walking around in this heat without it.'

'I have. I burn so easily that it's one of the first things I thought of. Wish I was more like Ross. He tans, whereas I just go pink like a lobster. Must be his Italian heritage.'

Ross, black haired and dark eyed, was Noah's half-brother, and it had to be said they looked nothing alike, though they seemed very close.

They came to a gate and Daisy unlatched it and walked through, holding it open for Noah. 'I burn, too, but my brother Tom doesn't,' she told him as she checked the gate was closed properly before she led him down a mud track towards a footbridge. 'So, I know how you feel. Not fair, is it?'

They crossed the water and began to walk along the riverside track. To their right the wildflower meadows were still in bloom, and she heaved a sigh of relief.

'We're not too late. I was a bit worried,' she admitted. 'They'll be gone this time next week. The farmers will have cut them down for the animals' winter feed.'

'This is stunning,' Noah breathed. They stood still for a few moments, gazing around them.

'It would have been even better in June,' she told him. 'But at least we haven't missed them entirely.'

'What sort of flowers are they? Do you know? I can see lots of buttercups, daisies and dandelions.'

'They're not dandelions,' Daisy told him. 'They're cat's ears —false dandelions. They do look similar, I'll grant you. See those gorgeous purple flowers? They're wood cranesbill, or woodland geraniums. And those lime-yellow, frothy flowers? Lady's mantle.'

Noah looked impressed. He pointed to some straight, yellow flowers. 'What about those?'

Daisy nodded. 'Yellow rattle. It's not my favourite flower, and a lot of farmers consider it a pest, but it's great for wildflower meadows, cos it suppresses dominant grasses and helps to recycle the nutrients in the soil. Those other, prettier, yellow ones are hawkbit.'

She continued pointing out the different flowers and telling him the little bits she knew about them, and he listened, seeming genuinely interested.

'You're a wildflower expert, Miss Jackson?'

Daisy laughed, embarrassed. 'Hardly that. But I did grow

up around here and the wildflower meadows are such a big deal in Upper Skimmerdale.' She took a deep breath and closed her eyes for a moment. 'It's good to be back.'

He didn't speak, allowing her a moment to just be. She was surprised and grateful that he didn't say anything and didn't urge her to get moving again. For a moment she simply stood, breathing in the scent of the wildflowers and taking in lungfuls of fresh air. Eventually, though, she thought he'd been patient long enough.

'Shall we continue?'

He gave her an understanding smile. 'Only if you're ready.'

'I am. Thank you.'

She cast a sideways glance at him as they walked, the path veering uphill, thinking there was something rather sweet about him. No matter how hard she tried she simply couldn't imagine him giving Isobel a hard time about her weight, or her calorie intake. As for breaking her fingers...

Then again, how many cruel men hid behind a facade of respectability? You just couldn't tell, and she had to keep that in mind.

'Why do you call me Miss Jackson?' she asked him impulsively.

He looked startled by the question. 'Isn't that your name?'

'My name's Daisy,' she replied. 'You're the only person I know who calls me Miss Jackson.'

He tilted his head, considering as he walked. 'I suppose I get used to it at work, with addressing the female staff as Miss or Mrs in front of the children all the time. Besides, it seems the polite thing to do. My aunt always made sure we minded our manners. She was quite a stickler for it.'

Daisy could imagine. She wondered what it must have been like to have been brought up by Miss Lavender but didn't like to ask.

'We're getting higher and higher,' he said, puffing a little. 'I thought this was an easy route?'

She smirked. 'It is! You're just out of condition.'

'I suppose I am. Too much time sitting at a desk,' he admitted.

'Don't worry. It's not as high as some of the routes round here. You're not struggling, are you?'

'Not really. I think I'll take my jacket off, though.'

'Good idea. Me too.'

They dropped their backpacks on the ground and shrugged off their jackets, stuffing them into their bags.

Daisy took the opportunity to take out a bottle of water.

'Have you got anything to drink?' she asked him.

'Yes, a bottle of water like you. And a flask of tea.'

She giggled. 'You're very well prepared. Bet you haven't got cake, though!'

His eyes widened. 'No, have you? Not that white chocolate and caramel cake?'

'No. Sorry. Orange and lemon cake. But there's a big wedge of it left over from yesterday. More than enough for two. We'll share it when we stop for lunch. I take it you've brought lunch?'

Noah looked embarrassed. 'Actually, no. I thought I'd grab something to eat at a pub or something.'

'Oh. Well...' Daisy shook her head. 'That's nowhere near as much fun. And I think we'll be starving by the time we get back to Camacker, don't you? Don't worry. I've got loads of sand-wiches and some quiche so you're welcome to share that, too.'

'Then I insist on sharing my flask of tea,' he told her.

'You don't have to insist, I'm not going to argue. Mind, I'll warn you now—once I start on the tea I won't stop. You'll have to snatch the flask from my greedy grasp.' She took a long swig of water then screwed the cap back on her bottle.

'I'll save the tea for lunch then,' Noah said, reaching for his own water bottle. 'It will help wash that cake down.'

'You're a bit of a cake fiend, aren't you?' she said.

'I am a bit partial,' he admitted. 'W-we don't have it at home so...'

Daisy wrestled with her conscience. Should she ask the question? It was none of her business, after all. But the truth was, she wanted to know. Was he really the control freak Isobel was making him out to be?

'Why don't you have it at home?' she burst out, then watched him closely, waiting for his reaction.

He looked a bit awkward. 'Well, it's a health thing really. If we had cake in the house we'd eat it. Best not to have it in. No temptation. Bad enough when I'm at work.'

She couldn't be certain what he meant by that. Was Isobel right? Was that why they didn't have cake at Peony Cottage? But that made him one heck of a hypocrite if that was the case, because most working days he visited The Crafty Cook Café and ate cake there. Was the house rule simply to control Isobel? And if so, how else was he controlling her?

It was a depressing thought.

'Come on,' she said, tucking the bottle inside her backpack. 'Best get walking.'

They continued in silence for some distance, the climb taking up a lot of energy. The Skimmer was just a stream far below them and they could see sheep, like toy farmyard animals, in the distance. Eventually the path began to snake its way down the hillside, and they dipped down into shady woodland, glad of the respite from the increasingly hot sun.

Noah gasped suddenly. 'Can you hear that?'

His blue eyes were bright with excitement and despite her earlier worries Daisy couldn't help but grin at him.

'The waterfall? Yes, it's coming up any moment.'

They hurried through the trees along a track, the sound of rushing water growing louder in their ears as they walked, until...

'Skimmergill Foss,' Daisy announced, waving an arm ahead of her.

They stepped onto a wooden footbridge over the river and rested their elbows on the rails, staring ahead of them at the waterfall.

'Wow,' Noah breathed. At least, she thought that was what he said. It was hard to hear him with the thundering sound of the water gushing onto the rocks in the river below.

'I can't believe you've never visited here before,' Daisy said, frowning. As he gave her an enquiring look, she raised her voice above the roar of the water. 'You're a Skimmerdale man, aren't you? You grew up here. How come you've never seen Skimmergill Foss before?'

Noah was silent for a few moments, then he shrugged and turned to look at her.

'It just wasn't on our radar really. Aunt Eugenie's life is in and around Tuppenny Bridge. I was either at Lavender House or at St Egbert's, and at home life revolved around homework or the museum. Then I went to university and country hikes in the Dales were the last thing on my mind. And th-there was Isobel...' He hesitated a moment. 'Hiking was never her thing. And I don't think she'd ever see the attraction of a waterfall to be honest.' He cleared his throat. 'Each to their own. She has a lot of interests that I don't share. We can't all like the same things, can we?'

'I suppose not.' Although Daisy couldn't help wondering what interests, if any, Noah and Isobel *did* share. Still, it was nothing to do with her, and the light had gone from his eyes, and he had that sad look about him again, so it was time to change the subject.

'Feeling cooler?'

'Much,' he agreed. 'It's amazing how little sunlight filters through into these woods, isn't it? I'm feeling miles better now.'

'Good,' she said, 'because I reckon it must be about time for something to eat. What do you think?'

'Here?' He looked around, clearly not convinced.

'Follow me,' she told him, and led him over the footbridge and along another path out of the woods.

They turned left and the path began to climb the hillside on the opposite side of the river from before. The sound of the rushing waterfall faded, and instead the occasional sound of bleating sheep was their only soundtrack as they walked.

Noah groaned as they reached a particularly steep section of the trail. 'Not again! I hadn't realised I was so unfit!'

'This is just the beginning,' Daisy told him. 'In a few minutes we'll reach the part of the hike that makes this look like a nursery slope.'

His eyes widened in horror. 'You're joking!'

Daisy giggled. 'Yes, of course I am! You're going to be so easy to wind up. Don't worry, we're nearly there.'

'Thank goodness for that,' Noah puffed. 'I hope this is going to be worth it.'

But the path led them to the ruins of an old farmhouse, much photographed by hikers, and a wooden bench nearby, and even Noah had to agree that the climb *had* been worth it for the stunning views.

'Here we go. Time for food.'

They settled themselves on the bench and shrugged off their backpacks. Daisy dug out the plastic lunchboxes she'd packed, and Noah found his flask of tea.

'Cheese or ham?' she asked.

'Whatever you like least is fine by me,' he told her, polite as ever.

There were four sandwiches, so they had one cheese and one ham each, plus a slice of tomato, basil, and parmesan quiche, and a wedge of orange and lemon cake, both of which Daisy carefully broke in half since she had no knife with her.

'If I'd known I was feeding you I'd have brought more,' she said with a sigh as she brushed cake crumbs from her T-shirt.

'Sorry,' Noah said immediately. 'You should have said. Honestly, I wouldn't have minded you not sharing.'

'Don't be daft!' Daisy burst out laughing. 'I think there was more than enough, don't you? Besides, what sort of person do you think I am? Any road, don't forget that tea, *Mr Lavender*. I'm just about ready for it now.'

'Please, call me Noah,' he said, a slight pleading tone in his voice.

And there it was again. Something about him—the expression in his eyes, the tiny downturn of his mouth, that wistful note in his words—something that made her heart lurch. Something that made her want to wrap her arms around him and reassure him that everything was okay.

But why?

She was being ridiculous.

'I'll call you Noah if you drop the Miss Jackson bit and start calling me Daisy,' she told him.

'If that's what you want,' he said, smiling.

'It is. Deal?'

'Deal.' He handed her the flask of tea. 'There you go, Daisy.'

She realised she liked the way he said her name. It made her feel funny inside. She wondered if she was getting sunstroke.

'Thank you.'

They sat in amiable silence, drinking tea and gazing at the incredible views of the Upper Skimmerdale landscape.

'I'd like to come here again,' Noah said thoughtfully. 'I know the wildflowers will be gone soon, but even without them the area is so incredibly beautiful.'

Daisy took another sip of tea, half wanting to suggest they come back another time, but she said nothing. She wasn't sure why. Maybe because it seemed presumptuous. After all, he hadn't said anything about returning with her.

But anyway, he was Noah. And he was Isobel's husband. It wouldn't be right. She knew all too well how people could talk. Look how they'd talked about her and Eliot. Assumptions could be made, and she didn't fancy going through all that again.

If she'd thought Beckthwaite was bad, she knew that the gossip in Tuppenny Bridge would be far, far worse. She'd heard enough about the Lavender Ladies—Miss Lavender and the Pennyfeather sisters—and their little sideline of running bets on the Bridgers' private lives to be certain of that.

'You should,' she said finally, when he didn't say anything else, and she had an uncomfortable feeling he was waiting for her reply. 'It will do you good, and besides, you need to build up your fitness.'

She smiled at him, and he smiled back. She noticed flecks of gold in his blue eyes, the glints of red in his hair where the sunlight was shining on him, and the dusting of freckles across his nose and sharp cheekbones.

'Have you finished with that?' he asked, nodding at the flask.

She swallowed, realising she'd been staring at him.

'Oh heck, have I drunk it all?'

'Don't worry, I've had enough,' he reassured her. 'And I've still got some water left.'

'Sun lotion!'

'Sorry?'

'We need to top up,' she said, taking the bottle from her backpack. 'Have you brought some with you?'

'No,' he admitted. 'I put loads on before I left the car though.'

'Not good enough,' she said sternly, smoothing lotion into her arms. 'And you a headmaster! You can borrow some of mine.'

'I'm not very well prepared, am I?' he asked ruefully, watching as she dabbed lotion over her nose and chin.

'No, but you'll know better next time,' she said, handing him the bottle.

He quickly applied another layer of lotion to his arms, face, and neck and gave her the bottle back. 'Thanks, Daisy.'

'We'd better make our way back to the car park,' she said, getting to her feet and stuffing the empty plastic boxes into her backpack.

'I suppose we better had,' he agreed.

They shrugged on their backpacks and set off downhill, over another footbridge and along the floor of the valley, passing ruined old barns and rusting agricultural machinery.

Daisy told him about the bothies that were scattered across the dales—little stone buildings with no electricity or running water. Originally built as shelters for the shepherds or accommodation for farm labourers, these days they were left unlocked to provide overnight shelter for anyone who needed it, though sometimes winter feed was stored in them. Some, though, had been repaired and done up as holiday accommodation, which Daisy thought was hilarious.

'You should see the prices some of them are rented out for. More money than sense, some folk.'

They squeezed through a narrow gate and followed the path through the fields, passing grazing sheep, then along a lane towards Camacker, with the wildflower meadows once again to the side of them, providing them with one last glorious burst of colour before they reached the village and turned, with some regret, towards the car park.

'I have to admit,' Daisy said as Noah, ever the gentleman, opened the car door for her, 'I'm really glad I don't have to face two bus journeys now.'

'Lucky we bumped into each other then,' Noah said, fastening his seat belt and starting the engine. He turned to her and gave her a bright smile, and Daisy thought suddenly that she was very glad he'd chosen today, of all days, to take a hike in the Dales. It occurred to her that she'd not worried about the café once since he'd joined her. Funnily enough, she wasn't even worrying about it now.

'Do you mind if we have the radio on?' he asked, as they pulled out of the car park.

'Ooh, no! I love a bit of music. Mind you,' she warned him, 'I do love singing along, so you might change your mind.'

For a moment he stared at her, and her smile faded as she wondered what he was thinking.

'I won't change my mind,' he said, and flicked the radio on.

They drove out of Camacker, accompanied by the strains of ELO's 'Mr Blue Sky', their laughter at the bemused looks they'd earned from a group of wandering sheep almost drowning out the cheerful song.

A moment of perfection in an imperfect world.

FIVE

'Well!' Caroline sank back in her chair and aimed a beaming smile at Noah. 'That's half a day gone. Just one afternoon to go and we're free. What will we do with ourselves?'

Noah had been wondering the same thing. It was the last day of term, and he should have been looking forward to the long summer holidays, but right now he wasn't sure what to think.

Isobel had jetted off to Portugal yesterday, full of excitement and so happy she'd even bestowed a long and lingering kiss on his lips at the airport.

Her grandmother had eyed them disapprovingly.

'Don't make an exhibition of yourselves,' she'd snapped.

Isobel had winked at him as she pulled away and his heart had leapt. For a moment there she'd looked like her old self—the Isobel he'd first fallen in love with so very long ago—and he'd wanted to grab her and beg her to stay with him.

Then the glint had gone from her eyes replaced by an expression that was far more familiar.

'Remember what I said. Word travels fast in Tuppenny Bridge. Behave yourself or I'll know about it.'

The warning was delivered in a low voice, but its meaning was crystal clear. Where, he wondered, had this suspicion come from? He'd never cheated on Isobel, and he never would. Why did she persist in checking up on him and making these threats?

'You have n-nothing to worry about,' he said wearily, his hope dying as quickly as it had flared. He would, he acknowledged with despair, be relieved when she stepped onto that plane.

Now he was facing the next fortnight alone and he really wasn't sure what to think about that. It would be a respite from the constant sniping and the oppressive atmosphere in Peony Cottage, but it would also give him time alone. Too much time. And he knew the way his mind started to work when he was alone for too long in that house.

He loosened his tie a little, already feeling restless. 'I'm popping out for lunch today,' he told the school secretary. 'I won't be long, though.'

Caroline eyed him sympathetically. 'Make sure you eat something filling. There's not a pick on you these days. You work too hard, I reckon.'

'We all work hard,' he pointed out. 'It's the nature of the job. And don't worry, I'll make sure I eat something every bit as hearty as any meal on offer here.'

Heading across Market Square ten minutes later, he took a deep breath, glad to be outdoors in the fresh air. It wasn't particularly sunny today, but it was reasonably warm. He hoped the weather would be kind for the next few weeks so the children could spend most of their time outdoors. Not, he thought ruefully, that most of them would want to. They were worryingly dependent on their phones and tablets and seemed to prefer sitting indoors staring at screens to exploring the countryside.

Not like in his day. He and Ross had practically had to be bribed to go indoors, he recalled. They'd been lucky to grow up in Lavender House, with those amazing gardens and a maze that was just ripe for some fantastic games, even though they'd been warned repeatedly that the main gardens were for visitors, and they should stay in the private family garden at the side of the house.

Ross might have been younger than Noah, but he was definitely the ringleader. Noah had been supposedly looking after his little brother. In reality, daredevil Ross had led Noah to do all sorts of things he would never have dared do on his own.

Noah smiled to himself, remembering. He missed Ross. Now that his brother was so loved up with Clemmie, as well as being busy with The Arabella Lavender Art Academy, he saw little of him these days. And, of course, Ross seldom visited Peony Cottage. Although maybe he would, now he knew Isobel was away.

It had pained him for years that Ross didn't like Isobel. Although his brother had never said as much he really hadn't needed to. It was obvious. Isobel, meanwhile, had shown no hesitation in telling him that she felt the same way about Ross, labelling him spoilt and selfish, and not worthy of their time and attention.

In recent years, Noah had grown to be grateful that Ross avoided Isobel. It made life so much easier all round. Maybe he'd get the chance to catch up with his brother next week, though. He'd like that.

He didn't even consider Market Café for lunch, heading directly to The Crafty Cook Café where he'd had the foresight to book a table. He knew it would be busy at this time of day and wasn't leaving anything to chance.

Daisy greeted him with a sparkle in her eyes and his heart lifted at the sight of the dimple in each cheek which always appeared when she smiled. He found them endearing. Round-faced, with large, soulful eyes and shoulder-length dark brown hair, he thought she looked young for her age. He'd been surprised when she'd admitted she was thirty-five, only two years younger than him. He couldn't deny that the sight of her cheered him up immediately.

'I've reserved table two for you,' she told him. 'Nice view of the market square for a change. Take a seat and I'll be over to take your order in a minute.'

He nodded his thanks and threaded his way through the tables to the one by the window. A quick glance around the room revealed there was currently no one he knew in the café. Well, no one he knew well anyway. A couple of his pupils' mothers were sitting chatting, cups of coffee in their hands, taking no notice of him. That didn't worry him. Anyway, he thought as he took a seat and picked up the menu, he'd done nothing wrong. He had nothing to feel guilty about.

It was just...

He sighed inwardly, knowing that he shouldn't be feeling so wary about visiting a café in his lunch hour. But if Isobel found out, if she got the wrong idea... And she seemed to get the wrong idea so often these days, no matter how much he reassured her that she had nothing to worry about.

Sometimes he seriously wondered if he was giving off signals that he wasn't aware of. She'd accused him of flirting, of encouraging some of the female members of staff at the school, even a few of the mums. He'd denied it because, as far as he was aware, he'd done no such thing, but he was starting to think maybe it was something he did on a subconscious level.

But then, at other times, he'd see that look in her eyes and he'd wonder... Was she making the whole thing up? Was it just something she used as an excuse to be angry? A stick to beat him with.

He didn't know any more and when he tried to process his thoughts it gave him a headache. He just went round and round in circles, getting nowhere. All he knew right now was that he was very glad Isobel was in Portugal and he could risk staying for lunch at the café this time instead of just popping in for a quick slice of cake.

Something, he thought, resting his chin in his hand, would have to change, and soon. Things couldn't go on this way. *He* couldn't go on this way. But how could he change what was happening? What was he supposed to do?

'Have you made your mind up yet?'

He jumped, startled by the voice so close to his ear. Daisy was smiling down at him, but her smile quickly died, replaced with a look of concern.

'Are you okay?'

There was a strange expression in her cocoa-coloured eyes.

'Of course. Why shouldn't I be?'

'I don't know. You looked like you had the weight of the world on your shoulders then.'

He managed a laugh. 'D-did I? Sorry.'

'No need to apologise to me,' she assured him. 'I was just worried about you, that's all.'

'You were?' His voice caught and, to his horror, tears pricked his eyes. Where the hell had they come from? 'Let's see what I'm going to eat today.' He snatched at the menu and studied it intently, hoping she hadn't noticed his display of emotion.

Daisy pulled out the chair opposite and sat down. 'Noah, are you all right? Seriously?'

'Of course I am,' he said brightly. 'Just can't decide what to eat that's all, and I'll have to get back to the school before you know it.' He glanced over at the counter. 'You have customers.'

She smiled gently. 'That's okay. I took Bethany's advice. I've hired Rowan and Tess while they're on holiday from college. Rowan's here on Mondays, Tess on Fridays, and both on Wednesdays for market day. We'll see how it goes. So, you see, I'm all right to spend five minutes making sure my loyal customers are okay. If Rowan needs me, she'll soon give me a yell.'

He nodded and pretended to read the menu again.

'I heard Isobel went away yesterday,' she said.

Noah rolled his eyes. 'Word gets round here, doesn't it?'

'I expect you'll miss her,' she said, sounding sympathetic. 'But cheer up. She'll be back before you know it.'

'She will,' he agreed heavily. 'What do you recommend?'

She blinked. 'Sorry?'

'To eat. What do you recommend?'

'Oh!' She shook her head. 'Depends what you fancy and how hungry you are.'

He realised bleakly that he'd totally lost his appetite. Hardly the sort of thing to say to a café owner when you'd just reserved one of her precious tables, though.

'As long as I leave room for a slice of cake I'm fine,' he joked.

'I've baked your favourite,' she told him with a smile. 'White chocolate and caramel.'

'Mm. I'll look forward to that.'

'I'll tell you what's popular,' she said suddenly. 'How about a bacon, brie and cranberry panini? They go down a real treat. Or I can do you a jacket potato if you fancy, with cheese, or chilli, or both if you like. Or you can have it with prawns, or—'

'The panini sounds great,' he said, trying desperately to inject some enthusiasm into his tone. 'And a coffee please if it's not too much trouble.'

'Of course it's not too much trouble,' she said, getting to her feet. 'Latte, was it?'

He nodded and she hurried off to the kitchen. He slotted the menu back into its stand and stared out of the window, wondering what Isobel was doing right now. Lying on the beach in one of her new bikinis he supposed. Not a care in the world.

He had to stop this. He knew it. Yet how could he change things?

Leave her before it's too late.

He mentally shook his head as the thought he was having with alarming frequency lately returned. He couldn't do that. He'd made his vows. He'd promised. And she'd be devastated, lost. It was, after all, what she feared most—being alone. Besides, he owed her. He could never fully make it up to her, but he could try. He would never stop trying. He just had to keep a lid on his emotions. Stop giving in to them. Focus. He couldn't put her through anything else. He just had to be a better man, make her happy, do whatever it took.

Daisy returned, carrying a tray. She put his coffee and panini on the table and gazed down at him. 'Everything to your satisfaction?'

'Of course. Thanks, Daisy.'

Her expression softened and she said softly, 'I get it, you know. Summer holidays start tomorrow and your wife's away for two weeks. You must be dreading it. Hey, are you going to Dolly's party on the twenty-seventh?'

He unfolded his napkin carefully, buying himself time to think. 'I shouldn't have thought so,' he said at last. Imagine what Isobel would say if she found out! God, it wouldn't be worth the hassle, especially as she'd thrown the invitation in the bin the moment it arrived, saying scornfully that hell would freeze over before either she or Noah attended any rubbish fiftieth birthday bash at The White Hart Inn.

'Oh, but why not? Surely it's better than sitting at home alone? And Ross will be there, after all.' She hesitated. 'And me.'

He looked up quickly, noting the slight flush of pink on her cheeks.

'I mean, if all else fails I'll talk to you,' she said lightly. 'To be honest, I'd be glad to see you there. I might have lived in Skimmerdale all my life, but I'm still an incomer as far as the

Tuppenny Bridgers are concerned, so it would be good to have someone who's guaranteed to chat with me.'

Something stirred within him, and he dismissed it quickly. She was just being friendly, and he was being ridiculous.

'Well, maybe I will then,' he said, not willing to make a solid commitment. 'I'll see how I feel nearer the time.'

She shrugged. 'Fair enough. You know when and where so it's up to you. Now, tuck in and enjoy. Give me a shout when you're ready for that cake.'

She winked at him and headed back to the counter and Noah stared at the panini, not even registering it. He was being stupid. Daisy was just a kind-hearted soul who would worry about anyone if she thought they were sad.

But that flush of pink on her cheekbones, and the embarrassed look in her eyes, as if she'd said too much, given herself away...

Oh, God! Was he really that desperate that he'd allow his imagination to play such stupid tricks? This was Daisy. Kind, chatty, always friendly. Definitely not interested in him in that way, and it was a good job because he loved Isobel and he would never, ever let her down again.

It was, he thought, the least he could do for her. The very least.

SIX

'I can't believe you came! You're the last person I was expecting to see.'

Ross clapped Noah on the back, and his delighted smile told Noah that his brother's surprise was genuine. He could hardly blame him for doubting him. He hadn't believed he'd be here himself, and right up until the last minute had dithered over whether to attend Dolly's fiftieth birthday party or not.

He couldn't help worrying what Isobel would say if she found out he'd attended and knew the chances of her not finding out were slim to non-existent. Even so, for some reason he'd decided to take the risk. He didn't want to think too deeply about why he'd made that choice.

The White Hart Inn was decked out with bunting and balloons, which proudly revealed that Dolly was, indeed, fifty today, although as the birthday girl kept insisting, no one would ever guess just by looking at her.

Dolly was dressed up to the nines, despite having officially been told by Clemmie that they were simply having a quiet birthday drink in the pub. She played the role of surprised guest of honour to perfection, but no one was fooled. Everyone had heard that this entire party was Dolly's idea, and that she'd organised every bit of it behind the scenes. Still, it was all part of the fun, and no one breathed a word to her that her secret was out.

Noah thought, not for the first time, how well and happy Ross looked. His brother was clearly loving his new role, running The Arabella Lavender Art Academy, and even more, his role as Clemmie's boyfriend. Even when they were on opposite sides of the room, Noah noticed their gazes straying to each other, and saw the loving smiles they exchanged often. It warmed his heart, while reminding him all too savagely how very different things were with him and Isobel.

He accepted a drink from Jonah with grateful thanks. His old friend was another one currently basking in the warmth of a loving relationship. His wife, Kat, was nearly six months pregnant, and Jonah was clearly happy and excited that their family was about to expand.

'Three kids, Noah,' Jonah said, shaking his head as he gazed into his pint. 'Can you believe it? Me with three kids. Who'd have thought it?'

'I'm happy for you,' Noah told him, meaning it. 'You've been so good with Tommy, and then taking on Hattie, too. You were born to be a father if you ask me.'

'Aw, thanks, mate.' Jonah hesitated as if about to add something else, but he clearly thought better of it.

Noah didn't have to think too hard to guess what he'd been about to say. Aunt Eugenie had ventured the same question many times over recent years: 'What about you and Isobel? Any plans for a family yet?'

It was an intrusive question, and not one he felt people should ask. After all, no one knew what might be going on in a couple's life. Things weren't always as they seemed, and a seemingly innocent question could lead to all sorts of heartbreak.

As it happened, Noah and Isobel had never tried for a baby.

Isobel had never brought the subject up, so he could only assume it wasn't something she wanted. As for him... He'd always thought he would love to be a father, but he didn't believe for an instant that the time was right, which was why he'd never brought the subject up either. The way things were between himself and Isobel, the worst thing they could do was bring a child into the world. Knowing the sort of relationship he'd had with his father—if you could call it that—he knew that, no matter how often the urge to become one himself appeared, it would be a bad decision and just another reason to feel guilty. And he carried more than enough guilt already.

'How are you managing without Isobel around?' Jonah asked.

Noah hid a smile, suspecting that Jonah was only asking him that to cover up the fact that he'd almost asked a much more awkward question instead. His friend rarely mentioned Isobel unless he had to.

It was hard to believe that, fifteen years ago, they'd all hung around together. Friends forever. Noah, Isobel, Kat, Jonah, and Leon. Inseparable. Or so they'd thought. Now look at them. Leon gone forever. Kat and Jonah married with children. Himself and Isobel...

'It's peaceful,' he said, making every effort to sound jokey. 'A house to myself for two weeks and no job to go to. It's every man's dream, right?'

'You're not kidding. Wow, I can't imagine what peace and quiet is like these days.' Jonah grinned. 'It's chaos in our house. I go to the forge to escape.'

His eyes twinkled and Noah knew that Jonah wouldn't swap places with him for anything.

'Mind if we join you?'

Clive, Bethany, and Daisy were at their table. Noah got to his feet. 'Please do.'

Daisy and Bethany exchanged amused glances and Clive

shook his head. 'Your manners are putting the rest of us to shame, Noah! Sit down for God's sake or they'll be expecting us all to brush up on our etiquette.'

'Well, it wouldn't do you any harm,' Bethany teased as they all sat down. 'We missed the beginning, didn't we? How did it go? Did Dolly act all surprised?'

'She did,' Jonah confirmed, 'and she was bloody good at it, too. It was funny, though. Kat said it reminded her of that episode of *Friends*. You know, the one where they don't know who knows and it gets more and more complicated and confusing? Does Dolly know that we all know that she knows about the party?' He chuckled.

'I'd never have had you down for a *Friends* fan, Jonah,' Clive said with a grin.

'Aye, well, living with Kat I've not got much choice.' Jonah didn't sound too unhappy about it, though.

'Hmm. I'll believe you,' Clive said in mock suspicion. 'As for Dolly, I doubt very much that she'd care who knew what one way or the other. As long as she's the centre of attention she's happy. Oh, and I see that young fella Reuben's back. Good to see he's been invited.'

'Who's Reuben?' Daisy and Bethany chorused at the same time.

'Clemmie's half-brother,' Jonah explained. 'Nice chap. Got married just before me and Kat actually. That's his husband over there, talking to Clemmie now. Matt, I think his name is.'

'I didn't even know Clemmie had a brother,' Bethany admitted. 'I can see there's still a lot I have to learn about Tuppenny Bridge.' She paused. 'Have you heard from Isobel, Noah? In Portugal, isn't she?'

Noah nodded. 'That's right. Sh-she'll be there for two weeks. I've not heard from her yet, but I expect she's b-busy sightseeing and the like.'

'Shame she couldn't have waited a few days so you could have gone with her,' Bethany remarked.

Noah thought he saw a look of irritation flit across Daisy's face, but it was gone before he could be certain.

'Ah well, her father's just moved there, and her gran was going to visit him so Isobel tagged along with her,' he explained, stretching the truth a little because it was easier that way.

'Oh, I see. That makes sense,' Bethany said.

Daisy smiled at Noah. 'I'm glad you came. I wasn't sure you would, and I think it's better for you to get out and about than be sat at home all alone watching television.'

'You're probably right,' he said. He took a sip of his beer, his eyes fixed on her as she gazed around the room. She looked lovely tonight, he thought. She seemed to have gone to a lot of trouble with her hair and make-up, and she was wearing a pretty shift dress in a bright orange colour that really suited her dark hair and eyes.

'We ought to wish Dolly a happy birthday,' Bethany told Clive. 'We've got her a present, too, though goodness knows if she'll like it.' She turned to the others. 'It's so hard to buy for someone you barely know, isn't it? And Clive was next to useless.'

'Aye, well, how do I know what a woman wants for her fiftieth birthday? Be reasonable. We'll go over there now and get it over and done with. I'll say hello to Jennifer while I'm at it. So good to see her here, isn't it?' Clive got to his feet and addressed Noah. 'Would you save our seats? Is Kat not here, Jonah?'

'Oh yes, she's just talking to Sally at the bar,' Jonah explained. He glanced over to where his wife was giggling with her best friend, Sally Kingston, who along with her husband, Rafferty, owned and ran The White Hart Inn. 'She'll be over soon, no doubt.' He drained his pint. 'In fact, I might go over there now and remind her that she's a married woman and should be attending to my every need.' He grinned. 'Not really.

I just need another drink. Noah, do you want one while I'm there?'

'I'm fine thanks. Next round's on me, though. I owe you one.'

'Don't be daft, mate.'

Jonah patted his shoulder and followed Clive and Bethany to the bar, where Dolly was holding court watched by an amused Jennifer, Sally, and Kat.

Noah gulped down some beer. This wasn't awkward at all. Just him and Daisy sitting opposite each other, clearly not knowing what to say.

'I really am glad you came,' Daisy said at last.

He raised an eyebrow. 'Are you? Thanks. I'm glad I came, too. I think.' He put down his glass and glanced around, not really sure why he felt so uncomfortable suddenly.

'I envy you really,' she told him.

'Me? Why would you envy me?'

She shrugged. 'Well, you know, six weeks off work. How fantastic is that?'

'Ah, if only. People don't realise that teaching staff still have work to do even in the summer holidays,' he explained. 'And for a headmaster—well, let's just say I won't be putting my feet up for a full month and a half.'

'That's a shame,' she said.

'To be honest,' he admitted, 'I don't mind. I have no idea what to do with myself most of the time. I like the order and the structure of work. Keeping my mind occupied. I really don't know what I'd do without my job to go to every day.'

Daisy sipped her wine thoughtfully. 'Well,' she said at last, 'we could always go on another hike. I mean, only if you want to, of course.'

The way his heart lifted at the thought of it rang alarm bells in his mind, but he ignored them. 'Are you sure?'

'Of course I'm sure. Why wouldn't I be?'

'Well...' He shrugged. 'I kind of foisted myself on you last time. There you were, out for a quiet stroll to see the wildflowers and then I landed and that was that. I even ate half your lunch.'

'And I drank more than half your tea,' she reminded him, grinning. 'Fair swap, I think. Besides, you gave me a lift home, which was exactly what I needed after all that walking. Honestly, I think I'd have keeled over if I'd had to catch two buses.'

'It was a great day, though,' he said wistfully, then gave her an awkward smile.

'It was. So, what do you think? I kind of liked having a walking companion. The wildflowers will be gone, of course, but we could go somewhere else. There's a great walk round East Midham. It passes near the castle grounds, and I haven't been there for years. Do you fancy that?'

Noah was silent as a dozen thoughts flashed through his mind. Hope, fear, excitement, dread, confusion, all vied for dominance in his brain. He pictured the interrogation he'd get from Isobel if she found out. Then he pictured spending another day with Daisy, taking in the scenery, walking, walking, walking—walking all his cares away. Isobel was still away. Maybe she'd never know. It wasn't as if he was doing anything he shouldn't after all. Even so...

Regretfully he forced himself to answer her. 'Daisy, I can't—'

He broke off as the song that had been blasting out for the last four minutes faded away, to be replaced by something else. Something fast and bouncy and utterly joyous.

His eyes met Daisy's and they smiled at each other. A shared secret. An unexpected bond.

'"Mr Blue Sky",' he murmured.

'What were you saying?' she asked, leaning across the table to hear him better.

'I was saying—' He took a deep breath. 'I was saying, that sounds brilliant, and I'd love to.'

She raised her glass to him. 'Well then, here's to our next adventure. Next Sunday okay? And don't worry. I'll bring cake.'

Dolly was having a fine old time. Egged on by Bluebell she'd downed copious amounts of champagne, waving her glass around as she took centre stage on the dance floor, and bestowed hugs and kisses on just about everyone in the pub.

At ten o'clock she finally blew out the candles on her birthday cake, and everyone sang 'Happy Birthday' to her.

'Make a wish!' Clemmie urged her excitedly, but Dolly insisted she couldn't think of anything to wish for.

'I've got everything I want and more,' she told her niece, in a slightly slurry voice. 'Can't ask for anything else.'

'But it's your birthday!' Jennifer protested. 'You must make a wish! It's the law.'

Dolly gave an exaggerated sigh. 'All right then. I wish that this cake is as good as it looks, cos if it's not I'll be coming for you, Daisy Jackson!'

Everyone laughed, including Daisy, who was watching the scene from beside the buffet table. She'd made Dolly a rasp-berry ripple cake—officially at Clemmie's request, but everyone knew it was Dolly's orders. She was confident Dolly would love it and had no fear that her wish wouldn't come true.

She smiled as a slightly tipsy Bethany wandered over and draped her arm around Daisy's shoulders. 'Bit of a waste of a wish, don't you think? That cake's guaranteed to be gorgeous.'

'Ah well, Dolly's very lucky,' Daisy said. 'Fancy being in the position where you've nothing left to wish for.'

'And what,' Bethany asked, eyeing her seriously, 'would *you* wish for?'

Daisy shrugged. 'No idea. A lottery win, maybe?' She laughed awkwardly.

'Hmm, so maybe you're as lucky as Dolly then.'

'Maybe I am.'

They were quiet for a moment, watching with some amusement as Dolly attempted to cut her cake into even slices, refusing all offers of help from Clemmie.

'Noah's looking good tonight, don't you think?' Bethany said thoughtfully. 'I'm so used to seeing him around town in his smart suit and tie, it's nice to see him wearing something a bit less formal.'

Daisy smiled. 'I'm just glad to see him here at all. I didn't think he'd get here.'

'Clive says he doesn't get out much,' Bethany admitted. 'He says he used to, but he's quietened down a lot over the years. I suppose that's what all the responsibility of being a teacher, then a headmaster does to you. He's quite young to have attained that position, don't you think?'

Daisy hadn't really thought about it. 'I suppose so. He must be good at his job. He strikes me as being someone who'd take their responsibility very seriously and put everything into the role.'

'Yes, I imagine he does.' Bethany took a sip of her wine and eyed Noah, who was sitting with Ross. 'You'd never think they were brothers, would you? They couldn't look more different. I mean, Ross is all broad and hunky and dark, and Noah is...'

When she didn't continue, Daisy gave her a sharp look. 'Noah is what?' she said indignantly.

'Oh, he's very nice, don't get me wrong. Just, he's so unlike his brother. Not so well-built, for a start. And a bit more—well, ordinary looking, I suppose.'

'I don't think he's ordinary looking,' Daisy said immediately. 'He's got lovely eyes. Really blue, with gold flecks in them, and

—' She broke off as she realised how she must sound to Bethany. 'Anyway,' she finished with a shrug, 'he has a really nice smile.'

'He probably has. He just doesn't smile very often, does he?'

'Like you said, he's got a lot of responsibility,' Daisy reminded her.

'No need to sound so defensive,' Bethany said. 'I wasn't attacking him. He's a nice-looking man in his own way. And I'm sure he's a nice person. You clearly seem to think so anyway.'

'What do you mean by that?' Daisy asked suspiciously.

'Nothing. Nothing at all.' Bethany swilled what remained of her wine around the glass, as if considering her next words. 'It's just... I wondered if you and Noah had struck up some kind of special friendship lately, that's all.'

Daisy's face burned. 'Special friendship? What does that even mean? What are you implying?' She glanced around, hoping no one was nearby who might have overheard Bethany's insinuations and got the wrong idea.

'Oh, Daisy, you must think I'm daft.' Bethany sighed. 'Okay, I'll come clean. I've been watching you this evening and if I didn't already have my suspicions about you two I certainly have now. What's really going on between you?'

Daisy was genuinely appalled. 'Nothing's going on! He's a married man.'

'Yes, but wasn't—' As Daisy's eyes narrowed, Bethany's expression changed to one of horrified embarrassment. 'I—I mean...'

'You were going to say, wasn't Eliot married, weren't you?' Daisy asked flatly.

Bethany's cheeks were pink. 'I'm so sorry. Look, I'm not criticising you, honestly. I care about you, Daisy, and I'd hate to see you get hurt again.'

'Noah's with Isobel and that's fine by me,' Daisy managed. 'He and I are just friends, that's all. Not even that, really. I barely know him.'

'That's partly my worry,' Bethany confessed. 'I've seen the way you look at him. I've noticed it the last few weeks to be honest, when I've been in the café, and he's come in. Your face lights up, it really does. It's okay, Daisy, I haven't told anyone, and I wouldn't.'

'It's not what you think,' Daisy protested. 'I just—I feel sorry for him if you must know. There's something so sad and wistful about him. I can't explain it.'

'Sad?' Bethany frowned. 'I don't know about sad, but what does worry me is what's going on behind the door at Peony Cottage. After what Isobel said about him controlling her, and then the incident with her broken fingers... Now it seems like he's flirting with you and—'

'Flirting with me?' Daisy gasped. 'Are you joking? Noah wouldn't know how to flirt. He's the most polite, respectful person I've ever met. It's not like that. *He's* not like that.'

Bethany shrugged. 'Okay, okay, if you say so. But I know how these things start, and I'm telling you, there's a spark there. I doubt anyone else has noticed but I've been watching you both and I've seen it for myself. I just wanted to warn you, that's all. Please be careful, Daisy. We really don't know what he's like as a husband, do we?'

'A saint, I should think,' Daisy said grimly. 'He'd have to be to put up with Isobel.'

Bethany considered the matter. 'I hear what you're saying,' she said at last. 'Isobel's a pain in the neck, it's true. But we don't know why she behaves in that way. What's making her so unhappy that she feels the need to lash out at everyone?' She gave Daisy a troubled look. 'I'd just hate for him to...'

'Hate for him to what?' Daisy drained her vodka and Coke. 'You really think he's capable of hurting her, don't you?'

'Don't you?'

They both stared over at Noah again. He was deep in conversation with Ross. Ross said something to his brother and

Noah laughed. It was so unexpected and so rare to see him laughing that Daisy's heart leapt.

'I'm sorry, Daisy, but if you think you're not interested in him in that way you're fooling yourself,' Bethany said quietly. 'You should have seen your face just now. It's obvious how much you like him.'

'He's a nice man,' Daisy said defensively. 'But I'm not looking to start anything with him, or anyone else. For one thing, he's married, and I've learnt my lesson there. For another, I'm finally in a good place. I'm living life on my terms and pleasing only myself. I don't want to throw that away, especially when it's taken me so long to get to this point.'

'So, you'll stay away from him?' Bethany asked hopefully.

'He's a friend,' Daisy said firmly. 'And I see him only as a friend. But I won't avoid him, if that's what you're asking me.' She couldn't explain to Bethany, or to anyone else. If they couldn't see it for themselves what would be the point?

There was something about Noah that made Daisy's heart ache for him. She really wasn't sure what it was, but there was something about him that made her want to protect him from— from what? She didn't know. She only knew that she couldn't believe that he was anything other than the polite, kind man he'd shown himself to be ever since she'd met him.

'You know, there's an old saying that goes something like, "The first time someone shows you who they are, believe them",' Bethany said carefully. 'We don't know what's really going on with Noah and Isobel, but we have enough information to be worried. Promise me you'll remember that, and you'll take it on board. I'm not saying Noah's the bad guy in all this, but I'm saying there are reasons to be concerned. Will you be careful? For me?'

Daisy nodded. 'I promise. And that's a good saying. It's by Maya Angelou, I think. I'll remember it.'

'That's all I ask,' Bethany said. 'I just want you to be happy, Daisy.'

'Then you're in luck,' Daisy assured her, 'because that's exactly what I am, and I have no intention of sabotaging that happiness for anyone.'

Bethany watched her for a moment then nodded. 'I'm glad to hear it. Come on, let's have a dance, shall we?'

They put down their glasses and headed onto the dance floor, where Dolly was leading everyone in the Macarena.

The first time someone shows you who they are, believe them.

Well, Bethany might think that would warn her off but, if anything, it only convinced Daisy more that her belief in Noah was right. He'd shown her what a gentle soul he was, while Isobel had demonstrated repeatedly that she was a nasty piece of work who loved to bully other people.

If anyone was vulnerable in that relationship it was Noah. Daisy would put money on it. He needed a friend, and she was going to be that friend. Nothing more, she told herself hastily. But there was a lot to be said for friendship after all.

SEVEN

Neither Noah nor Daisy had specifically said anything to each other about not meeting up in Tuppenny Bridge, yet somehow they both knew it wouldn't be a good idea. When, as they said goodnight at the party, Noah had casually offered to pick Daisy up on the Sunday morning, he hadn't stated where. But when Daisy equally casually mentioned that she'd be at the bus stop in Larkspur Common at ten o'clock, he'd not seemed surprised and had merely nodded and said he'd see her then.

As Daisy got off the bus and settled herself on a bench in the shelter—thankfully empty at this time of the morning—she had to admit that, if anyone knew about their arrangement it would look bad. No one would buy their just good friends routine. Not when they'd deliberately chosen to meet away from Tuppenny Bridge. The more she thought about it the hotter she felt, even as she repeatedly assured herself that they were doing nothing wrong. She and Noah genuinely were just friends. She wasn't expecting anything else, and she honestly didn't think Noah was the sort of man who'd engage in anything shady.

Even so, it made sense to keep their hiking trips a secret.

She wouldn't want to cause trouble for him with Isobel, and she thought Noah's wife wouldn't take kindly to him spending time with another woman, even though she would surely know her own husband well enough to believe there was nothing going on. Anyway, she didn't want to damage his reputation. People were always so quick to assume the worst. And in a town like Tuppenny Bridge gossip ran riot. It was the last thing either of them needed.

She was half expecting him not to show. Maybe, if she was feeling this uncertain, he was feeling just as unsure. Probably more so, because he was the one who was married, with a lot more to lose than she had, and because she knew how honourable he was.

She didn't ask herself how she knew that. She just did. People could say what they liked but she wasn't buying Isobel's story about him controlling her. It didn't add up.

When the car pulled up and she saw Noah waving to her, she ignored the little flutterings in her stomach and jumped to her feet, dragging her backpack with her.

'Bang on time! I hope you've brought that flask of tea,' she joked, climbing into the passenger seat. 'I think we'll need it today.'

Noah, in a fleecy jumper and jeans, grinned at her. 'Two flasks of tea,' he said. 'I thought I'd make one just for you because you drank nearly all my share last time.' He nodded at the sky. 'Not so hot and sunny today, is it? I hope we don't get rain.'

'Have you brought a waterproof just in case?' she asked.

'I have. I'm prepared this time. I've brought sandwiches and everything,' he assured her.

'You're learning. Come on then, let's get going.'

When they arrived in the pretty market town of East Midham around half an hour later, they weren't surprised to see how busy it was, even though the market wasn't open on Sundays.

First of all, the town itself was stunning; all pretty stone cottages and houses set on a slight incline which led up to the main focus of the place—East Midham Castle. The castle was owned and managed by ECHOES—The Enterprise for Conservation of Historic Old English Sites—and was a popular tourist destination in its own right.

As well as the quaint little shops, the castle, and several popular pubs, the nearby racing stable brought in many curious visitors, eager to catch a glimpse of the racehorses on the gallops. Then there was the stunning countryside all around the town. Pure Yorkshire Dales with its hills and woodland, rivers, and pastureland. And, of course, the walking trails which passed by and through East Midham, attracting thousands of eager hikers every year.

'Why do I come here so rarely?' Noah pondered aloud as they walked from the car park to the crossroads in the main street. 'I'd forgotten how lovely it is here.'

'I think it's easy to take a place for granted when it's on your doorstep,' Daisy admitted. 'It's only when I moved to Leeds that I realised how lucky I'd been to grow up in the Dales, and that was when the pining for home really set in. I can't tell you how relieved I am to be back.'

'I can imagine.'

She saw him looking at her and felt suddenly self-conscious, dressed as she was in an old turquoise sweatshirt and faded blue jeans, her dark hair swept up in a ponytail.

'I just can't picture you living and working in a city,' he admitted. 'You're a country girl through and through, and I can see how much you love it here.'

'Are you calling me a yokel, Mr Lavender?' she joked.

'No! God, no, I didn't mean...'

Clearly noticing the amusement in her eyes, he sighed. 'You're winding me up again, aren't you?'

'Told you you'd be easy,' she reminded him, nudging him.

He gave her a wry grin, a faint blush on his cheeks. 'So which route are we following then?'

'It's a circular route,' she explained. 'Not that long, but it will take us out into the fields, through the woods, and bring us back to East Midham, but at the north of the town. We'll end up a bit further up this street and we can pop into the castle for a look around before we head back down here to the car park.'

'Sounds good to me,' he said.

She looked up at the sky. 'Keep your fingers crossed that the rain holds off. Some of the paths will get very muddy if it doesn't and I haven't brought my wellies.' She grinned at him, and he thought that, even if it poured down, it would still be a fun day. Nothing could dampen the delight of being out in such an amazing place with such good company.

'Right then. Let's go.'

They headed right, away from the main street, and soon found themselves out in the countryside, with only the odd stone cottage to break up the views of open fields and distant hills.

As they walked, they chatted about Dolly's party, laughing again at her fake surprise, and wondering what extravaganza she'd plan for her sixtieth. Noah told her about his great aunt's eightieth birthday last year, which she'd only managed to keep quiet after bribing Rita and Birdie Pennyfeather with their own private party.

'She said she didn't want the whole town knowing she was turning eighty,' he explained, holding open a gate for Daisy to walk through. 'She reckoned if people got wind of it, they'd want to put her out to grass, and she's no intention of giving up her place on the parish council, let alone loosening her grip on anything else. But she knew the Pennyfeather sisters were dying for a party, so she promised them that if they kept their mouths shut, they could throw a party for her at Lavender House. She even let them have full reign over decorations and food.' He laughed. 'You can imagine what happened with that! Her living room looked like a rainbow had exploded. She was horrified!'

Daisy chuckled at the thought of it. 'Was anyone else invited?'

'Absolutely no one was there except Aunt Eugenie, Rita, Birdie, me and Ross. Even Kat wasn't told about it, and of course, it was before Ross got back together with Clemmie.'

There was one glaring admission there but neither he nor Daisy referred to it. Whatever reason Isobel had given for not attending he clearly didn't want to explain, and Daisy wouldn't ask.

'Well, however it looked I'm sure it tasted okay,' she said. 'I've heard the Pennyfeathers are pretty good at baking.'

'It wasn't too bad,' he acknowledged. 'Trouble was, they used food colouring in everything. Even the sponge cake was blue, which was a bit off-putting. Reminded me of eating mould. If you could get past that, though, it was okay. You just had to eat with your eyes closed.'

The broad grin on his face warmed her heart. It was good to see him looking relaxed for a change.

According to the website, the East Midham Circular Walk was supposed to take around three hours at a steady pace. They'd decided to stop for lunch after an hour and a half, but in the end, it was two and a half hours before they took a break, having enjoyed the scenery on the route, and being so busy chatting that they'd lost track of time. It was after one o'clock, therefore, before they stopped, deciding that the views from the hill were so stunning it would make sense to linger for a while.

Daisy had to acknowledge that Noah had thought of everything when he pulled a picnic rug from his backpack and spread it on the ground.

'Oh, wow. Look at you! How far you've come,' she said, impressed.

'I know! And I made all my own sandwiches too.' His eyes twinkled as he unpacked a plastic lunchbox and held it up in the air. 'Chicken salad, and ham and tomato,' he announced. 'I called at Maister's yesterday for supplies. I have crisps, too, if you fancy some.'

'I do,' she admitted. 'I can never say no to crisps. I've got ham and tomato sandwiches, too. Great minds, eh? And I've brought some slices of quiche Lorraine, and also something special—but I'll keep that a secret for now.'

'Not, by any chance, the fabled white chocolate and caramel cake?'

She widened her eyes in mock surprise. 'How on earth did you guess?'

'Daisy, you're a star,' he told her, laughing.

'I aim to please.' She bowed then sank down onto the picnic rug beside him. 'Oh, wow, Noah. Just look at that view.'

'It is incredible,' he admitted, as they gazed down upon the lush, green fields, the River Skimmer sparkling below them and, in the distance, the turrets of East Midham Castle, surrounded by the rooftops of the cottages and shops that had sprung up around it over the centuries.

'We're so lucky,' she said, meaning it. The short time she'd spent living in an urban semi-detached house, walking through city streets every day, had ensured that she'd never again take living in the Yorkshire Dales for granted. She'd had enough of concrete pavements, and skylines broken by blocks of flats, industrial chimneys, and huge, ugly factories and warehouses to last a lifetime.

'We are,' he said abruptly and bit into a sandwich. She saw the clouds pass over the sun and shivered.

'So, what was it like?' she asked, deciding to return to lighter subjects. 'Growing up at Lavender House, I mean. You must have had a field day, running around in such a big place. Were there any secret passages or anything else exciting?' She chewed her ham and tomato sandwich, watching him thoughtfully.

He hesitated a moment then said, 'It was all right.'

'All right? Is that it?' she teased.

'Well, it was a museum, remember,' he said. 'We knew perfectly well that most of the rooms were off limits, and at night they were all locked up and secured. There are security guards and alarm systems all over the place. Don't forget, we have some original paintings by Josiah Lavender in there. The insurance is sky high, so there's no way two kids were going to be allowed free run of the place.'

'Oh, yeah. I'd forgotten about that. Not such a fun place then,' Daisy agreed.

'But the bits we were allowed into were okay,' he said. 'And the grounds were great. We had loads of fun in the gardens, especially with the maze. Even so... It probably wasn't as much fun as you'd expect it to be. Luckily, we both made friends nearby and had a better time wandering around Tuppenny Bridge with them. We spent a lot of time at Monk's Folly— that's the name of the house where the art academy is now. Ross was friends with Ben Callaghan, and I—I hung out with his older brother, Leon, and with Jonah.'

'I heard about Leon Callaghan,' she confessed. 'Kat says there's going to be a memorial service at All Hallows for him in October. I'm so sorry about what happened to him.'

'Yes, well.' He gazed down into the valley below and shrugged. 'It was a long time ago.'

Daisy had also heard that Kat and Isobel hung out with the three boys, but clearly Noah hadn't wanted to mention that, so she said nothing.

'What was Miss Lavender like when you were little?' she asked, hoping it was enough of a change of subject.

She was relieved when the smile returned to his face, and

he glanced over at her. 'Probably nowhere near as bad as you're imagining,' he said. 'Yes, she could be strict, but she needed to be. Ross and I were a bit rowdy at times. After all, we were young and she was—well, not to put too fine a point on it—she was middle aged and set in her ways even then. She got landed with us after all. She'd never expected to be raising two children at her age, so I think she did amazingly well.'

'But she wanted to?' Daisy asked curiously. 'I mean, it was her choice to raise you?'

'I think so,' he said, sounding unsure. 'I don't honestly think our parents left her much choice. My mother skipped off to the US when I was very young, and Dad got stuck with me. He wasn't interested, even less so when he married again, and then Ross came along. My stepmother didn't want me either. I didn't take it personally. She didn't particularly want Ross, her own child. They were so absorbed in their mind games with each other they didn't have time to bother with children. Aunt Eugenie stepped in and saved us really. She offered to take us on, and they practically bit her hand off. We've rarely seen them since. I haven't seen my mother since I was a teenager, and Ross has only seen his mum a couple of times in the last few years. As for Dad—Lord knows what he's up to now. He's so irrelevant to our lives I don't think either of us cares.'

'That's such a shame,' Daisy said, so wrapped up in his story that she'd quite forgotten to finish her sandwich and was holding it aloft, half-eaten.

'Worse things have happened to other people,' he said casually. 'What about you? I know your dad passed away, but what about your mum?'

'Oh, she died years ago,' Daisy said. It didn't hurt to say that anymore. Far too much time had passed, and her mum was just a vaguely pleasant memory from long, long ago. 'I barely remember her,' she admitted.

'I'm so sorry,' he told her, but she merely shrugged.

'Have some quiche?' she offered.

They continued eating in silence for a while, watching the sheep on the hillside and the occasional birds swooping over the landscape.

'What was it like for you?' he asked at last. 'Growing up on a farm.'

Daisy hardly registered the question. 'Shall we get on?' she asked, casting a worried look at the sky. 'It's definitely darkening, and I've an awful feeling the rain isn't going to—' She broke off as a few spots of rain landed on her arm. 'Uh-oh. Told you.'

'We'd better pack up,' he agreed.

They scrambled to their feet, hastily putting what remained of the food and drink in their backpacks and dragging out their waterproof jackets. Noah rolled up the picnic rug and stuffed it away as Daisy zipped up her jacket.

Trying to ignore the heavy clouds and drops of rain they followed the path down the hill and along the valley, crossing the footbridge over the Skimmer and heading back towards East Midham.

'Oh, heck,' Daisy said, grimacing as the rain began to fall heavier. She pulled up her hood and glanced at Noah. 'We'd better pick up the pace.'

By the time they reached the north end of the main street they were drenched and abandoned all thoughts of exploring the castle ruins. Instead, they ran into The Castle Keep, a pub just a few minutes' walk from the heritage site.

It was heaving. Clearly, quite a few people had taken shelter in there, too. Daisy looked around and spotted a table in the corner of the bar that hadn't yet been cleared but seemed to be empty. She gestured to Noah and picked her way between the occupied tables, reaching it just as a rumble of thunder sounded overhead.

'Phew, just in time,' Noah said, dropping his backpack and shoving it under the table.

There were two empty beer glasses and a puddle of beer on the table, as well as a soaked beer mat.

Daisy unzipped her wet jacket and hung it over a spare chair.

'I'll get us a drink,' Noah said, 'and I'll ask for a cloth while I'm there. What would you like to drink?'

'Just a Coke will do fine,' she said. 'Thank you.'

He headed to the bar and Daisy glanced out of the window, noting that the street was almost empty of people now. The sky was dark and threatening, and even as she watched a flash of lightning momentarily brightened the sky.

Noah, she noticed, was standing at the bar, chatting to the barmaid. A moment later she handed him a cloth and said something else to him before he made his way back to the table.

'She's going to bring our drinks over to us,' he announced, carefully mopping up the beer puddle and wringing the cloth over one of the empty glasses. He wiped up the stains on the table and wrung the cloth again before putting it to one side.

Pulling a face, he rubbed his hands on his jeans and sighed.

'You just missed the lightning,' Daisy told him.

'Really? Good job we made it in here then. What a shame. It's not like the weather we had on our last walk, is it?'

'I still enjoyed it though,' she told him.

'Me, too,' he said. 'And there's always next time.'

Next time? Daisy's stomach did a somersault, and she bit her lip. What the hell was wrong with her? But he'd said it so casually, as if it was a given.

What *was* this anyway? Were they hiking buddies? Friends who happened to like walking? They'd gone from exchanging pleasantries in her café to... This. Whatever *this* was.

The barmaid came over with their drinks. Hands suddenly ridiculously trembly, Daisy managed to pass the empty beer glasses, complete with cloth, to her in exchange.

Unexpectedly feeling self-conscious in Noah's presence,

she took a gulp of Coke just as he said, 'So, what were you going to say?'

She swallowed hastily and stared at him. 'About what?'

He grinned. 'Well, to be fair it was a conversation we started ages ago. I asked you what it was like for you growing up on a farm, and you were about to tell me.'

She narrowed her eyes. 'Was I? Are you sure?'

'Oh, you don't get out of it that easily,' he said. 'I told you about growing up at Lavender House, so fair's fair. Where was the farm again? Somewhere near Camacker, right?'

'Just outside Beckthwaite,' she said heavily. 'Crowscar Farm. It was hard work, if you must know. Tom and I were out helping with the sheep from a very young age, and I remember having to help Mum clean the house, too. After she died, I was expected to take over looking after Dad and Tom, which I did. I still had to help out on the farm, though, and we were out in all weathers. It didn't leave much time for making friends or having fun.'

'I'm sorry,' he said quietly. 'Sounds like you had it much worse than I did.'

'It's not a competition,' she said lightly. She sipped her drink, remembering. 'I think it would have been fun if Dad had been different, but he was a miserable old bugger. I don't think I ever saw him smile.'

'Isn't that typical of Yorkshire farmers?' Noah said, amused. 'It's the stereotype, isn't it? The dour Yorkshireman who barely grunts at people.'

Daisy didn't smile back. Her thoughts were wandering to darker times, back to the misery of those early years at Crowscar.

'Are you all right?' Noah sounded anxious. 'I-I didn't mean to make light of things. I can see you have some unhappy memories.'

'Dad wasn't easy to live with,' she said shortly. 'And after

Tom left it was just me and him, day in, day out. I took on another job, working in a local pub. I didn't really have the time or energy, but I needed a life away from the farm. I needed to see and talk to other people and earn some money for myself.'

'Your dad didn't pay you?' he asked, shocked.

She looked at him through narrowed eyes. 'You're joking. Bed and board, he said, and that's pretty much what I got. I had a monthly allowance for "women's things" and my clothes got replaced as they wore out, but that's about it.'

'That's terrible,' he said, horrified. 'Where was your brother in all this?'

'Like I said, he skipped off to Leeds the minute he could. Got himself a job and started a new life. He hated the farm, and he never got on with Dad, so I don't blame him.'

'He just left you, though!' Noah's eyes flashed with anger. 'How could he do that?'

'You sound like Eliot,' she said with a sigh.

'Who's Eliot?'

Why on earth had she mentioned him?

'Another farmer who lived nearby. He was Tom's best friend when they were at school. I—I used to help him out with his kids and the house after his wife died.'

'On top of your work at the farm and working in a pub?' Noah shook his head. 'You were a saint.'

'I was far from that!' Daisy was quick to deny it. 'Anyway, it was a long time ago now. Dad's gone and so has Crowscar. Tom's happily settled in Leeds with a good job, a house, and a girlfriend. And I'm...'

'A successful businesswoman,' he said firmly, 'and a cracking baker.'

She laughed. 'Yeah, I'll take that.'

They clinked glasses together and she said, 'Parents, eh? Sounds like you and I had pretty dismal ones.'

'Very much so,' he agreed. 'Though I was lucky. I had Aunt

Eugenie who stepped in and took care of me. Even so,' he added wistfully, 'it never really leaves me. That sense of being abandoned, unwanted.' He was silent for a minute, then shook his head. 'Wow, this conversation has turned as gloomy as the weather, hasn't it?'

She glanced out of the window. 'Rain's stopped,' she said hopefully. 'And look, the clouds are rolling away.'

'So they are. Maybe the day will brighten up again after all.'

'What time is it?' she asked.

'Half past two.' He hesitated. 'Are you in a hurry to get home?'

She lowered her glass, wondering why he was asking. 'Not at all. Are you?'

'Hardly. I was just thinking, how about we finish our drinks then explore the castle? And after we've done that, I'll buy you dinner at The Farmer's Arms in West Colby. It's got a great reputation for food.'

'That would be lovely,' she said slowly, 'but what if...'

'What if?'

'Well.' Daisy felt stupid. He would think she was making assumptions, reading things into this that just weren't there. 'Thing is, Bethany and Clive went there last week because Bluebell recommended it to them. It seems to be very popular with some of the people we know. And don't Dolly and Clemmie live in West Colby?'

She could feel her face burning as she waited for his response.

She waited for him to laugh and say, 'So what? We're only having a meal, not a torrid affair!'

He didn't, though. He considered what she'd said, his fingers curled tightly around his glass of Coke as he stared at the table. Finally, he nodded. 'I see what you mean. Some people in Tuppenny Bridge have never let the truth get in the way of a good story, and if the Pennyfeathers get hold of this—well, you can imagine.'

She could, all too clearly, and it made her shudder.

'It was a nice idea, though,' she said quietly.

'It was.' He smiled at her then said, 'But look, just because The Farmer's Arms is a bad idea it doesn't mean we can't do the rest of it.'

'The castle?'

'Yes, the castle, but also having dinner somewhere! Why not? We've got to eat, haven't we? And you'll only be going home to your flat, and I'll only be going home to an empty house, so we might as well have our meal together. There are lots of pubs in this town.' He glanced around, wrinkling his nose a little. 'Not this one, but we can find another. One that does good food and looks a bit less rustic.'

She laughed. 'I know what you mean.'

'So?' He eyed her hopefully. 'You don't have to. If you'd rather go home, I'll take you. No problem.'

She thought about the gossip that would flood the town if this got out. It would be so embarrassing if people got the wrong end of the stick and started talking about her and Noah as if they were having an affair. And Noah had so much to lose. What would Isobel say if she heard?

'It's up to you,' she told him. 'You're the one taking the risk after all.'

Noah's eyes widened. 'Taking... Oh. Well.' He shook his head. 'We're just two friends having a meal after a day out. But you're right, it makes more sense to stay round here than risk being seen at The Farmer's Arms. It's just—well, if Isobel heard we were out together she m-might...'

His voice trailed off and Daisy said quietly, 'Get the wrong idea. It's okay, Noah. Let's forget it, shall we?'

'No. Let's not. We'll be fine up here, and I can drop you at the bus stop in Larkspur Common on the way home, if that's all right with you? I'll wait with you until the bus comes to make sure you're okay, obviously. But it's up to you. No pressure, whatever you decide.'

Daisy couldn't help but laugh. 'We're a right pair, aren't we? Okay, decision made. We'll visit the castle, eat dinner at a pub round here, then you can drop me at Larkspur Common. Deal?'

Noah's eyes twinkled. 'Deal.'

They clinked glasses again, his gaze meeting hers and holding.

Daisy looked away first.

Just friends. That was all they would ever be, and she mustn't get the wrong idea. The last thing she wanted was a repeat of what had happened with Eliot, when she'd let her imagination run riot and ruined their friendship forever.

She'd hate to lose Noah's friendship, too.

Because, the odd thing was, something was telling her that he really needed this friendship—probably even more than she did.

EIGHT

'Just make yourself nice and comfortable, love. There you go. Let's tuck that towel in properly. We don't want your neck to get a good soaking, do we?'

As Daisy shuffled low in her chair with her head tilted back over the sink, Bluebell adjusted the towel around Daisy's shoulders then picked up the shower attachment which had been spouting water into the basin, once Bluebell had got it to the right temperature.

'I'll say one thing for your luscious locks,' she said cheerily, as she worked the water through Daisy's hair, 'they grow bloody quick! Nice and thick an' all.'

'Tell me about it,' Daisy said. 'Needs trimming every four to six weeks or I can't manage it at all. Luckily my landlady also happens to be the best hairdresser in Tuppenny Bridge.'

Buttercup, Bluebell's eldest daughter, stopped sweeping the floor and called out, 'Oy! What about me?'

'You're the apprentice, I'm the master,' Bluebell said, laughing. 'You've a long way to go before you reach my standard, love. Are you *still* sweeping up? Put the kettle on and make us all a cuppa, eh?'

'Aw, Mam! Can't our Clover do it?'

'You know she's busy in the back room doing Mrs Palmer's nails,' Bluebell said, massaging shampoo into Daisy's hair. 'Go on, hurry up before you-know-who gets here.'

Daisy couldn't see Bluebell's face, but she could have sworn, by the tone of her voice, that she'd just rolled her eyes.

Buttercup tutted loudly but went into the kitchen.

'Who's you-know-who?' Daisy asked, curious.

'Would you believe Isobel Lavender?' As Daisy made a gasping noise Bluebell said, 'I know! Fancy Lady Muck deigning to visit my humble salon. Apparently, she couldn't get an appointment with her usual nail technician and it's an emergency. All that sunshine and hard work dossing by the pool have played havoc with her manicure, so she needs Clover to repair the damage. Thought Mrs Palmer would be done by now but if Clover doesn't hurry up Isobel will have to sit in here and wait, and I'm buggered if I'm making small talk with her. Can't be arsed, so it will have to be Buttercup's job.'

Daisy groaned inwardly. Of all the people!

Usually, she loved having her hair washed at the salon. Bluebell was so good at it that she almost fell asleep as first shampoo, then conditioner, was massaged into her hair. Now, though, she felt jumpy and tense.

'Tea or coffee, Daisy?' Buttercup called from the kitchen door.

'Oh, not for me,' Daisy said hurriedly. 'I won't be here long.'

Bluebell rinsed out the last of the conditioner and wrapped the towel around Daisy's head, gently patting her hair dry.

'Don't be daft. Cut and blow dry you're booked in for,' she reminded her. 'She likes coffee, love,' she called to Buttercup. 'Milk, one sugar.'

The doorbell jangled and Daisy's heart skipped. She pushed the towel up and peered over at the door, her spirits sinking when she saw Isobel standing there, looking around her with an expression that revealed she was less than impressed with the decor in Cutting it Fine.

'Oh, you're bang on time,' Bluebell said. 'How smashing to see you, love. You're looking well. Glowing in fact.'

Daisy thought Bluebell either deserved an Oscar for her performance, or she was the biggest hypocrite in Tuppenny Bridge.

'Move over to the other chair, Daisy,' Bluebell said. 'Clover will be with you in a minute, love,' she added to Isobel. 'Would you like a cuppa while you're waiting?'

'No thank you,' Isobel said. She stared at Daisy, who felt as if her face was on fire. 'Daisy.'

'Isobel.'

Buttercup brought two mugs of coffee through. 'Oh, hiya, Mrs Lavender. Would you like a coffee or a tea?'

'No, thanks.' Isobel gave her a polite smile. 'Will Clover be long?'

'No, she's just finishing Mrs Palmer's acrylics as we speak, so sit yourself down and she'll be with you in a minute.'

Isobel slipped her shoulder bag off and removed her jacket, then looked pointedly around.

'Just hang it on the coat stand,' Bluebell said, nodding towards the corner of the room where said item stood in full view. She rolled her eyes in the mirror at Daisy, who bit her lip. Isobel must have seen the stand, after all. You could hardly miss it. If Bluebell and Buttercup hadn't been busy, they'd have taken the jacket from her, but as they were, surely it wouldn't hurt Isobel to hang up her own jacket for once?

Isobel carried out the task, her mouth set in a tight line as if it was all too much trouble, then sat in one of the seats facing Daisy, her arms folded defensively.

She looked, Daisy thought, as if the holiday hadn't done her much good at all. She certainly wasn't any happier, judging by her expression, although she had a lovely tan.

'Did you have a nice time in Portugal then?' Bluebell asked politely, combing gently through Daisy's hair.

'I had a lovely time, thank you,' Isobel said stiffly. 'The Algarve is such a stunning area. Have you been there, Bluebell?'

'Can't say I have,' Bluebell admitted. 'You were at your dad's place, weren't you?'

'Yes. He's bought a house there. Five bedrooms, three bathrooms, extensive grounds.' Daisy's eyes met Bluebell's in the mirror as Isobel added, 'And a pool, naturally.'

'Naturally.' Bluebell shook her head. 'Aw, it's a shame poor Noah couldn't go with you, what with him being off work and everything.'

Daisy's heart thudded, her face growing hot at the mention of Noah. She wished Bluebell hadn't brought him up. She glanced at her reflection in the mirror, wondering if the guilt was visible on her face and considering whether she should just tell Bluebell she'd remembered she'd left the oven on in her flat upstairs and needed to go—wet hair or no wet hair.

'It was family time,' Isobel said with a condescending smile. 'I haven't seen my father for a while, and my grandmother was with me. We needed some time to be with each other.'

'Don't your lot get on with Noah then?' Bluebell asked, clearly genuinely curious. 'I can't imagine why not. He's a lovely bloke.'

Isobel glanced up as Buttercup hurried to her side.

'Clover's sorry to keep you waiting,' Buttercup said. 'Are you sure you wouldn't like a tea or coffee, Mrs Lavender?'

'I suppose a coffee would be all right,' Isobel said reluctantly. 'Black, no sugar.'

'A please wouldn't go amiss,' Bluebell murmured under her breath.

Buttercup nodded. 'Coming right up.'

'Right, Daisy, how much are we taking off?' Bluebell had

finished combing through Daisy's hair and was now looking enquiringly at her, scissors in hand.

'Maybe half an inch? It's my fringe that needs trimming the most,' Daisy said, pulling her fringe over her eyes to show how long it had grown.

Isobel laughed. 'You look like the old horse that used to pull the rag and bone cart through the town. Do you remember, Bluebell? Big, hairy lump with a shaggy fringe that covered its eyes.'

Bluebell's mouth fell open and Daisy took a steadying breath.

It's nothing personal. It's just the tactless way Isobel speaks to everyone. Stop panicking. She doesn't know.

Bloody hell, imagine if she did! Daisy could just picture the barbed insults that would wing their way to her if Isobel knew Daisy had been out hiking with her husband four times in recent weeks. Not to mention a visit to East Midham Castle, a meal in a pub, and a recent trip to the theatre in Kirkby Skimmer, where they'd enjoyed a touring production of *An Inspector Calls*. They'd seen a poster advertising it on a village noticeboard and, upon learning that it was one of Daisy's favourite films, Noah had booked tickets, admitting he hadn't seen a performance since he'd studied the text for A level.

'Yes, well, that's why I'm here for a trim,' she managed.

Bluebell's eyes flashed her indignation on Daisy's behalf, but Isobel was clearly oblivious.

Buttercup hurried back and handed Isobel a cup and saucer, with a biscuit to go with the coffee. Isobel pulled a face.

'I don't want this,' she announced, holding up the wrapped biscuit. 'I've eaten far too much in Portugal and I need to look after my figure.'

As they all stared at her she added, 'Noah likes me to stay trim.'

Daisy bristled with annoyance. Was anyone seriously buying this "poor Isobel" rubbish?

'Aw, never mind. I'll take it back. Did you have a good holiday then?' Buttercup asked politely, collecting the biscuit from Isobel.

'Yes. As I've already explained to your mother,' Isobel said with exaggerated patience, 'I've had a lovely time. It's just a shame it was only for two weeks. I would have loved to stay longer.'

'So why didn't you?' Bluebell asked bluntly.

'My father had business to attend to,' Isobel said coldly. 'He's as active as ever and couldn't take any more time off work. Really, how much longer is Clover going to be?'

'Surely you and your gran could have stayed there, though,' Buttercup suggested, ignoring Isobel's question. 'Maybe your husband could have flown out to join you. Keep you company.'

Isobel shrugged. 'Noah and I are going away in October anyway. Half term.'

Noah hadn't mentioned that! Daisy felt her stomach plummet with disappointment and chided herself immediately. Why should he? It was nothing to do with her!

'Ooh, where are you going?' Buttercup asked.

'Not sure. We've not booked yet. It was Noah's idea so I daresay he'll make the decision,' Isobel said. 'He usually does.'

Daisy's eyes narrowed. For goodness' sake!

'Aw, well, it will do him good to get away,' Bluebell said, snipping Daisy's hair. 'I expect he's missed you while he's been away.' She paused just long enough before adding, 'Mind you, he had a whale of a time at Dolly's birthday party.'

Isobel's head jerked up, causing her coffee to slosh into her saucer.

'Dolly's birthday party?'

Daisy didn't miss the sharpness in Isobel's tone, and she

tried her best to flash Bluebell a warning look. Bluebell, however, either didn't see it or chose to ignore it.

'That's right. Had a great time, didn't he, Daisy? It was good to see him letting his hair down for a change, and of course, his auntie and Ross were there, and Jonah, too, so he had plenty of company. You were sat with him for a bit as well, weren't you, Daisy?'

Daisy nearly choked. 'I was sitting with Bethany and Clive,' she said quickly, 'but we were on the same table for a while, yes.'

'I see.' Isobel's jaw twitched.

'Didn't you know he went?' Bluebell asked innocently, raising her eyebrows slightly. 'I'd have thought he'd have mentioned it. Sorry.'

'He didn't,' Isobel said tightly. 'But it hardly matters. I went to all sorts of events in the Algarve, and I didn't mention most of them to him because, why would I?'

'Mm. Exactly. Anyway, I'm sure he'll get round to mentioning it one day,' Bluebell said. She moved round the other side of Daisy so neither of them could see the expression on Isobel's face, but Daisy could imagine it. She felt a creeping nausea and realised her heart was thumping with anxiety.

The salon fell silent as Bluebell worked, and it felt like an eternity before Clover finally came through, accompanied by a beaming Mrs Palmer. 'Sorry to keep you waiting, Mrs Lavender. I'll just take payment then I'll take you through to the back room.'

'Oh,' Isobel said, evidently surprised. 'You take card payments?'

Mrs Palmer gave a hearty laugh as she tucked her debit card back in her purse. 'Of course they do! Doesn't everyone these days? Good job, an' all, cos I don't even carry cash any more. I'm like the Queen, God rest her soul. Thanks, Clover, love. You've done a smashing job with my nails.'

'You're welcome.' Clover gave Isobel a dubious look. 'Er, would you like to come through?'

Isobel placed her cup and saucer on the floor and jumped to her feet. 'Actually,' she said, 'since you took so long, I won't have time for a manicure now. I suppose I'll have to wait for my regular manicurist. Thanks for the coffee.' She nodded at her practically untouched drink, snatched her jacket and bag from the coat hook and followed Mrs Palmer out of the salon with barely a goodbye nod to them.

'Bloody cheek!' Clover said immediately. 'Did you hear that? *Oh, you take card payments?* Where does she think we are —stone age Britain? Stuck up mare. And that means I've rushed Mrs Palmer for nothing. Now I've got ages to wait for my next client.'

'Good,' Buttercup said. 'You can put them towels on to wash for me, since I've just made all the coffees.'

'Did you see Isobel's face when I mentioned Noah going to Dolly's party?' Bluebell asked gleefully. 'By heck, she didn't like that, did she? Serves her right, especially after that cart horse remark aimed at Daisy. Mind you, I reckon that husband of hers is going to get a good grilling when she gets home.'

'Why did you tell her then?' Daisy asked reproachfully. 'You've really dropped him in it! If he'd wanted her to know he'd have told her by now.'

'Oh, come off it,' Bluebell said dismissively. 'As if you can keep anything quiet round here. If I hadn't mentioned it, someone else would have, believe me. You can't keep secrets in Tuppenny Bridge. Not for long anyway.'

Daisy's hands twisted in her lap. That was what she was afraid of.

NINE

'Now, should I or shouldn't I?' Kat wondered aloud as she gazed at the covered glass cake stands on the counter, where an array of various confections was clearly calling her name. She rubbed her rapidly expanding baby bump, a wistful expression on her face. 'I mean, they do say you should eat for two. But that doesn't literally mean eating double the calories, does it? And I don't think cake is exactly necessary nutrition for a growing baby, but...' She sighed. 'That red velvet cake looks so yummy.'

Sally burst out laughing. 'It's not a major decision, love. If you want some cake have some bloody cake. It's not life or death.' When Kat continued to dither, she said firmly, 'Two slices of that red velvet cake an' all, please, Daisy. There,' she said, glancing at her best friend, 'that's you told. I'm taking control.'

'Fair enough.' Kat shrugged. 'I'm not going to argue with you.'

'Right, so now that's us sorted, you go and take a seat and I'll pay while I wait for our coffees,' Sally said firmly.

'You will not! I'm perfectly capable—'

'I remember when you were having Hattie,' Sally reminded

her. 'Those swollen ankles! I don't want to be responsible for your fluid retention, thanks very much. Go and sit down before... Ooh, look. Isobel's just walked in.'

Daisy, who'd been enjoying the banter between the two women, felt the smile slide from her face immediately. For goodness' sake, couldn't she escape the bloody woman? Now she was home again no doubt she'd be bumping into her occasionally, but this was two days running!

'Look at her in her sunglasses,' Sally murmured. 'I suppose that's to remind us that she's just been on holiday. Mind you, she's got a lovely tan.'

'It will be out of a bottle,' Kat said. 'Isobel's not daft enough to sit out in the sun without protection. Never mind skin cancer, she'll be worrying about wrinkles. Priorities and all that.'

Isobel, Daisy thought with some surprise, seemed very different today. She might be dressed as immaculately as always and have a Hollywood starlet thing going on with her designer sunglasses worn indoors, but she wasn't exactly striding into the café. She appeared quite hunched and nervous, if anything. She approached the counter almost at a shuffle.

It seemed Kat and Sally were thinking the same thing, as Sally said kindly, 'You all right, Isobel?'

Isobel gave them a faint smile. 'Fine, thanks.' She nodded at Daisy. 'These cakes look lovely, Daisy. Very tempting.'

'We're having the red velvet,' Sally told her. 'You should treat yourself, love.'

Isobel hesitated, as if considering it, then shook her head. 'I'd better not. Just a skinny latte to go for me, Daisy, when you're ready. Please.'

Daisy frowned. This humble politeness wasn't like Isobel at all.

'Let me get that,' Sally said, her kind heart clearly getting the better of her as she handed her debit card to Daisy.

'Oh, thank you, Sally. That's very sweet of you,' Isobel said, sounding uncharacteristically grateful.

'Not back at work yet then, Isobel?' Kat asked.

Isobel shook her head. 'I was supposed to be but... Well, anyway, Kelly's gran's offered to stay on for another week.'

'Ooh, nice. You can spend some time with Noah,' Sally said.

Daisy's eyebrows shot up in surprise as Isobel visibly cringed.

'Yeah. Yeah, I guess so,' she said quietly.

What on earth was wrong with her? Had she had a personality transplant or something?

'Are you sure you wouldn't like some cake?' Kat asked. 'You can join us if you like. Take ten minutes for a catch up. We'd love to hear about Portugal, wouldn't we, Sal?'

'Ooh, yes. I've never been to the Algarve, but I might be able to persuade Rafferty that we need a break from the pub.'

Isobel shook her head, her fingers holding her sunglasses in place as if she was afraid the sudden movement would dislodge them.

'I—I'd better not. Maybe another time.'

Daisy handed Sally her debit card back. 'Right, so one cappuccino, one decaf, and one skinny latte,' she said. 'Coming right up.'

As she turned to deal with the coffee machine, she could barely hear what the three women were talking about, but her mind was whirring. Isobel was behaving weirdly, even for her. When she thought about the arrogant, sarcastic woman who'd made such cutting remarks in the salon yesterday and compared her to the woman standing in her café now, they could have been two different people.

'There you go,' she said at last, placing the two cups of coffee on a tray and handing Isobel a takeaway cup holding her skinny latte.

Isobel reached for the coffee and Daisy's eyes widened in shock.

'Thank you, Daisy,' Isobel said quietly. 'And thank you, Sally. I really appreciate this.' She gave them all a weak smile. 'Enjoy your cake,' she said, then turned and headed down the stairs.

Sally's mouth was open, and Kat shook her head. 'Bloody hell. Did you see that?'

'I did,' Sally said grimly. 'And just how do we think she got those then?'

Daisy's heart was racing. 'It's not what you're thinking,' she said defensively.

'And what are we thinking?' Sally asked.

They all stared at each other.

'He wouldn't,' Daisy said. 'He's just not like that.'

'Daisy, did you not see them? Whopping great bruises all round her wrist and up her arm! And that's just what we could see. Who knows what her sleeves are covering?' Sally sounded horrified. 'How else would she have got them?'

'Do you think that's why she was wearing sunglasses indoors?' Kat murmured, her expression grave.

'Oh, my God! Of course! And no wonder she's got Kelly's gran to cover for her for another week. She can hardly serve in the shop with a black eye, can she?' Sally shook her head. 'This is awful. What do we do?'

'Nothing!' Daisy cried. 'I'm sure there's another explanation for all this. Noah—I mean, he just doesn't seem the type, does he?'

'Most of them don't seem the type,' Sally said.

'And just what is the type anyway?' Kat asked sadly. 'They don't exactly wear big signs around their necks, do they? *Warning: violent thug. Keep away.* I wish.'

She clutched Sally's arm. 'Remember when she had her fingers all strapped up last October, Sal?'

'I do,' Sally said nodding. 'I remember thinking at the time there was something fishy about her story, but we were all too preoccupied with supporting Ben and Jennifer, weren't we?' She turned to Daisy. 'It was the anniversary of Leon's death, you see, and we all met up at the Garden of Ashes in the churchyard.'

'What did she say had happened?' Daisy asked, hoping it was a plausible story.

'I can't honestly remember,' Kat admitted. 'But I think maybe she said she'd fallen or something. But I do remember Noah trying to put his arm around her and her moving away from him.'

'Ooh, you're right, love. I remember that, too.' Sally shook her head. 'Should we call the police?'

'For what?' Daisy asked, aghast. 'You can't just accuse Noah of doing something like that. You have no proof.'

'But we have to protect Isobel,' Kat said. 'I mean, she's not my favourite person, and I don't think she's got many friends in this town, but that doesn't mean she deserves this.'

'Daisy's right, though,' Sally said. 'Supposing we call the police and Isobel refuses to give a statement. What might he do to her once the police have gone? We'll have to be careful about this. We need to coax her into admitting what's going on.'

'And how do we do that?' Kat asked. She bit her lip, her eyes troubled. 'I really don't like this. It's horrible. You think you know someone...'

'But that's surely the point?' Daisy asked, feeling increasingly desperate. 'You *do* know Noah! You've known him for years. Can you honestly believe he'd do such a terrible thing?'

'Trouble is, love,' Sally said, 'the most unlikely people do the most awful things. And what goes on behind closed doors— well, it would make your hair curl.'

'I don't want to think it of Noah either,' Kat said gently. 'I always liked him, whereas Isobel's always got on my wick, to be honest. But maybe there's more to the story than we realise. Maybe that's why she's so prickly and downright horrible sometimes. Even sweet little puppies bite if they're wounded or afraid.'

Sally picked up the tray bearing the coffees and the cake. 'Come on, let's go and sit down before your ankles balloon,' she said. 'We'll think of a plan to befriend Isobel. Figure out how we can get her to trust us and confide in us. It's the best we can do for now.'

She smiled at Daisy. 'Thanks for these, love. Hey, don't look so sad. I know it's horrible but we're on the case now. We'll protect Isobel, whether she realises we're doing it or not.'

She and Kat headed over to a table leaving Daisy staring incredulously after them. What was wrong with them? Daisy had only been in this town for a few months, but she already knew Noah wouldn't inflict those injuries on his wife. He just wouldn't.

Yes, the bruises were pretty vivid. And yes, it was odd that Isobel was wearing sunglasses indoors and taking more time off work. And yes, the broken fingers last year were worrying, but...

Icy fingers trailed along Daisy's spine, making her shiver.

If even the people who'd known Noah for years were having doubts, he could be in real trouble. Somehow, someone had to get to the bottom of this before things went very badly wrong.

The hallway in the vicarage was long and rather gloomy, despite the colourful Victorian tiles on the floor, and the white walls.

Noah supposed it was because there was no window in here. He leaned against the old, cast-iron radiator, feeling sick. What was he even doing here? He was wasting his time. Wasting Zach's time. As if a vicar didn't have enough to do.

Ava, he realised, was eyeing him with some concern. 'Are you all right? You've gone terribly pale. Should I fetch you a glass of water?'

'No, honestly, I'm fine. I just—I wondered if Zach was free for a chat. Just for a few minutes.'

Ava smiled, her hazel eyes twinkling. 'Oh, he'll always make time for a chat,' she assured him. 'Follow me.'

She led him to the study door, which she opened without knocking and popped her head around.

'Darling, Noah's here to see you. Can you spare him a few minutes?'

Noah realised he was holding his breath and wondered what he was hoping Zach's response would be. When he heard the vicar cheerfully state that he could indeed, he wasn't sure whether to be glad or sorry.

'Told you,' Ava said with a wink.

She held the door open and ushered him into Zach's study. Zach was sitting at his desk, laptop open in front of him. As Noah entered Zach closed the laptop and gestured to him to sit in one of the two old armchairs that were facing the fireplace.

'Noah!' he said, moving away from the desk. 'This is a pleasant surprise. What can I do for you?'

Zach glanced at Ava who gave a slight shrug, which Noah didn't miss. He felt terrible. He shouldn't have come. Why had he, anyway?

He sat down and rubbed his face, weariness overwhelming him. Ava gave a discreet cough.

'Tea, Noah? Coffee? Or would you like something stronger?'

'Not for me, thank you.' He couldn't stomach it. Not even a drink.

'Perhaps later, love. Thanks.' Zach's broad Yorkshire tones were rich and warm and somehow soothing. They reminded

Noah of Daisy's accent. There was something very comforting about that.

Ava closed the door quietly behind her and Zach sat down in the other armchair.

'You seem troubled, Noah,' he said gently. 'It's not your aunt, is it?'

'Oh no! No, she's fine.' He studied his hands intently. 'I just thought... How are the plans for the sheep fair coming along?'

Zach frowned. 'Is this Eugenie checking up on me?' he asked, his tone gently teasing.

'Not at all! I was just wondering, that's all. I thought—I thought I'd pop in and ask, seeing as I never seem to contribute much to this thing. Do you—I mean, if you need any help...'

'Well.' Zach rubbed his chin thoughtfully. 'I mean, there's always something to do if you really want to be involved, although it strikes me you've got enough on your plate running that school of yours. By the time the fair comes around you'll be up to your eyes in it with the autumn term.'

Noah nodded. 'Hmm. Guess so.'

They were both quiet for a long moment. Noah heard the old-fashioned clock on Zach's mantelpiece ticking loudly.

'Have they decided who the recipient of the Tuppenny Bridge Fund is going to be this year?'

Zach shook his head. 'No, not yet. Why, have you any thoughts?'

Noah's mind blanked. 'Not really,' he admitted sheepishly.

'I see.'

Zach was clearly puzzled, and Noah couldn't blame him. He should leave. Get out of here before he made an even bigger fool of himself. He got to his feet. 'Well, if everything's okay maybe I'll—'

'Please don't go,' Zach urged. 'Look, I'm going to have a coffee and a biscuit. Why don't you join me? I'd love the excuse to take a break from sermon writing for a while.'

Noah hesitated. 'I wouldn't want to impose on you, or Ava.'

'You're definitely not imposing on me. And anyway, I'll make the coffee and fetch the biscuits myself. I'll make Ava one, too, so you'd be doing her a favour, an' all. What about it?'

Noah felt he could hardly refuse, so he nodded.

Zach beamed at him. 'Smashing. I'll be right back.'

As he left the study, Noah leaned back in his chair and closed his eyes, wondering what on earth had made him seek out the vicar of all people. It wasn't as if he was particularly religious.

Even so, there was something reassuring and comforting about Zach. Noah thought that, even if he hadn't been a vicar, he'd have been his friend. He was kind and easy to talk to. And maybe the fact that he *was* a vicar would mean he was even less likely to judge. He didn't want judgement. He just wanted someone to listen while he tried his best to work out this mess in his mind.

Good luck with that.

He wasn't sure how long he waited, nor how many times he nearly got up and left the vicarage, his nerve almost failing him on countless occasions. It was a relief when Zach finally opened the study door, his face set with concentration as he balanced a tray on one arm and manoeuvred a tricky door handle with his free hand.

'Right, that's that done,' he said cheerfully, placing the tray on a round table between the two armchairs. 'I've pinched the packet of KitKats out of the fridge before our Bea gets her mitts on them. That's the trouble when the kids are off school. All the good stuff gets eaten before I even see it.'

He sank into the armchair and smiled. 'Help yourself to milk and sugar, and have as many KitKats as you like. As long as you leave me at least four,' he added, laughing.

He was always such a nice man, Noah thought. Tuppenny Bridge was lucky to have him.

They sat in amiable silence for a while, the only sound the occasional ruffling of KitKat wrappers and the odd slurp of coffee from Zach.

'So,' Zach said at last, 'Isobel's back then. How did she enjoy Portugal?'

It was an innocent question, but to Noah it felt like an interrogation had begun.

'O-okay, I think. Her d-dad seems to love it over there. She's on about going back to see him in October.'

'Oh?' Zach raised an eyebrow. 'Half term, is it? You're going with her next time?'

Noah swallowed. 'No, I don't think so. She doesn't get to see much of him, so she'd prefer to go alone. J-just so she can devote all her attention to him,' he added hastily.

'Right. I get you.' Zach gave him a thoughtful look but said nothing, busying himself with opening yet another KitKat.

'I was wondering...' Noah paused, not sure why he'd blurted that out.

'Aye?' Zach's expression was encouraging, and he replaced the KitKat on the tray as he waited for Noah to finish.

Noah took a steadying breath. 'It's—it's about me. Me and—well, me and Isobel.'

'O-kay.' Zach leaned back in the chair and steepled his forefingers under his chin. 'What about you and Isobel?'

'We've been having—problems.'

'I see.' Zach nodded. 'And how can I help?'

Noah gave a short laugh, finally meeting Zach's gaze. 'Honestly? I don't know that you can. I don't know that anyone can.'

'Why don't you tell me what's brought you here today?' Zach asked. 'There must have been something that made you think you needed to talk to me.'

'I suppose...' Noah shrugged, feeling helpless. 'Do you think everything can be forgiven, Zach?'

Zach's eyebrows shot up in evident surprise. 'Are you asking me as a vicar, or as a friend?'

Noah wasn't entirely sure. 'Both, I suppose. Is there a difference?'

Zach considered. 'Well, I suppose... Jesus teaches that all sins are forgiven if we repent and accept Him as our saviour. That's what's meant by grace, after all. If you turn to the Lord and you're truly sorry for your sins then, yes, they're washed away by the sacrifice Christ made on the cross.' He sighed. 'As a friend, I'd say I know it's not always that easy, and sometimes it's bloody hard to believe that forgiveness is deserved. I struggle, too, when I hear certain things on the news. I think, how can that person possibly be forgiven? But I have to believe in the grace of God, or what's the point?'

'Even—even sins that are against another person? Even if you've *hurt* another person?'

Zach frowned. 'It doesn't matter what the sin is. The same applies. Christ has paid for our sins already. Noah,' he leaned forward, his forehead creased with concern, 'what's all this about?'

Noah shook his head. 'Just—just wondering aloud, that's all.' He glanced around the study, noting the framed photos on the wall of Zach and Ava, Ava on her own, the children, the whole family together. Sparkling eyes. Wide smiles. How happy they looked.

'Do you and Ava ever argue?' he asked, without thinking. Realising what he'd said his face burned with embarrassment. 'Sorry. None of my business. Ignore me.'

Zach smiled. 'Of course we argue,' he said. 'We're human beings, with very different upbringings, and all the stresses that come with modern life. Not to mention two teenage children who drive us nuts at times. Heck, there'd be summat up with us if we didn't argue.' He shook his head. 'There's nothing wrong with arguing in a healthy marriage, Noah. I'm guessing you and Isobel are experiencing difficulties at the moment?'

'You could say that.'

'Has this been going on long?'

Noah sighed. 'Yes.'

'Right. And can you pinpoint where it all started to go wrong?'

He felt his stomach tighten with dread. *So long ago. The first time I let anger win. It's just got worse and worse since that moment, and I don't know how to fix it. God knows, I've tried to put things right, but I just can't...*

'Not really,' he said. 'You know what it's like. These things escalate without you even noticing at first. Then one day you look around you and you realise there's no joy left. Only misery and guilt.'

'Guilt?' Zach asked. 'Guilt about what?'

'It doesn't matter. Do you think there's a point where there's just no going back? No way of saving things? And when you hit that point, is it okay to walk away? Even if it's you that started the rot, I mean? Even if it's all your fault? Is it better to admit that you can't put things right, no matter how much you wanted to, and that you need to get out for both your sakes?'

Zach shook his head, clearly confused. 'I—I suppose so. Well, yeah, of course. The church teaches that marriage is for life, and in an ideal world that still holds true. But nowadays we recognise that sometimes it's better to separate and find some happiness either alone or with a new partner. But,' he added, holding up one hand as Noah opened his mouth to speak, 'that advice comes with a caution. The problem we're seeing so much of is that people tend to give up on marriage far too quickly nowadays. The marriage vows are still sacred and should never be made lightly. We really shouldn't give up on our marriage until we've exhausted every possible way to make it work.' His eyes expressed sympathy. 'Are things really that bad, Noah?'

'I should go,' Noah said, half rising.

'Go? No, no of course you shouldn't,' Zach told him. He nodded at Noah's mug. 'Come on now, you haven't even drunk your coffee. And if you don't help me with these KitKats, I'll eat the lot.' His eyes twinkled, but there was clear concern in them, too. 'Why don't you tell me what's going on, eh?'

Noah sat down again and took a steadying breath. 'I think,' he said slowly, 'that all I do is hurt Isobel constantly. I—I broke her heart once and it seems at that moment I also broke any chance we had of happiness. Any chance *she* had of happiness. What she is now is what I made her, and I don't think I can ever forgive myself. But it worries me. She's so insecure. You know, her parents were divorced when she was very young, and they used her as a weapon all through her childhood. She's always had to fight for their time and attention. Even now they rarely bother with her unless they want something, or to score points with the other. As a result, she seems terrified of being alone. Terrified of going through a divorce herself. I sometimes think she's only with me because of that fear, not because she loves me any longer. If she ever did.'

'I'm sure that's not true,' Zach began, but Noah shook his head.

'It *is* true, Zach. And maybe—maybe if I'm honest, I'm only with her out of fear, too.'

'Fear of what?' Zach asked gently. When Noah didn't reply he leaned towards him, his hand resting on Noah's arm. 'Come on now, mate. What is it you're afraid of?'

'I'm afraid that...' Noah stopped, unsure suddenly how to explain. He hadn't put into words before the fear that sometimes made him wake up in the middle of the night, drenched in sweat, heart thudding with a memory he couldn't bear. 'I suppose I'm afraid that if I walk away from Isobel, my only chance to atone for my sins will be gone.'

Zach's eyebrows knitted together. 'That sounds very serious. You sound more like a vicar than I do,' he added, trying to inject some lightness into the conversation. 'Come on, how bad can things be? All this atone for your sins lark. What have you done that can be so bad?'

'Like I said,' Noah said heavily, 'I broke her heart.' He stood, determined to get out of here before he said something he'd regret.

'*Once*,' Zach pointed out. 'You said you'd broken her heart *once*. Sounds like it was some time ago, and look how long you've been together. It's got to be worth the effort to mend it, hasn't it? Sit down, mate, and let's try to figure out how we can fix this for you both.'

'I need to go,' Noah protested.

'You came here for a reason,' Zach said. 'You've come this far. Why walk out now? Besides, if you don't drink your coffee I'll take it as a personal insult.'

Noah reached for his coffee mug and sat down again, taking a large gulp of coffee and waiting for the vicar's verdict.

Zach was silent for a moment as he contemplated what Noah had said. 'Have you thought about counselling?' he suggested at last. 'Marriage guidance counselling can work wonders. It might—'

'She would never agree to that,' Noah said heavily. 'She's a very private person, and a very proud one. And the problem is, there are things we could never admit to another person. Things we haven't even admitted to each other, and I doubt we ever will now.' He ran a hand through his hair and gave Zach a rueful smile. 'Not making much sense, am I? Sorry.' He took another long gulp of coffee as if it would somehow help calm his nerves. 'The top and bottom of it is, I want Isobel to be happy, but I don't think I can make her happy. I don't think I've made her happy for a very long time. But she's too afraid to let go and I don't want to hurt her any more than I already have, so...'

'And what about you, Noah? What about *your* happiness?'

'The truth is, Zach, I don't think I deserve happiness. I really don't.' He drained the last of his coffee and set the mug back on the tray.

'Everyone deserves happiness,' Zach said kindly. 'I think you're being way too hard on yourself, Noah. Whatever you did that hurt Isobel so much, she's clearly forgiven you or you wouldn't still be together. And you've been a good husband. It's been a good marriage. You've both worked hard, you've built a lovely home together, supported each other in your careers.'

Noah shook his head in wonder. Was that really how it looked to outsiders? If they only knew...

'You're saying I should give this marriage another try,' he said dully.

'I can't tell you what to do, Noah,' Zach said. 'Only you know what's in your heart. All I will say is that you and Isobel have been together a long time, and it would be a shame to walk away after all those years. It seems to me that you've got some sort of burden you're carrying, and you need to deal with that before you can start to work on the marriage.'

Noah gave him a weak smile. 'You could be right,' he said. He nodded at the clock on the mantelpiece. 'I really had better go. I've taken up more than enough of your time.'

'Honestly, I don't mind. Stay as long as you want,' Zach assured him. 'I'd like us to get to the bottom of this if we can. Figure out a way forward for you both.'

Noah didn't reply. He headed to the door, his hand reaching for the handle.

'Will you at least consider the counselling?' Zach pleaded. 'If not for the two of you then maybe for yourself. It seems to me you might need it. Or I'm here, any time you want to talk.'

'Thank you.' Noah shook his head slightly, staring at the carpet. 'You're very kind.'

He wrenched open the door and left the room, the lump in his throat threatening to choke him.

TEN

They'd met up on the Saturday, even though Noah only had a couple of hours to spare.

'I promised Aunt Eugenie I'd help her in the garden, and if I don't turn up she'll say something which might get back to Isobel,' he explained. 'I'm sorry. I wish we could have the whole day.'

'It's okay. I get it. We can still have a nice time, getting away from it all for a couple of hours,' Daisy reassured him. 'Where shall we go?'

Noah thought about it. 'There's a village called Little Whitsun. It's about half an hour's drive away. I know that won't leave us long but there's a gorgeous park there with a lake, and there's a teashop. We could get a drink and a sandwich, walk around the lake...'

'Sounds perfect,' she said.

He wondered at how easy to please she was. She never made a fuss or complained. It was as if she could find the positive in anything. He'd never met anyone quite like her before.

The drive to Little Whitsun was, thankfully, without incident, and they ordered sandwiches and tea at the teashop and ate them at an outside table, admiring the views of the park. It was far too nice a day to be stuck indoors.

As they walked round the lake, they talked about silly little things. Things of no real consequence, like if they'd ever been on a rowing boat, what their favourite flavour of ice cream was, and when was the last time they'd ridden a bike. Noah couldn't remember when he'd last felt so relaxed, despite everything.

Daisy, he realised, couldn't be more different from Isobel. Being with her was so undemanding, in a good way. So joyful.

They sat on the grass and watched the ducks swimming along in the lake.

'Have you got sun lotion on?' Daisy asked suspiciously.

He laughed. 'Of course!'

'That's all right then,' she said. 'I wouldn't want you to burn.'

He watched her as she shaded her eyes with her hand and gazed out over the water. God, she was so beautiful! Every time he looked at her his heart seemed to leap up into his throat, as if it wanted to escape his body and make a new home with her.

His eyes drank in every detail of her, from her neat little nose to the curve of her chin, from her thick, dark hair which was just begging him to run his fingers through it, to her soft lips which looked so inviting they were pulling him in. There was a moment when he half hesitated, asking himself what he thought he was doing, but even so he knew he couldn't stop himself.

He leaned over and gently turned her face to his.

He caught the surprised expression in her eyes, but then his gaze dropped to her mouth, and finally he did what he'd been longing to do for far longer than he'd admitted to himself.

For a moment she was still, then she put her hand on the back of his neck and kissed him back, while his heart thumped with joy and excitement and all thoughts of right and wrong scudded away like clouds being chased by the breeze.

Until he remembered...

. . .

'I'm so sorry, Daisy. I shouldn't have—' Noah looked stricken as he pulled away from her.

Daisy blinked away the tears that had threatened at his words. She stared fixedly at the ground, dimly registering that some sort of beetle was scurrying away from them through the blades of grass.

Eliot had never kissed her. Never shown any signs of wanting to, however much she'd longed for him to do so. But Noah... She'd honestly thought for a moment that this meant something, but now here he was rejecting her and basically telling her it was a huge mistake. And the worst—the most frightening—thing was, it hurt even more than Eliot's indifference to her had. She'd wanted Noah to kiss her. She realised now she'd wanted it for a long time. But he'd ruined it. Where did they go from here?

'Daisy?' He cupped her chin and tilted her face to look at him. 'Oh, God, you're crying! I'm so sorry.'

Daisy shook her head, confused. 'What did you expect when you've just said it was a mistake?'

It was Noah's turn to look confused. 'I never said it was a mistake.'

'Did you want to kiss me or not?'

Noah cupped her face in his hands. 'What do you think? Of course I wanted to kiss you! But that doesn't make it right, does it? I'm a married man.'

She couldn't argue with that, even though the hollow pit in her stomach told her she wanted to. Desperately.

'So why did you do it?' she asked heavily.

'Because...' He gave an exasperated sigh, running a hand through his hair and gazing around him in frustration. 'I—I wanted to. That's the truth of it. I need you, Daisy, and I know that's horrible and selfish and deeply unfair, and that's why it won't happen again, and why I'm so very sorry.'

His words were lost as Daisy threw her arms around him and kissed him hard. All she'd heard was that he wanted to kiss her, and that he needed her. Nothing else mattered.

His arms enfolded her, and he pulled her to him, kissing her with a desperation that left her breathless until suddenly he let her go and sprang to his feet.

'I can't! This can't happen!'

Daisy buried her face in her hands, feeling completely stupid. He was right. Of course he was! Hadn't she learned anything from her long years waiting for Eliot to see how badly wrong his relationship with Jemima was?

'You still love her,' she said flatly. 'I should never—I'm sorry.'

There was a long silence, then Noah said, 'I don't love her, Daisy. Not anymore. That's not what this is about.'

She stared up at him, not understanding, even though his words had given her a sudden flare of hope. 'Then…?'

He held out his hand and helped her to her feet. They stood facing each other, both pink faced and a little embarrassed.

'I don't know how I can explain things to you,' he confessed. 'I don't even know if I understand them myself. The point is, I have to draw a line here, even though I don't want to.'

'Don't you?' Daisy asked. 'Because I don't either.'

She wished she hadn't said that when she saw the look of anguish in his eyes.

'I can't offer you anything, Daisy. I can't make any promises. Everything's such a mess and I don't know how to get out of it.'

'Get out of what? You mean, your marriage?'

He nodded, biting his lip.

'Do you—do you *want* to get out of it?'

'Yes,' he said, so quietly she had to strain to hear him. 'I do. But it's really not as easy to walk away as you might expect.

There are so many complications, not least hurting Isobel. She's more vulnerable than you'd think, and I don't want to cause her any more pain. She doesn't deserve it. But the thing is, she and I —it doesn't work. It hasn't worked for a long, long time. Knowing it and doing something about it are two very different things.'

She wondered what he'd say if he knew what she'd witnessed at the café. How would he have reacted to Sally's and Kat's veiled accusations? She was torn between wanting to tell him what was happening and wanting to protect him. He would be devastated if he knew how people were jumping to conclusions and judging him so harshly.

Looking into those sad, blue eyes, she was more certain than ever that they were wrong. Noah was a kind, honest man, who wanted to protect his wife even though their marriage was deeply troubled. And he was looking out for Daisy, too. This man had no violence in him, she would swear to it.

'She seems—difficult.' She didn't want to appear eager to badmouth his wife but couldn't help wishing he saw her as she did. Even those who were worried about Isobel didn't particularly like her.

'Huh!' He rubbed his neck, a humourless smile on his face. 'That's one way of looking at it. But then,' he added with a shrug, 'I'm not perfect. The truth is, the Isobel you see now—I made her like this. Well, me and her parents. She didn't have the easiest childhood. Oh, she was rich and wanted for nothing as far as material things went, but the lack of love left its mark. I can't really go into that. It's not my place to tell other people her business. It wouldn't be right. And I don't mean that you're just *other people*,' he added quickly, as if he'd read her thoughts. 'You're far more than that to me. But it would be disloyal to talk about Isobel's family life to anyone, even you. Especially to you. Do you see?'

She did and nodded slowly. 'She just seems so bitter.'

'She has every right to be.' He held her gaze for a long time, as if trying to work out what to tell her. 'Daisy, I can't talk about Isobel. And the thing is, I don't want to. These days with you, walking in the countryside, visiting the castle and the theatre, going to the pub together, they've been so precious to me. An escape from home and all the problems there are there. I can't tell you how much you've come to mean to me. I wanted a friend and I found one in you. But somehow, you've become more than that. My feelings for you aren't just feelings of friendship any longer.'

Daisy's heart raced. 'But it's the same for me! Exactly the same!'

'Except it's not. You're free to have those feelings, whereas I'm not. I never thought this would happen to me. It's all such a mess.'

Daisy put her arms around him and, after a moment's hesitation he rested his chin on her head and held her tightly.

She was lost in his embrace, but her common sense told her she couldn't stay this way forever. She should walk away now. He'd just made it very clear that he couldn't leave his wife, so what was the point? And yet...

'This isn't what I expected when I bumped into you that day in Camacker,' she admitted.

'I know,' he murmured. 'I'm sorry.'

'Are you? Because I'm not.' She realised she wasn't. However difficult this relationship was she was glad it had happened. Her feelings for Noah were stronger and more real than anything she'd experienced before and knowing that he felt the same way about her made everything worthwhile. And if he was so unhappy with Isobel—well, it couldn't last forever, could it? Their marriage had to end at some point, surely? One day Noah would realise that being with his wife was far too painful to endure any longer and he'd walk away. She was sure of it.

And when that happened they could start their relationship

over, on new terms. Daisy understood Noah well enough to realise that, while he was with Isobel, she would never get to know the part of him that he considered belonged only to his wife. He just wasn't that sort of person, and although it hurt she realised that's what made him so special.

If she let him go now, if she gave up on him, lost patience, she could lose him for good, and she didn't think she could bear that. In fact, she knew she couldn't.

'I'd wait for you, if you told me there was any hope.'

'One day,' he said wistfully. 'But I don't know when that will be, Daisy, and how can I ask you—'

'You haven't asked me, though. I've volunteered. I'll wait, Noah, until you're ready. You'll know when the time's right.'

'That's not fair on you,' he said miserably. 'What sort of life would that be? You could find someone else. Someone who deserves you.'

'I just want you,' she said, meaning it. 'I think I knew from that day we met up in Camacker, and you hadn't brought any lunch, but you had a flask of tea and you let me drink nearly all of it without saying a word. There was something about you that day. I started to see you differently. I tried not to, but I couldn't help it.'

'I think I knew from the moment you started singing along to "Mr Blue Sky" in the car,' he said softly, his eyes shining. 'And whenever I hear that song now that's what I picture. You and me in that car, driving home, singing our heads off and frightening the sheep.'

He gazed around him, perhaps hoping to see a solution to their problems written in the peaceful landscape of the park. 'What I really need is a friend. The truth is, I can't tell you how this is going to play out because I don't know. My head's in bits, Daisy. I'm a wreck, and the last person in the world you should saddle yourself with. I can't start anything with you. Do you understand that? I couldn't live with myself, and I don't think you could either. Besides, apart from anything else, I'm so messed up I don't think I could cope with it.'

She gazed up at him, wondering what was really going on and longing to ask, but afraid to push him. Something was tormenting him and the last thing he needed was her nagging at him. Right now, she needed to be patient and let things unfold in their own time. Noah would tell her when he was ready. 'Whatever you want.'

'You'd really be happy with that?'

'Honestly? If friendship is all you can offer me for now, I'm happy with it.'

Well, perhaps happy was too strong a word, but she could deal with it. They'd figure the rest out in time.

'It won't be forever, Daisy. I'm not stringing you along, I promise you. I just need you in my life, but if it's too much I'll totally understand if you walk away.'

She put her finger on his lips. 'I'll wait for as long as you need. There's no pressure. Let's just see what happens, shall we?'

She wrapped her arms around his waist, and they held each other tightly. Who knew what lay ahead of them? Right now, it didn't matter. They had each other. For the time being it was enough.

ELEVEN

Daisy hadn't meant to tell Bethany what had happened between her and Noah, but when it came to it, she needed someone to confide in, and there was no one she trusted more.

They were having a girly night at Daisy's flat, binge watching *Bridgerton*, eating pizza, and making their way through a bottle of wine, and Daisy kept sneaking glances at her friend, longing to tell her the big news.

Ever since she'd got home after that fateful meet-up in Little Whitsun, she'd hardly slept a wink as her mind replayed what had happened. She'd woken up the following morning, her stomach in knots as she wondered if Noah had changed his mind or regretted what he'd said to her.

She knew he wouldn't risk coming into the café, so wasn't expecting to have any sort of assurance from him that day, but in the event, he'd called her before she'd even set off to work, his voice little more than a murmur as if he was making sure Isobel didn't overhear. It jarred with Daisy, she couldn't deny it, but nor could she deny that she was relieved and excited to hear from him. He'd clearly wanted to check how she was feeling in the cold light of day.

'If you've any regrets just say so now. I'll understand.'

'I haven't,' she'd assured him. 'What I said to you yesterday —I meant every word. I'll wait, Noah, but for now we're friends. Just friends. And that's okay.'

'Oh, Daisy...' He'd fallen silent for a long moment, then he'd said, 'I don't know what I've done to deserve you, but I'm so grateful we met that day in Camacker.'

She'd genuinely meant what she'd told him, but it was hard not to wonder where they went from here, and as her chaotic thoughts chased each other around her exhausted brain she knew she needed to talk over the situation with her friend, or she'd go mad.

'I can't believe it,' Bethany gasped. 'He kissed you? Oh blimey, this calls for another bottle. What was I thinking, only bringing one?'

'There's another in the fridge,' Daisy said, her stomach swishing with nerves as she tried to gauge how her friend really felt about the situation. 'I knew we'd need it.'

'Good call.'

Bethany headed into the kitchen, returning moments later with the bottle. 'Right, don't say when because I'll just ignore you.'

Glasses topped up, they leaned back on the sofa, *Bridgerton* on pause, and stared at each other.

'So, you've been sneaking off to meet up all this time?'

'Don't say it like that. It really wasn't like that. The first time we met up was a fluke. We'd both gone to see the wildflowers, that's all.'

'But after that?'

'Well, yes, but it was purely as friends. He seemed... lonely.'

'Oh, Daisy!'

'It's true! And anyway, he's good company. We get on really well, and we have lots in common.'

'Like?'

'Like how much we both love hiking, and being out in the Dales, and white chocolate and caramel cake.' She couldn't hide her smile. 'And singing along to the car radio.'

Bethany's eyes widened. 'Oh, wow. You sound smitten. Far be it from me to pour cold water on your romantic fantasies but, are you sure about this, Daisy?'

Daisy folded her arms. Was this where Bethany tried to talk her out of it? Where she tried her best to persuade Daisy that she was making a huge mistake?

'We genuinely care about each other,' she said, almost daring Bethany to challenge her. 'He's such a nice man, he really is. A gentleman. We just clicked. We talk for hours, and we have such a good time together.'

'A good time? Maybe for now, but it's not going to be much fun for you long term, is it?' Bethany swirled the wine in her glass. 'He has a wife, however much you'd like to pretend otherwise. Is he going to leave her?'

'Not for the foreseeable future,' Daisy admitted. 'There are complications. He doesn't want to hurt her.'

'Bit late for that,' Bethany said grimly. 'Especially when you think about the rumours. Because the rumours *are* growing, you know. People are talking.'

'Rumours!' Daisy tutted in disgust. 'Idle gossip. Anyone who really knew Noah would dismiss them out of hand.'

'And how well do *you* know Noah?' Bethany asked. 'Sorry to play devil's advocate, but you haven't been here long. How can you be sure? For all you know he could be stringing you along, playing with your feelings.'

'He cares about me,' Daisy said stubbornly.

'So he says.'

'He's not what you think he is,' Daisy said. 'Really he isn't.'

'What, married?' Bethany gave her a pointed look.

'I meant—'

'I know what you meant. It was a joke. Although it's not

funny, is it?' Bethany sighed. 'I know how much you like him,' she said, 'and if you say he cares about you, too, I believe you. But at some point, the two of you are going to have to decide what happens next, because if you don't, you're going to spend the rest of your lives sneaking off to meet up away from Tuppenny Bridge, feeling wretched and miserable and full of guilt. That's no life for you. Either of you.'

'It's not up to me, though, is it?' Daisy said. 'This has to be Noah's decision. He's the one with the wife, after all.'

'And he's not being fair to either of you,' Bethany said bluntly. 'Look, I'm willing to believe that whatever's happened to Isobel, the rumours are just that, with no basis in fact. I'll buy that Noah's not hurting her, physically at least. But if she knew about you and him, it would definitely hurt her emotionally. I should know. Been there, done that.'

'We're not having an affair,' Daisy reminded her. 'Nothing's happened. Well, we've kissed, but that's it. We wouldn't. He wouldn't. We're keeping it at friendship for now and—'

'Do you seriously believe that just because you haven't had sex this isn't an affair?' Bethany shook her head. 'In a way, that makes it worse. I remember when Ted and Helena confessed that they were together. They went to such pains to assure me that it had been ages before they got physical. That they'd just spent a lot of time talking to each other, making each other laugh. They honestly thought that made it better! It didn't. It hurt me so much more. Sex is sex. It can be utterly meaningless. But when a couple wants to be together because they love each other's company... Oh my God, that really hurts! You and Noah being such good friends, enjoying being together even without the physical side, don't you realise, you could break Isobel's heart? You don't have to be sleeping with him, Daisy. Trust me.'

'I know.' Daisy stared into her glass.

Bethany sighed. 'I'm sorry. I didn't mean to rain on your parade. I'm just worried about you. All of you. Especially you. I remember when you told me about how you got so involved with that farmer chap, Eliot.'

Daisy's head shot up. 'That was different!'

'Was it? He was married, wasn't he?'

'But Eliot never said he loved me. That was all in my head!'

'Noah's said he loves you?'

Daisy's face burned. 'Well, no. Not in so many words. But we like each other a lot.' She shook her head. 'Oh, I can't explain! Look, I know I messed up with Eliot, believe me. But this truly isn't like that. Eliot was a friend and I let my imagination run away with me, wanting far more than he could ever give. He didn't see me in that way. Not at all. But Noah...'

'How much can *he* give you, though, Daisy? If he's not prepared to leave Isobel, where does that leave you?'

'It's way too early to talk about him leaving Isobel,' Daisy protested. 'I wouldn't expect him to. I wouldn't ask!'

'So, like with Eliot, you want more from him than he can give?'

There was silence.

'You're always telling me what a decent, honourable man Noah is,' Bethany reminded her. 'Always defending him. Always seeing the best in him. But is this being decent? Is it honourable to lead you on when he has a wife at home? And look, I know we have no idea of the true facts, but you can't deny there's something odd going on between him and Isobel. Enough to make people start to wonder if he really is as honourable as you'd like to believe.'

'Not that again,' Daisy said. 'I told you, he wouldn't hurt her! He wouldn't hurt anyone.'

'And I say again, how well do you really know him? Oh, Daisy, I'm sorry!' Bethany put down her glass and wrapped her arms around her friend. 'I'm not saying this to upset you, really I'm not. I'm just worried sick about you, that's all. I don't want you to get hurt. Not after everything you've already been through. Just when you've made a new start and you're finally getting your life together.'

Daisy's glass joined Bethany's on the coffee table, and she took her friend's hands in hers, meeting her gaze with quiet determination.

'You said to me that if someone shows you who they are, believe them,' she said. 'Well, Noah has shown me who he is. I understand that you don't really know him, and I know it's easy to listen to gossip, putting two and two together to make five. But you do know me. Can you just trust me when I tell you that my every instinct is telling me that he's a good man? He's everything I keep telling you. I would bet my life that he's not someone who would hit his wife.'

Bethany's eyes revealed how deeply troubled she felt. 'Thing is, Daisy, you might actually *be* betting your life. If you're wrong...'

'I'm not wrong.' Daisy blinked away tears. 'Noah's not that person. I don't know what's going on, and I don't know how this is going to play out, but I do know he needs me, and we care about each other. The rumours about him are unfounded, and one day we'll prove it.'

Bethany shook her head, then smiled, her own eyes glassy with unshed tears. 'He's really got under your skin, hasn't he? But you're right. I did tell you to believe someone when they showed you who they are. Once upon a time I didn't listen to my instincts, and I lost my brother, gave far too much time to people who didn't deserve it, and almost lost Clive. So, I can't tell you to ignore your own instincts. If you truly believe he's the man you think he is—well, all I can do is support you and wish you luck.'

'Thank you,' Daisy whispered.

It meant the world to her that Bethany was willing to back her, even if she clearly had reservations.

She had the feeling that she was going to need her friend's

support. She trusted Noah, and she knew he cared for her and needed her. But where this was going she had no idea. They'd started something and it couldn't be stopped. This was going to play out and they'd just have to go with it and see where they ended up.

It was far too late to walk away now.

TWELVE

Kat's baby shower took place on the first Saturday of September in the flat above The White Hart Inn. Sally had offered to host it for her best friend, since Tommy and Hattie would be asleep in Forge Cottage, Kat and Jonah's home, and their parents were worried the noise would disturb them. Plus, it meant Kat didn't have to turf Jonah out of the house, whereas Rafferty was already working behind the bar and safely out of the way.

Daisy had dithered about accepting her invitation, but Bethany had persuaded her to attend.

'The chances of Isobel being there are practically zero. You know that. Why miss out? Besides, if you ask me, you need some fun in your life. You might be in love, but you'd never know it from your face.'

'I never said I was in love,' Daisy said.

Bethany raised an eyebrow. 'You didn't have to,' she replied.

Daisy couldn't deny her feelings for Noah had deepened over the last couple of weeks, even though they'd only spent two days together in that time. Isobel had gone back to work for the last week in August, and Daisy had swapped Tess's Wednesday shift to the Tuesday, enabling her to take the Tuesday off and head out into the Dales with Noah.

They'd hiked and talked and eaten lunch in a village café, but they hadn't kissed, or even discussed Isobel. It was as if what had happened between them had been a dream, and Daisy was beginning to wonder if it had been, until she glanced up from picking at her lunch and caught him looking at her. The expression in his eyes melted her heart and she'd smiled back at him. They hadn't said anything, but they hadn't needed to. They knew.

Then, on Thursday evening they'd taken a bit of a risk. Isobel had gone straight from work to see her granny in Harrogate. It was pouring down with rain, so Noah had finally braved the flat above Cutting it Fine.

By then, all the shops were closed, and the market square was deserted. Even so, they were both nervous, and Daisy couldn't let him in fast enough, so anxious was she that he wasn't seen.

She couldn't help feeling self-conscious as she showed him round the small flat, knowing he and Isobel shared Peony Cottage. Their home looked stunning from the outside. It overlooked the village green and had a beautiful front garden full of gorgeous flowers. It stood out from the nearby buildings as it was rendered and painted white, and with its mullioned windows, gabled roof, and pretty pastel blue paintwork it reminded her of the houses she'd read about in her Enid Blyton books when she was little.

Noah, though, hadn't seemed to notice how cramped the little flat above the hairdresser's was. After his initial nervousness about being there at all, he'd relaxed quickly, and had seemed very much at home.

Nothing had happened between them. They'd eaten home cooked shepherd's pie, watched a film on television, and talked —mostly about the work Noah had to do before term restarted, and how things were going in the café. He didn't say a word about Isobel, and she was glad of it.

Yesterday he'd sent her a text message:

> Hey you! Isobel has arranged to visit her mother next week. She'll be going straight from work next Saturday night. Weather forecast for the Sunday is good. How do you feel about tackling the Kirkby Skimmer to High Denton walk? It's a toughie but I'm up for a challenge. How about you? x

She'd barely taken in his words at first, so fixated on that single kiss and wondering what it meant. Then she realised he was challenging her to one of the toughest hikes in Upper Skimmerdale and grinned to herself. Oh, she was up for it all right.

> Challenge accepted but be prepared for defeat! You bring the tea and sandwiches and I'll bring the sausage rolls and cake. Deal? See you then. x

Noah had gone back to work on the Tuesday and had been too busy with the first week of term to visit the café for lunch, and Daisy was shocked at how much she missed him. She had to agree with Bethany that it would be better for her to mix with her friends at Kat's baby shower than to sit at home alone all evening, thinking about Noah and wondering what he was doing. Apart from anything else, she didn't want to be *that* person. She'd started to build a life for herself here, and she didn't want to throw that away, no matter how much Noah meant to her.

They arrived at The White Hart Inn at seven o'clock, to find Jennifer, Ava, and Bluebell already there, along with Eugenie Lavender and the Pennyfeather sisters.

Kat, who was positively glowing and had never looked lovelier according to Sally, gave them an apologetic look as she ushered them into the kitchen to get them drinks.

'Sorry,' she whispered. 'I know the Lavender Ladies aren't everyone's cup of tea, but Rita and Birdie are my great aunts, and they'd be so hurt if I didn't invite them. And where they go, Eugenie goes, so...'

'Honestly,' Bethany assured her, 'it doesn't bother me. They've all been really kind to me ever since I arrived in this town. Besides, it's your baby shower. You don't have to apologise.'

'Aw, thanks.' Kat poured them both wine. 'I just don't want everyone to think they have to watch what they say. We all know what gossips the Ladies are, but I've warned Rita and Birdie that what's said in here tonight stays in here. I know what happens when some of the people here have a few glasses of wine. Mentioning no names—but Bluebell and Dolly.' She laughed. 'Here, enjoy. I, meanwhile, will be on soft drinks for the foreseeable. Good job I like this elderflower cordial, right?'

'Bloody hell, the Wyrd Sisters are here again then!' Dolly burst into the kitchen, her voice trailing off as she saw Kat standing there. 'Oops, me and my big gob. Sorry, love. I didn't mean anything by it. You know I think the world of them really, don't you?'

Kat grinned. 'I'll believe you. Thousands wouldn't. Help yourself to a drink, Dolly. I've got plenty of soft drinks for me and Clemmie. I know she doesn't like alcohol.'

'I know! You'd never think she was related to me, would you?' Dolly shook her head and grabbed a glass. 'Ooh, I see Rafferty's been doing the catering again,' she said, glancing at the table where all sorts of delicious snacks were on display. 'Love his vol au vents. I'd marry him myself just for those, and that's me who'd rather have me eyes poked out with a sharp stick than get married.'

Sally gave her a mock indignant look. 'Hands off, madam. He's taken.'

Clemmie and Summer wandered into the kitchen. 'Isobel's here,' whispered Summer. 'How awkward.'

The blood seemed to drain from Daisy's face, and she put down her glass of wine, suddenly feeling sick. Bethany gave her a sympathetic look and took charge.

'So what? Why should you feel awkward?' She didn't wait for an answer which came as a relief to Daisy, who didn't want to hear anyone's opinions on the state of Noah's marriage. 'Hey, have you seen all this fabulous food that Rafferty's prepared? I can't wait to tuck in.'

'Me neither,' Clemmie said, smiling. 'I haven't eaten my tea so I'm ready for this.'

'I didn't think she'd come,' Summer said, stubbornly refusing to acknowledge the change of subject. 'She so rarely does, does she? And I wouldn't have thought a baby shower would be her thing. Although, come to think of it, she was at Kat's other one when she was expecting Hattie.'

'I invited her,' Kat explained quietly. 'In fact, your mum and I badgered her until she agreed, didn't we, Sal? It's not good for her to be isolated from other women. She needs to realise we're not the enemy—that way if she needs to offload to anyone she can.'

Bethany and Daisy exchanged glances. Daisy bit her lip, so tempted to tell Kat and Sally how very wrong they were in their assumptions. But how could she? For one thing, she had no proof, and for another the last thing she wanted to do was draw anyone's attention to her feelings for Noah. Oh heck, this was going to be a long and fraught evening.

People drifted in and out of the kitchen, helping themselves to food and drink and exchanging news with their friends and neighbours.

Miss Lavender eyed Daisy keenly as she finally sat down on the sofa, plate of food in hand.

'Well, Daisy, how are you settling in at Tuppenny Bridge?' she asked politely.

Daisy was chewing a sausage roll so couldn't answer, but Bluebell called across, 'She's settling in smashing, aren't you, love? That café's doing right well from what I've seen. Might have to put the rent on the flat up.' She burst out laughing as Daisy shot her an alarmed look. 'Only joking, don't worry!'

'You like the flat above the hairdresser's, Daisy?' Miss Lavender asked politely.

Daisy swallowed the sausage roll and nodded. 'I really do. It's the first place of my own I've ever had, and I love it there. And of course, it's really handy for work. I couldn't get any closer, could I?'

'Indeed not,' Miss Lavender said, her faded blue eyes narrowing. 'I should imagine the flat's very convenient for lots of things.'

Daisy had been about to take a sip of wine, but she paused, the glass halfway to her lips. Her face began to heat up as she thought for one awful moment that Noah had been spotted going into her flat, but then Miss Lavender said airily, 'Not least the fish and chip shop. I can think of two people who wished they lived closer to Millican's.' She turned her gaze on Rita and Birdie. 'Can't I?'

The Pennyfeathers grinned and nodded. 'I do love a battered sausage,' Rita said innocently.

'Have you seen the cake Daisy's made for me?' Kat asked, having just entered the living room and clearly catching her great aunt's remark. She gave Rita a knowing look. 'I hope you two are behaving.'

'Naturally!' Rita clutched her chest dramatically. 'There might be some naughty buggers in this room but me and Birdie are good as gold, aren't we, Birdie?'

'And in answer to your question,' Birdie said in a dignified tone, while cleverly avoiding her *sister's* question, 'yes, we *have* seen the cake. Is it one of them gender reveal cakes again? Like you had for Hattie?'

'It is.' Kat beamed at them.

All eyes turned to Daisy. 'So, you know what gender the baby is?' Birdie asked eagerly.

Before Daisy could answer Kat said firmly, 'Yes, she does, and no she's not going to tell you. She promised!'

'And I'm quite sure we can trust Daisy,' Miss Lavender said. 'She's just not the deceitful sort, is she?'

There it was again. A sort of barbed undertone to her words. Daisy wondered if she was being paranoid. It wouldn't surprise her. After all, she was a bag of nerves already, what with the guilt and then the shock of Isobel's appearance at the party.

At least Isobel didn't look like a downtrodden housewife tonight. In fact, Daisy had to admit, she looked stunning. She couldn't help but compare herself to Noah's glamorous wife and find herself wanting.

Evidently, Miss Lavender was thinking along the same lines, as she turned her attention to Isobel and said, smiling sweetly at her, 'You do look lovely, my dear. That dress really suits you.'

Isobel glanced down at her bubblegum pink dress and shrugged. 'This old thing? Thank you.'

'You're looking well, Isobel,' Kat said kindly, taking a seat in a comfy armchair, a plate of food resting on her baby bump. 'You still haven't told us about Portugal, by the way. We'd love to hear about it.'

'Oh!' Isobel waved a hand at her. 'That's not important. This is your baby shower and that's what really matters. I've put your gift with the others in Sally's spare bedroom, by the way. I hope that's okay.'

'Ooh!' Kat beamed at her. 'You've got me a gift?'

'Well, for the baby really,' Isobel said. 'I do hope you like it. You seem to have lots of presents already.'

'I know! People are so lovely. Do you remember when I was having Hattie? All the presents I got then! I barely needed to buy a thing for her, which was a real blessing because I didn't have a lot of money to spare at the time. To be honest, we've still got most of the stuff we got for her, so it will come in handy for this one.'

'Did you ever find out who bought you that pram?' Sally asked, reaching over and nabbing a sandwich from Kat's plate, receiving an indignant, 'Oy!' in exchange.

'Ah yes, the mysterious pram!' Ava's eyes widened. 'Such an intriguing mystery.'

'Pram?' Bethany glanced round at them all. 'What do you mean? You actually got a pram and you don't know who it was from?'

'That's right.' Kat shrugged. 'It was just left on my doorstep with no explanation.'

'Wow!' Bluebell puffed out her cheeks. 'I'd have thought someone would have admitted to buying it by now.'

'But surely,' Isobel said, frowning, 'it was from Hattie's father?' She glanced around at everyone. 'At least, that was what I was given to understand.'

Kat bristled and Daisy couldn't help but feel a little pleased that Isobel had obviously annoyed her. 'I don't know who told you that,' she said stiffly. 'People do like to jump to conclusions, don't they?'

'It's a bloody good pram, an' all,' Sally said, waving her half-eaten sandwich around. 'It will do lovely for the new baby. Top of the range. Whoever bought it for you must think a lot of you.'

'Which makes the puzzle even more intriguing,' Jennifer said thoughtfully. 'You'd think whoever it was would want to take credit.'

'Are you sure it's not young Hattie's dad, love?' Dolly asked, as blunt as ever. 'He might have decided to do something good for her, even if he isn't part of her life.'

'Can we change the subject?' Kat asked, clearly uncomfortable.

'Yes,' Miss Lavender said firmly. 'Let's.'

'Of course,' Isobel said. 'I just can't believe whoever it is hasn't come forward, that's all. How peculiar.'

Kat gave a heavy sigh and put her plate on the chair arm. 'All right,' she said, looking round at them all. 'I can see I'm not going to get any peace until I tell you all. If you must know, I don't know *who* Hattie's father is. Okay?'

Daisy noticed the shocked look on Miss Lavender's face, and the twinkle of amusement in Bluebell's eyes, while Dolly raised her glass in Kat's direction.

'Good for you, love. Play the field. That's what I'd do if I looked like you. If I could be arsed.'

'I don't mean like that,' Kat said patiently. 'If you must know, I got pregnant through a clinic, using a sperm donor. That okay with everyone?'

There was a stunned silence as everyone absorbed this information, then Bluebell said, 'Well, bugger me! That means our Buttercup's won thirty quid.'

'I'm sorry?' Bethany asked, as the rest of the women started to laugh.

'There was a sweepstake on who the father was,' Dolly explained. 'I'm gutted. I had twenty quid on Zach.'

As Ava spluttered her wine Dolly shrugged. 'Nothing personal, love, but you know what they say about the quiet ones being the worst. Besides, it would have made a great plotline in one of my books. I couldn't resist.'

'Zach!' Bluebell hooted with laughter. 'As if! I'd put a tenner on it being Ross. I mean, if anyone was the favourite...' Her face fell as she remembered Clemmie was in the room. 'I mean, the old Ross,' she said hastily. 'Not the loved up, romantic fool he is now he's back with you, love.'

Clemmie giggled. 'It's okay. I know what you mean. Although Ross never deserved his reputation, just for the record. People have completely the wrong idea about him.'

'Quite right, Clemmie. Ross was always a gentleman,' Miss Lavender said firmly.

'Well,' Isobel said slowly, 'that did surprise me, I must say. But if the baby's father didn't buy the pram, who on earth did?'

'I reckon it's something we'll never know,' Sally said with a shrug. 'Whoever they are, they've a heart of gold. Now, are we going to cut this cake and find out if you're having a boy or a girl?' She gave everyone an indignant look. 'Can you believe she hasn't even told me? Her best friend!'

'Shall I get the cake?' Summer called from the kitchen doorway.

They all turned enquiring eyes on Kat. 'Oh, go on then,' she said, clearly relieved that no one seemed to have taken her admission badly. 'And can you bring me a knife, too, please?'

Daisy couldn't help but feel proud as Summer settled the cake on the coffee table and they all leaned forward to look at it. She'd taken a lot of care and attention with this creation, wanting it to do justice to Kat and Jonah's big news.

'Oh, it looks lovely, Daisy,' Jennifer told her.

'You've done a smashing job, love, I'll give you that,' Dolly agreed.

Summer handed Kat the knife. 'Go on then,' she said. 'We're all on tenterhooks here!'

Kat raised an eyebrow. 'Hmm. And I can guess why.' She turned to her great aunts. 'Running another bet, are we?'

Birdie pursed her lips. 'I have no idea what you're talking about.'

'It's all in a good cause,' Rita added, not in the least embarrassed. 'The Tuppenny Bridge Fund has done quite well out of you and your shenanigans, Kat.'

'Charming.' Kat laughed and plunged the knife into the cake without further ado.

'Blue!' Sally shrieked. 'It's a boy!'

Daisy couldn't help but remember Noah's comments about Miss Lavender's blue birthday cake and how it had reminded him of mould. Her mouth curved into a smile before she could stop herself.

'Something amusing you?'

Miss Lavender's tone was unexpectedly frosty, and Daisy's smile faltered.

'No,' she said carefully. 'I was just smiling at the good news, that's all.'

Miss Lavender looked away but not before Daisy saw something in her eyes that alarmed her. If she didn't know better, she would swear that was a look of disgust. But what had she done to earn the old lady's contempt? Absolutely nothing. At least, nothing Miss Lavender was aware of.

She felt goosebumps break out on her arms and swallowed down her panic. Unless Miss Lavender had somehow learned about her and Noah. But how? Surely, Noah hadn't confided in her? But then, she'd confided in Bethany, so maybe...

No. She was being stupid. Overthinking things because she was feeling so guilty. She forced herself to calm down and listened as everyone congratulated Kat and chatted excitedly about baby boy's names, and how Jonah had reacted to the news, and whether Tommy and Hattie were excited about having a little brother.

Miss Lavender handed her a plate with a slice of cake. 'There you go, Daisy. And I must say, Jennifer's quite right. This really does look beautiful. Well done.'

Oh, Daisy, you're going to have to get a grip! Daisy took the plate and smiled her thanks. Her imagination was running riot again. She'd have to be more careful in the future or she was going to give away her guilt at some point.

Miss Lavender was consulting with the Pennyfeather sisters about who had put money on the baby being a boy, and clearly had no concerns about Daisy and Noah.

As for Isobel... She was picking at her cake but showed no signs of actually eating it. In fact, she seemed miles away. What was she thinking?

It was a problem for another day. Daisy picked up her fork and smiled at Kat. 'Congratulations, I'm so happy for you. It's brilliant news!'

THIRTEEN

It was Saturday morning, and the market square was heaving as Noah threaded his way between the jostling crowds and the various stalls, on his way to Lavender House. Despite telling himself not to, he couldn't help but glance over at Pennyfeather's, his eyes straying to the first floor and the windows of The Crafty Cook Café. Daisy would be rushed off her feet, even with Tess and Rowan's help.

He was half tempted to call in but knew he didn't have the time. Aunt Eugenie had been insistent when she telephoned him earlier that morning.

'I need your help with the dogs. I'm not well and Ross is so busy with the art school that he can't spare me any time.'

'You're not well?' he asked, alarmed. 'What's wrong with you?'

Aunt Eugenie wasn't one to discuss her health issues, and she certainly wouldn't mention them if she hadn't been forced to. Just how bad was she feeling?

'It's simply a cold,' she said dismissively. 'Nothing to make a fuss about but I don't feel able to leave the house. Please, Noah, come and take my little angels for their walk, and then we can have a nice chat and some elevenses.'

Since Isobel was at work, and he'd only been intending to mow the lawn, he didn't mind staying a few hours at Lavender House, and he was concerned enough about his aunt to set off as soon as he was ready. If nothing else, it wouldn't do to keep Boycott and Trueman waiting.

He was waved straight through at the reception of Lavender House, and seeing they were busy with summer visitors already, and with concerns about his aunt's health upmost in his thoughts, he didn't stop to chat to them as he usually did. He strode purposefully to her private quarters, punched in the key number and made sure the door was safely locked behind him before proceeding to her apartment door.

'Come in, Noah!' Her voice sounded reassuringly strong when he knocked, and he opened the door, to be immediately pounced on by her two yapping Yorkshire terriers.

'Okay, okay. I'm here now,' he said, shaking his head in amused exasperation as they danced around him on their hind legs. He was amazed they had the energy, given how plump they both were, despite the frequent lectures Ben gave their owner on healthy diets for dogs.

Aunt Eugenie was sitting on one of her chintzy sofas, looking surprisingly well. As elegant as always in a soft grey dress, her short, white hair neat and stylish, she fixed him with a piercing gaze as he entered the living room.

'Boys, boys,' she said, addressing Boycott and Trueman. 'Do behave yourselves or I'll put you in the garden for the rest of the morning and see how you like that.'

Noah glanced at the small table in front of her where a pot of tea waited, along with a plate of buttered scones. He frowned.

'I thought we were eating after I'd taken the dogs out?' he queried.

She patted the sofa next to her. 'Come and sit down, dear. I really need to talk to you.'

Noah sat next to her. 'You're not ill at all, are you?' he asked.

'Never felt better,' she admitted. 'Well, physically anyway. I do, however, have anxiety issues at the moment.'

'Anxiety issues?' Noah couldn't imagine his great aunt ever suffering from anxiety. 'What's brought this on?' He raised an eyebrow as Trueman yapped loudly. 'Do they need their walk?'

'Oh, they're trying it on with you,' she said, smiling fondly at the dogs. 'I've already taken them for a long walk this morning. Let them out into the garden, dear. It will give us a chance to eat our scones and have a civilised chat without them interrupting us.'

Wondering what on earth was going on, Noah headed over to the French doors and opened them up, gazing out for a moment at his aunt's pretty, walled garden, with its generous expanse of lawn which the dogs loved. He didn't even have to call for them, as they charged past him, tumbling onto the grass with yaps of delight.

He closed the doors and rejoined Aunt Eugenie on the sofa.

'All right,' he said heavily. 'So, you've got me over here on completely false pretences. I can see that now. What's going on? What are you up to?'

She eyed him steadily. 'That, dear boy, is what I was about to ask you.'

Noah's heart thumped, and his face burned as guilt seared through him. Then he remembered that he hadn't actually done anything and had nothing to feel guilty about. Except, he'd kissed Daisy, and he'd wanted so much more, and—oh, hell. He had a *lot* to feel guilty about. But what, exactly, was Aunt Eugenie referring to? Because she couldn't possibly know about Daisy. Could she?

'I'm afraid you'll have to be more specific,' he told her, reaching for a scone.

'Really?' She poured tea from the pot into two china cups, added milk and sugar, and pushed one towards him. 'Very well. What's going on between you and Daisy Jackson? Is that specific enough for you?'

Noah stared at her in dismay. How could she possibly know about Daisy?

'You're not going to deny it outright,' she said flatly. 'I suppose that's something. I am disappointed enough in you, Noah, without you lying to my face.'

'How did you...?'

'You have Rita and Birdie to thank,' she told him. She took a sip of tea and eyed him, with some reproach, over the cup. 'Can you imagine how I felt? There I was, minding my own business, when the walkie-talkie crackled into life. Birdie had gone to Millican's for fish and chips, and she spotted you, skulking around in the rain. She couldn't believe her eyes when you went into Daisy's flat. Naturally, she told Rita immediately—they always have their walkie-talkies on them—and Rita felt it only fair that she tell me.'

'How very altruistic of her,' he said drily.

'Don't go passing the buck,' she snapped. 'I'm ashamed of you, Noah. I really am.'

'For visiting a friend?' he asked. 'Do you never visit friends?'

'I've been making some enquiries,' she continued, as if he hadn't spoken. 'That is, Rita and Birdie have been making enquiries on my behalf. Subtle ones, naturally. We wouldn't want to draw attention to this matter, would we?' She sounded as if the whole subject was distasteful, which made him want to ask why she was so insistent on talking about it. 'It seems you make a habit of frequenting The Crafty Cook Café, and you've struck up quite a friendship with Daisy. Your passion for her, er, cake is well known among the regulars.'

He glared at her. 'Are you seriously telling me that the Pennyfeathers, of all people, have been asking people about me?

Can't you see how damaging that is? What if Isobel heard about all this?'

'It's Isobel I'm thinking of,' she said sternly. 'Which is more than can be said for you.' She shook her head sadly. 'What happened to you, Noah? You were always the sensible, loyal one. Steady. Reliable.'

'Like Binks,' he said bitterly, referring to her previous dog, a yellow Labrador who she often talked about with great fondness.

'Don't be facetious. We need to nip this in the bud at once. You must stop seeing Daisy Jackson immediately.'

He stared at her incredulously. 'I beg your pardon?'

'You heard me! If you must frequent a café, go to Market Café. Better yet, take a packed lunch to work if you won't eat one of the school meals.'

'You're asking me to drop my friendship with Daisy? Why should I?'

Her gaze seemed to pierce his soul. 'Friendship? Is that what you call it!'

'Yes!'

'So, you have no deeper feelings for Daisy?'

His face burned again, and he wished he could get better at hiding his emotions, especially from his aunt who was almost telepathic.

'Oh, Noah,' she murmured, shaking her head. 'I knew it!'

'It's not what you think,' he said, wondering how many times cheating men had said the same thing. 'We're not having an affair. I swear it.'

'Then what is this thing?' she demanded. 'Have you touched her? Kissed her?'

'I hardly think I should be discussing my private life with my great aunt,' he said uncomfortably. 'With all due respect, Aunt Eugenie, it's none of your business.'

'I'll take that as a yes then,' she said, replacing her cup on the table and folding her hands in her lap. 'Well, this is a pretty pickle, isn't it?'

'It was one kiss,' he said dully. 'Well, two. But that's it! We've both agreed to...'

'To what?' she asked, narrowing her eyes. 'What have you agreed to, Noah?'

He swallowed. 'To wait,' he said at last. 'We've both agreed to wait.'

'Wait for what?' She glared at him. 'Oh, this is too much! You're planning to leave Isobel for this woman, aren't you? Are you completely insane?'

'You know nothing about it,' he said. 'And don't call Daisy, *this woman*! It's not her fault. None of this is her fault.'

'She kissed a married man. Twice.' Aunt Eugenie sniffed. 'Whose fault is that?'

He placed his half-eaten scone on the plate and got to his feet.

'Where do you think you're going?' she demanded. 'Sit down.'

'I think we're done here,' he said.

'I said, *sit down!*'

Noah dropped back on the sofa. When all was said and done, she was the closest thing to a mother he had, and he owed her his respect. He couldn't just walk out on her, however much he'd like to.

'You'd better tell me how this all began,' she said, sounding suddenly tired. 'And then we'll figure out what we should do about it.'

He wanted to tell her that if she could figure it out, he'd personally recommend her for a medal, but he didn't. Slowly and carefully, he told her about that first fateful meeting in Camacker with Daisy, and how they'd walked the wildflower trail, and eaten lunch, and sung along to 'Mr Blue Sky'. She listened without interrupting as he told her about their other trips into the countryside, their visit to the theatre, how they talked and laughed and enjoyed each other's company.

'And you can't do all that with Isobel?' she asked, when he'd finally brought her up to date.

He gave a short laugh. 'Isobel's hardly the hiking in the Dales type.' And he couldn't remember the last time they'd laughed together. Seriously.

'So, you find something that you'd both enjoy,' she said with a shrug.

'Like what?'

'I don't know, Noah! Anything! Figure it out. Can't you see how dangerous this is? You're risking your marriage for a woman you barely know!'

'Yet I feel as if I know her better than I ever knew Isobel,' he said quietly.

'I'm sorry but this has to stop,' she said firmly. 'I've listened to what you have to say and it's flim flam. The pathetic cry of every cheating husband. *My wife doesn't understand me. I wasn't happy at home.* Boo hoo. You made your vows, and you need to do everything in your power to make your marriage work.'

'I don't think this marriage has ever worked,' he said. 'And I certainly don't think it can be fixed now.'

'Excuses! You haven't walked out and neither has Isobel. That means there's something keeping you together, and you must figure out what that is and build on it. The trouble is, you've let your head be turned by this newcomer with a pretty face. She's shown you some attention and you've fallen for it. Men do, don't they? But women like her are only out for one thing and if you don't drop her, you'll lose Isobel for good.'

'You don't know anything about Daisy,' he said angrily. 'She's a good person, and she makes me happy. Or doesn't that count for anything in your book? Would you rather see me miserable for the rest of my life as long as you can hold your head up in this bloody town?'

'Noah!'

'I'm sorry, Auntie, but it's true. All you really care about is your reputation, and the name of the Lavenders. If I'm unhappy, what does that matter? Right? You honestly expect me to throw away the one person who's made me want to get out of bed in a morning for the first time in years, and I can't do it. I just...'

He broke off, blinking away tears at the thought. She was seriously expecting him to give up Daisy, and the thought of it broke him.

'I'm sorry,' he said. 'I won't.'

'And if I decide to tell Isobel?'

Noah thought about it. He could imagine how Isobel would react. Imagining the scene made him feel physically sick and he knew he'd never have the courage to tell her himself. Maybe it would be better if his aunt did tell her. Yes, he was a coward, but at least it would be over. Finally. One way or the other.

'You must do what you feel best,' he said, getting to his feet. 'I will say this. I am not having an affair with Daisy. Neither of us want that. If our relationship is to develop it will be when we're both free to pursue it. I can't deny I hope that day comes soon. In the meantime, we'll continue to be friends and if you don't like that—well, as I said, you must do what you think best.'

When she stared up at him, clearly shocked, he bent down and kissed her cheek. 'I'm sorry, Auntie,' he murmured. 'I really am.'

Leaving her speechless for once in her life, he left Lavender House, his head held high but feeling sick to his stomach as he pondered what might happen next. But her demands had shown him one thing. He couldn't turn his back on Daisy. She was the one thing in his life that made it worth living. He would just have to face whatever came next.

FOURTEEN

'Will you be going?'

Daisy glanced up at the sound of a familiar voice, frowning in confusion as she saw Rita Pennyfeather standing in front of her, smiling.

'Sorry?'

'To that.' Rita nodded at the bench beside Daisy, who, looking down realised someone had dropped a leaflet advertising the annual sheep fair at the end of September. 'You weren't here for the last one, were you? Or were you?' She shook her head. 'My bloody memory's shocking. You could have been standing right next to me and I wouldn't remember.'

'I hadn't moved here then,' Daisy reminded her gently, 'but I did visit. I came with my brother and his girlfriend.'

Then did a runner because I saw Eliot on the stage, showing one of his sheep, and worse than that, he saw me!

'Ah, right. So you know how much fun it is then.'

Rita picked up the leaflet and sat down next to Daisy on the bench in the market square. It was Monday afternoon, and Daisy had escaped the café for ten minutes, leaving it in Rowan's capable hands. The lunchtime rush had long since

quietened and her assistant had sent her outside to soak up the
early September sunshine, breathe in the fresh air and, hopefully, chase away the headache that had been building for the
last hour.

'Maybe a storm's coming in,' Rowan had said, nodding
sagely. 'My mam always gets a headache just before one strikes.'

Daisy couldn't imagine a storm was on its way, but it had to
be said that the nights were drawing in and the clocks would be
going back next month. Some of the business owners had
already started to decorate their premises for autumn. The
market square had splashes of colour as pubs and shops were
festooned with garlands of gold and orange foliage, fake pump-
kins, and rich, red berries.

These were the dying days of summer. Dark evenings, and
cold and rainy days would be upon them before they could
blink. And then what?

It would make it so much harder to go for hikes in the countryside. She had Sunday's walk to look forward to but after
that... She'd hardly seen Noah since before he'd started back at
school, and she could only see things getting more difficult for
them. It was hard to stay optimistic.

'Don't look so glum,' Rita said, nudging her. 'I won't make
you go if you don't want to.'

'Huh?' For a moment Daisy was baffled, then she realised
Rita was still talking about the sheep fair and laughed. 'Oh,
it's okay. I enjoyed it. Mostly. Besides, I'm hardly going to be
able to avoid it, am I? This whole market square will be taken
over by it, and since my café's just there I'm not going to
miss it.'

'Well, I'm glad,' Rita said, patting her arm. 'All work and no
play makes Daisy a very dull girl, and we don't want that.'

'Er, no. We don't.' Daisy wasn't sure how to respond. Rita
was behaving rather strangely.

'So, do you like it here then?' Rita asked, evidently determined to spend some time with her. Daisy sighed inwardly. So much for taking a break for peace and quiet.

'I do,' she said, massaging her temples. 'It's a smashing town, and I love my flat and the café. I feel really lucky. Everything just came together so perfectly.'

'Yes, almost like fate,' Rita said thoughtfully. 'If you believe in such things, naturally.'

'You're in a very odd mood today, Rita,' Daisy said, eyeing her curiously. 'Is everything okay?'

'Oh yes, everything's fine, love. Ignore me. I'm a daft old bugger as anyone will tell you. Eugenie's always saying so, and you know her. She's not backwards in coming forwards, is she? Mind you, sometimes she's not that bright herself. Misses things. Thinks she knows it all, but she doesn't.' She tapped the side of her nose. 'Although, that might be because she doesn't want to see it, don't you think?'

Daisy had no idea what to say to that, so she just made a vague, 'Mm,' sound.

Rita hesitated then she said quickly, 'No, I can't do it! Bloody subtlety was never my strong point. Birdie told me to keep out of it, but I said to her, if that was our Kat I'd want her to know.'

'Know what?' Daisy asked, alarmed.

'The fact is, love...' Rita glanced around her then leaned closer to Daisy. 'Eugenie knows,' she said solemnly.

Daisy's forehead creased in confusion. 'Knows what?'

Rita sighed and sat up straight again. 'Well, what do you think? About you and Noah.'

Daisy's heart raced as the horror of what Rita had just said sank in. 'Wh-what?'

'She had a polite word with him, so she says. But knowing her she's read him the riot act. She'll have been laying down the law, no doubt about it. Telling him to stay away from you or else. Oh, I can just hear her, and I think it's all wrong. He's a grown man and he should make his own decisions. Besides,' she added, nudging Daisy, 'you're a much better match for him than Miss Snooty Drawers. What he ever saw in her I will never understand.'

Daisy swallowed. 'Rita, there's nothing going on with me and Noah.'

'Oh, don't do that. Don't kid a kidder.' Rita shook her head. 'Birdie saw him sneaking into your flat one evening. She fancied some fish and chips and went out in the rain, even though I warned her she'd catch her death. She was over the moon when she got back. She was so excited she let her chips go cold.'

'Oh no,' Daisy murmured.

'She did! Don't worry, we stuck them in the microwave. And the thing is, love, I'll hold my hands up, I'm a gossip. I like to know what's going on, and sometimes it pays off. Ask the vicar. We've given quite a lot to the Tuppenny Bridge Fund over the years with our little sideline. But I couldn't resist telling Eugenie what Birdie had seen. I mean, she *is* our best friend, God help us. And he *is* her nephew. Well, great nephew. She loves him to bits, like we love Kat, and she'd want to know. But of course, she reacted badly. Can't see the wood for the trees, you see, and it's all about the precious Lavender reputation.'

Daisy's mouth felt dry. 'So, you told Miss Lavender that Noah visited me at my flat? And she's spoken to him about it?'

'Yep. Saturday. She called him round and although she didn't tell us what was said, I can imagine. She wasn't too impressed, put it that way. But you know, she doesn't see what we see, because she doesn't want to. I mean, that Isobel. Who does she think she's kidding?'

'What do you mean?'

'We've heard the rumours. Noah's beating her up!' She snorted. 'Is he buggery! But that's what she'd like us to believe, and I'll tell you why. Because she's a nasty, vindictive bully, that's why, and she's done nothing but try to isolate him since she married him. You never knew him before then, but he was such an outgoing, happy young lad. And I'll tell you something else, he hasn't got a bad bone in his body, so there you go.'

Daisy could have hugged her, even though she'd admitted to telling Eugenie about Noah's visit to the flat. 'You don't believe he's hurting Isobel! Oh, thank God. I don't either.'

'Most people round here don't. Even the ones who are talking about looking out for her. Deep down, they have their doubts but what can they do? And they're right, of course. They *should* look out for her. Fair's fair, we wouldn't want to see any woman go through that, would we? But no one really believes it.'

'Kat does,' Daisy said. 'And Sally. And who knows who else?'

'They're just trying to be open minded,' Rita said. 'Too daft if you ask me. Me and Birdie—we keep our eyes and ears open, and we know there's summat very wrong with that lass. Isobel, I mean. Course, with her background she hasn't had much of an example of happy family life, but that's no excuse. You pick your own path in this life. You make a choice to be good or bad, and she's rotten if you ask me. Noah would be happier with you, and I've no doubt he knows it. But Eugenie won't see it because that would mean opening her eyes to how bloody miserable he's been all these years, and she can't face that.'

She sighed again. 'We all want what's best for our kith and kin, and sometimes we make big mistakes because we've read the situation all wrong. Now what I think is—' She broke off and stared over Daisy's shoulder. 'Ey up, what's going on there then?'

Daisy turned to look and saw a crowd gathered outside Pennyfeather's Craft Shop.

Rita got to her feet. 'It's our Kat!' she cried. 'What's happened?'

Daisy's heart leapt into her throat. Oh no! Not the baby,

surely? But then she heard Kat yelling, 'When I get my hands on them, I'll swing for them! You just wait and see.'

Weak with relief, she followed Rita over to the shop, where Kat was surrounded by passers-by who'd stopped to hear her rant. Jonah was looking grim-faced but was trying to calm his wife down.

Dolly had clearly heard the commotion as she'd joined them, leaving Clemmie to mind the shop. 'The miserable sods,' she said angrily. 'By, there's some bad buggers in this world, but this takes the biscuit.'

'We'll sort it,' Jonah soothed, putting his arm around Kat. 'Don't get yourself worked up, love. Think of your blood pressure!'

'My blood pressure!' Kat cried. 'It's not *my* health you want to be worrying about. I swear, I'll murder them!'

'Whoa, what the heck's going on?' Rita pushed her way through the crowd and appeared to be staring at something in shocked dismay. Daisy managed to join her and followed her gaze. Her hand flew to her mouth.

'Oh, my God! What happened?'

'That,' Jonah said, 'is what we intend to find out.'

They all gazed down at the pram—or what was left of it. It was soaking wet, covered in mud, and had been slashed to ribbons, as if someone had attacked it with a knife.

'Oh, Katherine,' Rita said mournfully, so upset she'd used Kat's Sunday name for once, 'who would have done this?'

'I fished it out of the river ten minutes ago,' Jonah explained. 'We haven't used the carry-cot bit—you know, the bit that converts it into a pram—since Hattie outgrew it. She's always in her fold-up buggy these days, you see, so I thought I'd take it out of the spare room and get it all cleaned up and ready for the baby's arrival. I gave it a good scrub and cleaned the pram frame and put them in the garden to dry, but when I went out back later to fetch it in, I found the gate open and the pram missing.'

He nodded at what remained of the expensive pram that the mystery donor had bought for Kat. The pram she'd been talking about at her baby shower just days ago.

'I got in the van and went looking for it and found it. Someone's chucked it into the river from the bridge by the look of it. Took me ages to get it out.'

'I don't get it,' Daisy gasped. 'Who'd want to do that to it? Why?'

'Morons!' Kat said bitterly. 'Bit of fun. They probably broke into the garden hoping to raid the shed for expensive tools or something, but when all they found was this pram, they decided to take out their frustration on it. Now look at the result. And that means we'll have to buy a new pram, which is just what we need.'

'For this to happen in Tuppenny Bridge, of all places,' Rita said. 'Things like that don't happen here. Aw, Kat, love, I'm that sorry. But don't worry, we'll all chip in. We'll get you a new pram, I promise.'

'That's not the point.' Kat's anger seemed to leave her suddenly, and she dissolved into tears. 'Who'd do this? My lovely pram.'

'Oh, Kat! What on earth's happened?'

Daisy spun round, her stomach flipping as she saw not only Isobel but Noah standing behind her. Noah's eyes briefly flitted to hers but then he looked back at the pram, shock clear on his face.

'Someone stole it from the garden and dumped it in the Skimmer,' Jonah explained curtly. 'Looks like they've had a field day first, cutting it to ribbons.'

'Kat, I'm so sorry.' Isobel shook her head. 'This is awful. You don't expect something like this to happen in this town, do you?'

Daisy noticed she was wearing her shop overall, with the Petalicious logo embroidered on it. Out of the corner of her eye she saw the Petalicious delivery van parked in the market square. Isobel must have been on her way to deliver some flowers and spotted the crowd. As for Noah...

She glanced at the clock on the church tower and realised it was gone four. Bloody hell! She should have shut the café up by now. Maybe Rowan had already done it? Noah had obviously left work for the day. Maybe he'd been coming to see her? Her heart did a little skip at the thought, but she ignored it. This wasn't the time when poor Kat was so upset.

'I'm really sorry about this, Kat,' Noah said, sounding choked. 'You too, Jonah. It just doesn't make sense. There are some terribly cruel, selfish people around.'

'There are,' Isobel agreed, nodding vehemently. 'I feel a bit scared thinking about it. I mean, your children play in that garden, Kat. What if they'd been there when whoever it was broke in? Tuppenny Bridge used to be such a quiet little town, but when something like this happens it makes me wonder if we should think about moving, Noah. Somewhere I'd feel safer. Maybe we could discuss it later.'

Noah looked shocked but kept his eyes firmly averted from Daisy's. She didn't blame him because the last thing they needed was for Isobel to notice, but it was hard standing so close to him and pretending he meant nothing. It was also deeply uncomfortable with Rita at her side, knowing what she knew. Fortunately—or rather, unfortunately—Rita seemed far too distressed to notice.

'Have you called the police?' Dolly asked.

'What would be the point?' The fight seemed to have gone out of Kat completely. She sounded exhausted. 'And we hadn't taken out insurance for theft from the garden so that's that.'

'I'm sure everyone will chip in,' Rita said eagerly. She cast pleading eyes on everyone who was standing round. 'Won't we?'

'Of course,' Noah murmured.

'Naturally,' Isobel said at once. 'I'm sure everyone who loves you will be only too eager to buy you a replacement.'

'It's all right,' Jonah said gruffly. 'Thanks for the offer and that, but we'll manage fine. I can buy my own baby a pram, don't worry.'

'Oh, I'm sure no one was meaning to imply that you couldn't,' Isobel said hastily. 'After all, things are very different this time around. Money was an issue when Kat was expecting Hattie, what with the father being—well, not on the scene. But now she has you and naturally you want to provide for your own. Still,' she reached out and ran her hands along the tattered, muddy pram apron, 'it is a shame. You just never know, do you? The things that are in people's hearts, I mean. What they're capable of.'

'Right, let's get you home, love,' Jonah said briskly. 'No point in hanging round here, and you're looking done in.'

Kat glanced at the shop. 'But I haven't finished—'

'I'll step in for now,' Rita said. 'It's only another hour, and I can lock up. You get off home and put your feet up.'

'I'd better be going back to the shop,' Dolly said apologetically. 'I told Clemmie I'd only be a minute.'

'I should go, too,' Isobel agreed. 'Kelly will be wondering where I am. I've just got back from delivering a bouquet to a house in Lingham-on-Skimmer. Are you going straight home, Noah?'

He nodded. 'Yes. I've got lots of work to do.' He patted his briefcase.

'Oh, really? Shame. I was hoping for one of your delicious spaghetti Bolognese for dinner tonight. I really don't feel up to cooking, and I haven't had one of your specialities for ages, but it's okay of course. I'll cook something for us when I get home.'

Noah cleared his throat. 'N-no, if you want spaghetti Bolognese then of course I'll make it. I'll pop to Maister's for the things I haven't got in.'

'Are you sure?' Isobel's eyes widened. 'I wouldn't want to put you to any trouble.'

'No trouble,' he said flatly.

'Oh, thank you, darling. You're very kind.' She kissed him on the cheek.

Daisy couldn't stomach this display any longer. 'Right, I'd better get the café closed up,' she said loudly, and pushed her way through the crowd to the door, pausing to squeeze Kat's shoulder. 'I really am sorry about the pram.'

As Kat nodded, Daisy's eyes met Noah's. She could see the apology in them but there was something else, too. Something she couldn't put a name to.

Sadly, she turned away and headed back to work.

FIFTEEN

Dinner smelled delicious as Noah stirred the Bolognese sauce before glancing at the clock. Isobel should be home any moment. He'd better drain the spaghetti.

He wished he could say he was looking forward to eating his share of the meal, but he wasn't. There was something bothering him. Something he didn't want to think about too closely.

As he dished the meal onto two plates, his stomach turned upon hearing the front door open and close. Isobel came into the kitchen, her face bright. His heart lifted a little and he thought maybe he'd got it all wrong after all.

'Just in time,' he said, smiling. 'Unless you want to get a shower first? I can keep it warm for you if you do.'

'Oh! You made it. You absolute star!' She beamed at him, and he relaxed. 'No, it's okay. I think I'll have a shower afterwards. I really can't wait for this another moment.'

'You go into the dining room, and I'll bring it to you,' he offered.

She nodded and headed into the dining room, while Noah sprinkled some parmesan on the Bolognese and carried the two plates through. Isobel was sitting at the head of the table, which he'd already set in advance, and he put her meal in front of her.

'Oh no! Don't sit over there,' she said, as he turned to sit at the opposite end of the table. 'Come and sit next to me.' She patted the chair and, trying to quell the nerves that had suddenly returned, he did as she requested.

'Shall I pour the wine?' she offered. Before he could answer she reached for the bottle he'd put on the table earlier and poured them both two full glasses of red wine.

'What a day!' She leaned back in her chair, making no attempt to eat, and sipped her wine thoughtfully. 'Isn't it awful about Kat's pram? Who on earth would do such a thing?'

'I have no idea,' he said quietly. 'There are some strange people about.'

'There certainly are.' She hesitated. 'Maybe it was Hattie's father. Maybe he's back on the scene and he's angry that Jonah's raising her as his own, and that they're having another baby. What do you think?'

Noah frowned. 'I wouldn't have thought so.'

'Wouldn't you? Why? Do you know who the father is?' she asked, leaning closer to him.

Noah tried to wrap the spaghetti around his fork, but his trembling hands made it almost impossible. 'No idea,' he said.

'Do you know,' Isobel told him, her eyes wide, 'Kat actually told us at her baby shower that he was an anonymous donor from a sperm clinic! Can you believe that? Did she really think we'd fall for such a ludicrous story? She must think we're stupid.'

Noah said nothing, deciding it was best all round if he kept his mouth shut.

'I reckon she's lying when she says she doesn't know who bought her that pram. I mean, come off it, Kat! Someone buys you a top of the range pram and leaves it on your doorstep and you have no idea who it's from? As if! What I think is the baby's father bought it for her, and she can't say anything because—oh, I don't know—he's married or something. What do *you* think?'

'If Kat says she doesn't know I don't see why she'd lie,' he said faintly.

'Don't you?' She took another large gulp of wine. 'Don't you, Noah? Really?' She got to her feet, slamming the glass on the table. 'Well, I'll show you one good reason she might keep her mouth shut, shall I?'

He watched in alarm as she hurried over to the windowsill, where she'd dumped her handbag for some reason, instead of hanging it up in the hall as she usually did. She rummaged around inside it and returned to the table, slapping something down beside his plate.

Noah stared at it and genuine dread unfurled deep within his stomach.

A piece of paper that he'd forgotten all about.

'Do you know what that is?' she demanded, jabbing it with her finger.

He swallowed. 'Yes.'

'What is it, Noah?' she asked. When he said nothing, she bent over, her face inches from his, and hissed, 'I asked you a question. What is it?'

'A—a receipt.'

'A receipt. And where is it from?'

He closed his eyes for a moment. 'From J-Johnson's Baby Store in Kirkby Skimmer.'

'Th-that's r-right,' she said scornfully. 'And can you see what the receipt is for?'

He didn't even have to look. 'For a pram,' he said heavily.

She snatched up the receipt and glared at it. 'Not just any pram, Noah. A very special pram. A very expensive pram. Paid for with cash, funnily enough. Any idea how that could have happened?'

His heart was hammering in his chest. 'It's not what you think,' he told her.

'Really? So why was this receipt hidden away in your desk drawer? Why did you never tell me about it? And why did you buy a bloody pram for Katherine Pennyfeather in the first place? Do you really think I'm that stupid? How dare you take me for a fool?'

If she'd shouted, he'd have been less worried, but he knew that quiet, menacing tone. Before he could gather his thoughts, she grabbed her plate and tipped the spaghetti Bolognese all over his head.

'That's all that's fit for. I really couldn't believe how easy it was to get you to make it for me. I had a lovely hour at work imagining doing this to you as soon as I got home.'

Noah got to his feet. 'If you'd just listen to me! It's not what you think. I'm not Hattie's father!'

She wasn't even listening, and he saw the darkness in her eyes and knew she'd made up her mind.

'Stop lying! You paid for it in cash because you know I check your credit card receipts. How sneaky and underhanded can you be? Does Jonah know? Is this some big secret you've all been keeping from me? Or is he as much in the dark about it as I was? Although, you weren't as clever as you think. I had my suspicions from the start. Oh, how long I've wondered! While those old crones were taking bets on who the father was, I've wanted to scream. You always did like her, didn't you? Even when we were teenagers hanging out together at Monk's Folly. You always fancied her. Don't try to deny it.'

The injustice of her accusations took his breath away. He stared at her, unable to comprehend her thinking.

'Don't you dare look at me like that!' Enraged she snatched up the wine bottle and slammed it against his side, dark red wine spattering over the table and floor like blood.

He gasped and headed quickly into the kitchen, spaghetti

and sauce dripping from him, his ribs aching. He grabbed some kitchen paper and tried to clean himself up at the sink, but Isobel was at his side within moments.

'How long was it going on, eh? How long were you screwing that bitch? Go on, tell me!'

'I never—it wasn't like that. Kat was just a friend, nothing more.'

'A friend you love so much you're willing to spend over a thousand pounds on a pram for her brat? *Your* brat! Admit it! Go on, I dare you!'

Noah shook his head. 'Hattie's not mine,' he repeated dully, knowing she wasn't even listening, and he had no chance of convincing her.

Isobel's eyes ranged over the draining board and her gaze fell on the pan he'd cooked the Bolognese in. He'd filled it with soapy water, leaving it to soak.

She grabbed the handle, tipped the water out of it, and swung it down between his shoulder blades. He lurched forward, gasping, as the breath was knocked from his body. He barely had time to register what had happened before she hit him again, on his shoulder this time. He fell to the floor as she hurled obscenities at him, telling him what a waste of space he was and how much she hated him, her sentences punctuated with another swing of the pan.

He wasn't sure how long it was before she finally dropped her chosen weapon and strolled to the door.

'I'm going for a shower,' she said coldly. 'Make sure the dining room is tidy when I come downstairs, or else.'

The door closed and he slumped against the sink unit, dazed and shocked.

But not surprised. No, he'd known the minute she started talking about Kat what was coming. Even if she hadn't found that receipt, she'd have found some reason to accuse him. And once he'd realised that was in her head, he'd known there was no avoiding what was coming for him.

It wasn't as if it was the first time after all.

Somehow, he pulled himself to his feet and leaned on the draining board, trying to take deep breaths even though his ribs throbbed, and he felt like he'd been hit by a bus. He couldn't think about it now. He had to get the kitchen and dining room cleaned up, because if it wasn't and she came downstairs and saw the mess...

Her temper might be washed away in the shower. It sometimes happened that way. She might come downstairs in ten or fifteen minutes, smiling and pretending nothing had ever happened. There wouldn't be an apology. They'd stopped years ago. But there wouldn't be another attack.

On the other hand, she might come downstairs angrier than ever, spoiling for another fight. God help him if she was in that mood today. He couldn't give her any more ammunition.

He closed his eyes, wincing at the pain, but realising he had no choice. Better get on with the cleaning then.

The message from Noah on Saturday morning was brief and to the point:

> Sorry, really not feeling up to a hike tomorrow.
> Another time?

Daisy stared at the screen of her phone, then pushed it into the pocket of her apron, a sinking feeling of disappointment in her stomach. Oh well, if he didn't want to meet up with her...

Maybe Isobel had changed her mind about visiting her mother? Or maybe Noah had had second thoughts about spending time with Daisy after all? It was fine if he had, she told herself. She'd understand. Except, he could have been honest with her.

'Right,' she said aloud, aware that she was, for the moment, alone in the café kitchen. 'That's good. No, really, it is. The flat needs a good clean anyway. I'll have a productive Sunday at home, polishing and hoovering. And I can get some baking done if I have enough time.'

What she wasn't going to do was sit around moping about Noah. No way. It wasn't as if they were in a relationship. Just friends, they'd agreed. She'd done her share of pining for someone who couldn't give her what she needed. She wasn't going down that road again. She'd be fine. She didn't ask herself why the thought of going hiking on her own—something she'd done many times—held no appeal now.

At home that evening she was just about to take a shower when her phone—which had been infuriatingly silent all day since Noah's message—beeped.

Daisy's heart leapt and she closed her eyes, knowing she'd been lying to herself. It mattered that he'd cancelled their plans. Noah mattered. He shouldn't but there it was. Too late to protect herself now.

She snatched up the phone from where she'd thrown it on her bed and read the message:

> I was wondering if you fancied a trip to the coast for a change? Just a lazy day by the beach, chilling out. It's been a tiring week at work, and it would be good just to relax. x

Hating herself for her weakness, Daisy found herself immediately responding.

> That sounds great. Not been to the coast for ages. Where were you thinking? x

It was almost half an hour before he replied, by which time Daisy had showered and changed into her pyjamas and was now sitting on the armchair in her living room, flicking mind-lessly through the television channels.

> Starfish Sands. Do you know it? x

Daisy frowned.

> Never heard of it! x

Another quarter of an hour, then:

> You'll love it. It's very private. Meet me at the usual place at ten tomorrow. Don't bother with lunch. We'll eat out. My treat. x

It's very private. That, more than anything, was what leapt out at Daisy. She put her phone on the arm of her chair and curled up, hugging her knees.

They weren't having an affair, and in the three months since they'd started this relationship, they'd only exchanged two kisses, and had agreed nothing more could come of it until he was a free man. Yet still, this had an unsavoury feeling to it. She couldn't deny it made her feel ashamed, somehow, even though technically she'd done nothing wrong.

'You could break Isobel's heart,' Bethany had warned her.

Daisy didn't like Isobel. She couldn't pretend that she did. Even so, she'd never deliberately set out to hurt another woman in that way, and she didn't want to be responsible for causing Isobel so much pain. She knew Noah felt the same, but where did that leave them?

He would either have to hurt his wife or call an end to this—whatever it was—with Daisy. He couldn't have them both, and she had a feeling this was torture for him already. There'd been a stricken look in his eyes the other day when he'd been outside the café. Obviously, he'd been as shocked as they all were over what had happened to Kat's pram, but there'd been something else. A look she couldn't quite decipher.

And it had been horrible seeing him with Isobel, she couldn't deny that. How much longer could this go on? Right now, she was in limbo, not sure which way this was going to go, and worse, not sure which way she wanted it to go. She really, really liked Noah. Maybe if she'd allow herself to, she would say she loved him. But did she want to be responsible for breaking someone's heart? No. No she didn't. So, what was the solution?

'Call it off now before it's too late,' she murmured. 'Text him back and tell him you can't make it. This isn't fair on any of you.'

It's already too late. I can't do it. I can't let him go.

Gulping down tears, Daisy picked up her phone.

> Sounds great. I'll see you tomorrow x

I'll tell him then, she thought. When we're face to face. I can't let him down with a text.

Liar.

Daisy put down the phone, knowing the time was coming when she'd have to make a decision, because she couldn't imagine Noah ever making it for them.

One day at a time.

It was all she could deal with right now.

SIXTEEN

Starfish Sands, as it turned out, was a quiet little village on the North Yorkshire coast, not far from Filey. It seemed to consist of a few cottages, a shop, a hotel, and a pub, although on closer inspection they discovered the pub had been turned into apartments.

The Sea Star Hotel was still open, though—a modern building with lots of plate glass windows and chrome, and spectacular views over the sea, as they discovered when they took their seats in the sunny dining room.

Noah had been very quiet on the journey, which had taken almost two hours. He'd smiled when he saw her sitting at the bus stop and had been as welcoming as ever, but she thought there was something different about him.

When he turned on the radio, she noticed he didn't sing along to any of the songs, which meant she felt unable to. Although, she had to admit she wasn't feeling much like singing. She had a nagging sense of unease, and it occurred to her that maybe Noah had been having the same thoughts as she'd had yesterday. Had he invited her here to tell her it was over?

Not, of course, that it had ever really begun. Even so, she had a feeling there was something very wrong. He wasn't himself, and she steeled herself for bad news as they perused the menu. Her appetite had deserted her, and she could tell he wasn't particularly hungry either.

In the end they both went for sandwiches. Daisy thought they could have brought a packed lunch and eaten it on the beach. It would have been far cheaper and a lot less formal than this place.

Maybe, she thought, he'd decided to break up with her in public so she wouldn't cause a scene? But surely, he knew her well enough by now to realise she never would anyway?

She watched him, concerned, as he nibbled listlessly at his sandwich, his mind seemingly somewhere else.

'Is there something you want to tell me, Noah?' she asked, unable to stand it any longer.

He looked startled. 'Sorry? Oh!' He shook his head. 'I was miles away. Sorry.'

'You already said sorry,' she told him, managing a smile. 'Just, you wanted to come here so I thought it must mean a lot to you, but you seem very distracted. Has something happened? Or did you—I mean, did you bring me here for a reason?'

'A reason?' He looked puzzled. 'Like what?'

He seemed genuinely perplexed by her question, which was reassuring. Maybe he wasn't about to end things then?

But you said you wanted him to. If not him, it will have to be you, remember?

Looking at him now, she couldn't imagine ever saying those words to him. Yet again she found herself wanting to reach out and stroke the frown lines from his forehead. He looked so lost. So sad. She hated to see him this way.

'What made you change your mind about the hike?' she asked, deciding he needed cheering up. 'Don't tell me you chickened out! I knew those hills would be too much of a challenge for you.'

He smiled faintly. 'You've got me. I realised I'd never make it up there, and I couldn't face the humiliation. What can I say?' He shrugged lightly then winced.

'Are you okay?'

'Oh yes, fine. Just a trapped nerve, I think. So, you've really never been here before? To Starfish Sands I mean, not The Sea Star Hotel specifically.'

'No, I haven't. To be honest, I've hardly been to the East Coast at all. We had one holiday that I can remember, but that was in Grange-over-Sands. Tom and I went to Blackpool a couple of times when we lived in Leeds, but apart from a couple of day trips to Scarborough when we were little that's about it for travel. I know. Pitiful, right?'

'Mum liked it here,' he said quietly.

Daisy stared at him. 'You came here with her?' she asked. 'How old were you then?'

'Well, she left when I was seven so... We came here a few times. At first it was just me and her. We used to come for the day or, sometimes, as a special treat, we'd stay the night. We paddled in the sea, and ate fish and chips, and made sandcastles...' He sighed. 'Then one day we arrived here, and I discovered we had company.'

'Oh? Who?'

'The man she later married,' he said wryly. 'American businessman. It was like I wasn't even there. They met up here a few times after that, using me for cover, I guess. They'd stay in their hotel room and send me off on my own to amuse myself. In a seaside village, in a caravan park full of strangers, with the sea on my doorstep. I was a little child! Can you imagine the danger I might have been in?'

Daisy watched him, her heart aching for him.

'It wasn't the same after that and I started dreading our

visits. Not least because she'd always warn me all the way home not to say anything about that man. She cleared off to the US with him just after my seventh birthday. I haven't heard a word from her since I turned sixteen.'

'You must have some happy memories, though,' Daisy said. 'Otherwise, why would you come back here?'

'I spent so many years pining for her,' Noah said, pushing away his plate even though he'd barely touched his food. 'I kept wondering what I'd done wrong. Why she didn't want me. When Dad left it didn't hurt me nearly as much. I was quite glad to see the back of him, to be honest. But her!' He gave an abrupt laugh. 'When I got out of the car earlier and looked around, all I could see was betrayal and pain.'

'Then why come back here?' she asked softly.

He considered the question for a few moments. 'I think I was just wondering if you can turn something bad into something good. Could I come here today and see something different? Some hope perhaps.'

Daisy wasn't sure what to say to that. All she knew was that, right now, he was in a very bad place emotionally, and she had no idea how to help him.

'There's always hope,' she said, reaching for his hand.

'Do you think?'

'Bad memories,' she said firmly, 'can be replaced by good ones.'

He gazed at her, unsmiling, and she could see he was far from convinced.

'Right,' she said, pushing back her chair. 'That's enough of this. Let's go and prove it.'

'Prove what?'

'That bad memories can be replaced by good ones. Let's go and make some good memories of Starfish Sands. Come on!'

Noah's eyes brightened as he smiled. 'Seriously?'

She held out her hand. 'Coming?'

He got to his feet and took her hand. 'Lead the way.'

After settling the bill, they headed out into the car park.

'Right,' Noah said, 'let's follow the path down to the beach. It's quite long and steep, though.'

'After the hills we've climbed in the Dales that will be a piece of cake,' she told him. She slipped her arm through his. 'Ready?'

He nodded, and they began their descent down to the sands. Noah had been right, though. It was a very long, winding, and undeniably steep path. Daisy thought it would take some energy to climb back up again and marvelled to herself at the sight of two joyful spaniels running full pelt up the hill, followed by a couple of laughing children and, a few minutes later, by their red-faced and clearly flagging parents.

She thought Noah was slower than usual. He seemed to be moving quite stiffly.

'Are you okay?' she asked, puzzled.

'Oh yes. Like I said, trapped nerve. I just hope I can walk back up here!'

'If not, I'll give you a piggyback,' she joked, and he laughed, which made her heart lift.

'Nearly there,' he said at last. 'Prepare to be amazed.'

They rounded the final corner and stepped onto the beach, and Daisy gasped. It was an incredible sight. A vast expanse of golden sand, an empty horizon, huge blue sky, and to the left, the long arm of Filey Brigg stretching out into the North Sea.

Apart from a few solitary dog walkers, three young families, and one or two couples, there was no one else on the beach.

'They'll all be at Filey,' Noah said, nodding towards the Brigg when Daisy voiced her surprise at the lack of tourists. 'Or in one of the other coastal villages round here. There's not much for people to do here, is there? No amusements or funfairs. Not even crazy golf. And some people don't like the fact that dogs are allowed here all year round. You know,' he added, 'you can walk to Filey from here. You just go along the beach.'

'Seriously?'

'Yep. Doesn't take long either.'

Daisy beamed at him. 'What do you think?'

'Walk to Filey? Now?'

'Why not?'

He frowned. 'We'd need to check the tide times.'

'Okay.' Daisy looked around then pointed to an information board that was standing just behind them at the foot of the path. 'Missed that because we were looking at the view.'

She pulled him over to the board and they studied the tide timetable that was pinned behind the glass.

Noah checked his watch. 'We'd have time to walk it there, but we might not have time to walk it back.'

'So we return by bus!' She whooped with excitement, determined that this was going to be a day Noah would remember with happiness instead of sadness. 'And just think, you won't have to climb back up that path. You're so slow today I think it would be dark by the time you made it up there, so that can only be a good thing, right?'

He hesitated, then his face broke into a smile. 'Go on then.'

Daisy bent down and unbuckled her sandals, and to her delight Noah removed his socks and trainers.

'We must be mad,' he said, laughing.

'Here.' She opened her shoulder bag and dropped her sandals inside. 'Put your stuff in here.'

'Are you sure?' he asked doubtfully.

'Of course! There's nothing in there to be damaged. Only my purse, sunglasses, and sun cream. Which, by the way, I meant to ask you about. Have you got any on?'

He nodded. 'Yes. Put some on before we set off.'

'Sunglasses?'

He patted his shirt pocket then put them on.

'You see? You're quite the experienced adventurer these days,' she teased, putting her own in place. Taking his hand she added, 'Ready for our next adventure then?'

The walk along the sands took less than half an hour, and it was glorious, even though it felt like quite an arduous task at times.

'Do you know, walking on sand burns off double the calories than walking on another surface,' Daisy told Noah, as they paddled ankle deep in the waves.

'Really? Is that a fact or are you just hoping that's the case?' he asked her.

'It's true!' She giggled. 'Well, I think it is anyway. I'm sure I read it once.'

'Here, let me take that bag,' he said. 'You shouldn't be carrying it all this way.'

'All this way?' She looked back to where they'd started their walk and puffed out her cheeks. 'Wow, it's further than I realised. But look!' she added, turning back towards Filey, 'I can see the slope up to the seafront. Not long now. And no, you don't need to carry the bag. It's not heavy, so don't be daft.' She lifted her sunglasses and peered upwards. 'Mr Blue Sky,' she said, smiling.

Slowly, he put his arm around her shoulders. 'Thanks, Daisy,' he said quietly.

'For what?'

'For making new, happier memories of Starfish Sands with me.'

For a moment, she was almost sure he was going to kiss her again and her heart thudded with anticipation. But he didn't. Instead, he dropped his arm and nodded towards the slope. 'Come on then. Let's go and get an ice cream.'

The beach became busier with people the closer they got to Filey. When they reached the slope, they sat down, brushing sand from their feet.

'Ugh! This is the worst bit,' Daisy said. 'It gets stuck between your toes and it's such a horrible feeling. Must make sure you've got it all off.'

Finally satisfied, they replaced their shoes and got to their feet.

'Very peoply,' Daisy said, observing the crowds not only on the beach but above them on the seafront.

'It is. But when you look at this amazing beach are you surprised?'

This part of Filey was, Noah told her, one of his favourite bits. One day, he added, he'd love to take her for a walk along Filey Brigg itself, which was a long, narrow, rocky peninsula with high cliffs, stretching out into the sea. But not today as the tide was coming in.

Daisy shivered, realising the day was turning colder. She'd been about to remind him of that ice cream but thought maybe a hot chocolate might be a better bet now. This area of the seafront was busy, with amusements, shops, and cafés. There were boats on trailers all along the front, and young children carrying buckets and spades, nagging their parents for a stick of rock or money for the arcades.

She and Noah found an empty table in front of a row of beach shops selling a variety of food and drink. There were burger stalls, a seafood stall, seaside rock shop, ice cream, waffles, fish and chips... You wouldn't go hungry here, that was for sure.

Even so, neither of them was hungry, and Noah bought Daisy a hot chocolate while he settled for a coffee. They removed their sunglasses and put them in Daisy's bag, then sat in companionable silence for a while, sipping their drinks and people—and dog—watching.

'I'd love a dog,' Daisy admitted wistfully, admiring a handsome golden retriever that was sitting patiently by its owner, its head tilted to one side as it took in the sights with interest. 'No chance in a flat, though. Plus, it wouldn't really be fair with me being at work so much.'

'I suppose not,' he agreed.

'Have you never thought about getting a dog?' she asked curiously.

'At times,' he admitted. 'It would be nice. I grew up with dogs, after all. Aunt Eugenie loves them. But, I suppose, like you, I'm thinking it wouldn't be fair, what with my job.'

He didn't mention Isobel's feelings on the subject, she noticed, but didn't remark on his omission. Why spoil things?

'It really is lovely here,' she said, looking around. 'I can't believe this beach! It's amazing.'

'I'll take you up into the town after this, if you like,' he offered. 'It's really pretty and not too commercialised. Or we can go for a stroll along the seafront if you'd prefer. It's a very good walk, and the views are great, obviously.'

'I'm easy,' Daisy said, with a shrug. 'I'm happy to go wherever you want to be.'

She looked up, smiling as the clouds rolled away and the sun returned. 'Yay! Ooh, that reminds me, time to top up.'

She took the bottle of sun lotion from her bag and dabbed some on her face, chest, neck and arms before passing the bottle to Noah. 'There you go. Better safe than sorry.'

He dutifully applied the lotion to his arms and face then handed the bottle back to her while Daisy rubbed the lotion into her skin.

'You should do your neck and chest,' she told him. 'They can burn too.' She frowned as she peered at the skin that was just visible under his shirt. 'What's that?'

Noah swallowed. 'What's what?'

'You've got something on the edge of your collarbone. It looks like...' She leaned forward, curious. 'Can I see it?'

'It's nothing,' he said quickly.

Daisy saw the look in his eyes, and something twisted in her gut. Nothing? Somehow, she didn't think so.

Her hand reached out to move his shirt collar out of the way but she immediately dropped it when she saw the look on his face. She barely had time to register the shock and fear in his eyes, or the way he reared away from her instinctively, before he sat up straight and tried desperately to look as if nothing had happened.

'What—what was that?' she murmured. 'You flinched.'

Noah's face was pink with embarrassment. 'Sorry. Just instinct.'

'Did you think...' Daisy's voice trailed off as memories of her childhood flashed through her mind. The frequent slaps and smacks from her father had taught her to be on alert for a flying hand, and to be ready to duck at any moment. Noah had that same look about him. He couldn't just say it was instinct. She'd seen the genuine fear in his eyes. He'd been *expecting* something awful to happen, and she couldn't dismiss that.

'Noah?' she asked gently.

'Shall we go on up to the town?' he asked, looking away from her.

She carefully reached out and laid her hand over his. 'Noah,' she repeated firmly. 'Look at me.'

'I don't want to talk about it, Daisy,' he said quietly.

'But we can't just pretend—'

'Please!' He turned to look at her finally, a plea in his eyes. 'Can we just forget about it? I think we should get the bus back to Starfish Sands. The bus station's in the town. It's not too far from here. Come on.'

He clearly didn't want to discuss the subject and she was torn between not wanting to push him and feeling she couldn't possibly let this go. Suddenly a lot of things were beginning to make sense to Daisy: why he always seemed so sad, so vulnerable;

why she'd been drawn to him from the first, sensing something within him that she now recognised as being something from her own past. She'd been beaten and bullied by her father for years. She knew what that felt like and she'd seen the same look on his face. Someone was hurting him, and she wanted to know who.

Though she had a pretty good idea of the culprit.

'Come on,' Noah said, getting to his feet. He winced again and she felt an icy coldness as she realised that maybe his "trapped nerve" wasn't a trapped nerve at all. Oh, God! What had he been going through?

Somehow, she had to find out. How could she help him if she didn't know what had been happening to him?

The main thing, though, right now was to make sure he knew he wasn't on his own with this any longer.

She took his hand in hers and squeezed it gently, letting him know that no matter what, he had her now, and she would always be on his side.

SEVENTEEN

Noah barely spoke on the bus ride back to Starfish Sands, and somehow, they both seemed to accept that their day out was over, as he led her straight to the car park rather than back to the beach.

The journey home was awkward and almost silent. Noah didn't even put the radio on, and Daisy wondered if she should say something or keep quiet. She didn't want to embarrass him, but she couldn't just pretend it had never happened.

They were almost back in Tuppenny Bridge when Noah finally spoke. 'I understand you must have a lot of questions.'

'I do,' she admitted. 'The thing is, are you willing to answer them?'

He didn't reply for what felt like ages. 'I'm sorry I ruined the day,' he said at last.

Daisy turned to him, aghast. 'You didn't! Not at all. I had a lovely time, and the way it ended wasn't your fault.'

'If I hadn't been so stupid!'

'Stupid?' Daisy stared at him. 'You're seriously calling yourself stupid for flinching like that?'

He didn't reply, keeping his eyes focused on the road ahead.

'Your shoulder,' she said sadly. 'It's not a trapped nerve, is it?'

'Daisy...'

'I don't want to push you. God, that's the last thing I want to do, believe me. But you have to understand how worried I am about you. I've been there, Noah. Where you are. I've been through it.'

Now he did glance at her, concern in his eyes. 'What? When?'

'When I was growing up,' she said miserably. 'My dad. He wasn't just verbally abusive.'

'Oh, my God, Daisy. I'm so sorry!' His hands clenched the steering wheel. 'It makes me feel sick. How could he treat you that way?'

'And that's how I feel about you,' she explained. 'How you've just reacted to what I said, well, that's how I'm reacting to the way you behaved earlier. I can't just pretend it never happened, Noah. Someone's hurting you, aren't they?'

He didn't reply and she took a steadying breath.

'It's Isobel, isn't it?'

She thought he was going to ignore her, but after a few moments he said in a resigned tone, 'Yes.'

'How long has this been happening?' she asked tearfully.

'I can't talk about it here,' he said.

'But I can't just forget—'

'It's okay. I get it. But not while I'm driving.' He glanced at the clock on the dashboard. 'Aunt Eugenie's having afternoon tea with Zach and Ava at the vicarage. Are you up for a quick stop at Lavender House?'

She nodded and Noah took a different route into Tuppenny Bridge, entering the town from the northern end where Lavender House stood not far from the border.

They swept up the drive and parked in the car park, then Noah hurriedly led her, not to the main front door of the museum, but to a side gate. He produced a bunch of keys from his pocket and unlocked the gate, glancing around him and ushering her in. Daisy was surprised to find herself in a large, walled garden which was clearly private and off limits to the visitors to the museum. To the left were two sets of French doors, and Noah unlocked one of them, which immediately set off an excited Boycott and Trueman who'd been lurking inside.

'Aunt Eugenie?' he called.

There was no response, other than increased yapping from the Yorkshire terriers, and Noah nodded at Daisy.

'It's safe. Come in.'

Feeling like an intruder, Daisy followed him into what was clearly Miss Lavender's living room. It was larger than she'd have imagined, if she'd given much thought to it, but just as chintzy as she would have expected.

Noah let the dogs fuss over them both then looked sheepishly at Daisy. 'Do you want anything? Tea? Coffee?'

She shook her head. 'Just answers really. If you feel ready to give them.'

He hesitated, then nodded. 'Come with me.'

He led her out of the room, leaving a disappointed Boycott and Trueman behind, and down a corridor to a bedroom.

'This used to be my room,' he told her, gazing around at it, a wry smile on his face. 'The Power Rangers posters have gone now, though, thank goodness,' he added with a wink.

She smiled, noting the single bed, wardrobe, desk and chair, bookcase, and chest of drawers. It was neat and tidy and just what she'd have imagined Noah's childhood room to be like. 'Has it changed much?'

'Hardly at all,' he admitted. 'Sometimes, in my darkest moments, I've thought about how easy it would be to just pack up and move back in here. It's like it's waiting for me.'

She wasn't sure how to respond to that, sensing that he

needed to talk this out in his own time, without her urging him on.

'Do you mind?' She indicated the bed and he nodded.

'Please, sit down.'

They both sat together on the bed and Daisy glanced nervously at the door. 'Are you sure your aunt won't be back any time soon?'

'She'll stay all afternoon at the vicarage,' he reassured her. 'They'll be going over the fundraising events at the sheep fair and making final plans.'

'Good job,' she said. 'I don't think she'd be best pleased to find me here, do you?'

He sighed. 'You heard then?'

'That she called you round to warn you off me? Yes. Rita Pennyfeather filled me in.'

He half laughed. 'That's rich, considering it was Rita who tipped Aunt Eugenie off in the first place.'

'I know, but she did apologise. Her heart's in the right place, but she admitted she can't resist a bit of gossip.' Daisy hesitated. 'Was she—was she very angry? Your aunt I mean.'

'She wanted to impress upon me that I made my vows, and that it's my duty to make my marriage work,' he said. 'She thinks it best that you and I have no contact with each other. I should stop frequenting The Crafty Cook Café and go to Market Café instead.'

'Oh no!'

'Yes! And can you imagine them serving up white chocolate and caramel cake in that place?'

He'd tried to make a joke of it, but she could hear the despair in his voice.

'Yet you still took me to Starfish Sands,' she reminded him.

'I did.' He gazed at the carpet for a long moment then turned to her. 'I can't give you up, Daisy. You're far too important to me.'

She hardly knew how to respond to that. Was he saying what she hoped he was saying? Or did he simply mean as a friend?

'You're—you're very important to me, too,' she said. 'But, Noah, you have to understand how worried I am about you.'

'I know. I get it, I really do.'

'Does anyone else know about this? Your aunt? No, I'm guessing not, or surely she wouldn't want you to stay in that relationship. Ross then? Have you told Ross?'

'I haven't told anyone,' he confessed. 'You're the first person.'

'But why not?'

'How many people did you tell about your father beating you?' he asked her gently.

Daisy bit her lip, understanding. 'No one,' she said at last. 'But even so, I was a kid back then. I just thought it was normal. You're an intelligent, educated adult. You must realise this isn't acceptable behaviour?'

'Who would I tell? What would I say?' He gave a bitter laugh. 'I can just imagine it, can't you? *A grown man getting beaten up by his wife? What are you, a man or a mouse? What kind of weakling lets his wife hit him?*'

'Have you never fought back?' she asked, tears stinging her eyes.

'Of course not! I—sometimes I try to stop her, when it gets really frightening. I try to prevent her from lashing out by holding her wrists. But it doesn't help really. It seems to make her even angrier and more violent. Besides...'

She waited until he composed himself again.

'She—she threatened to tell people I was hurting her,' he said, his eyes troubled. 'There were bruises, you see, from where I'd restrained her, and she said she'd tell everyone I was hitting her.'

'Someone told me she'd broken her fingers last year,' Daisy said carefully. 'Is that true?'

'*Someone told you?*' He frowned. 'Are they talking about my marriage then?'

She didn't want to upset him any more than he clearly already was, but she wasn't about to lie to him either.

'Yes,' she admitted reluctantly. 'Isobel came into the café recently wearing sunglasses, which made people wonder, and then we noticed bruises on her wrists and up her arm. Some people put two and two together and made five.'

'And you?' he asked anxiously. 'What did you think?'

'That you'd never hurt her,' she said immediately. 'Never any question in my mind.'

'Thank you, Daisy.' He rubbed his forehead. 'She did break her finger last year. *She* broke it, not me, and she did it by hitting me. They call it a boxer's fracture, actually. It's a break in the fifth metacarpal, the little finger. It had to be strapped up and it made her work at the florist's really difficult for her, which made her even more furious with me. Her knuckle still looks a bit weird, to be honest.'

'She's very clever, though, Noah,' Daisy burst out. 'Kat and Sally said she seemed wary of you after it happened. At Leon's burial place, they said you tried to put your arm around her, and that she moved away from you. And in the café, she was very careful not to accuse you of anything, but her whole attitude was one of fear. She was acting like the downtrodden wife who's afraid of her husband but won't speak out against him.'

Noah's face was pale. 'So, she's carrying out her threat,' he murmured. 'And Kat and Sally believe her?'

'I thought they did,' Daisy admitted, 'but Rita told me they don't really. Everyone knows what Isobel's like, and they know you. It's just—it's hard, isn't it? No one wants to dismiss it out of hand in case they're wrong. Kat and Sally have been trying to befriend Isobel so she knows she can turn to them if she needs to, just in case. Not that they're having much luck,' she added, trying to keep the disgust from her voice. 'Isobel's hardly the friendliest person, is she?'

'Who else thinks I might be hurting her?' he asked sadly. 'Jonah?'

'I doubt it,' she said, wishing she'd not started this line of conversation. 'Anyone who really knows you both wouldn't believe it of you, would they?'

'Has Ross heard about this?'

'I honestly don't know. But I do know Rita definitely doesn't believe it. She doesn't trust Isobel at all, and she's got a very high opinion of you. I expect Birdie feels the same.'

'Have they mentioned this to my aunt?'

'I wouldn't have thought so, because she'd have surely confronted you about it, wouldn't she? Miss Lavender's never struck me as someone who's afraid to speak her mind,' she said.

'No. Perhaps not.' He slumped, clearly stunned that all this had been going on behind his back. 'Can you imagine if some of the parents heard about this? Or the staff. My job! My God, I could lose everything! Why would she do that to me?'

'Why would she do *any* of this to you?' Daisy asked, taking his hand. 'Noah, I don't want to push you, but how bad is it? What's really going on?'

Noah didn't seem able to focus on what she was saying at first, his mind clearly too preoccupied with the information she'd already given him, and his fears about his job and reputation. Then, gradually, it seemed to dawn on him what she was asking.

He released her hand and, slowly and hesitantly, removed his shirt.

Daisy had been expecting signs of injury, but nothing prepared her for the shock of what she was now looking at. Noah's back was a mass of huge, purple and black bruises, some of them turning yellow or green at the edges, stretching from just above his waist, covering his ribs and heading up to the shoulder. No wonder he'd been so slow and stiff walking down that hill today.

She tried to be stoic but failed dismally. Tears rained down her cheeks—tears borne not just of sadness for him, but of anger and frustration, too. He'd been suffering like this for who knew how long, and that woman had been creeping around like she was the injured party.

'I want to kill her,' she said honestly, her voice cracking with emotion. 'Oh, Noah!'

She put her arms gently around him and held him, ashamed that it was he who was having to soothe and comfort *her*. He stroked her hair as she sobbed.

'It's okay, it's fine. I'm all right, honestly.'

'It's not okay,' she said, her voice muffled against his bare chest. 'It's very, very far from okay.'

She finally raised her face to his, barely able to see him through her tears. 'Please, please, promise me you'll walk away. You can't put up with this! No one should have to! Noah, she's insane. She could kill you!'

'I've thought that myself a few times,' he admitted. He dug out a handkerchief from his trouser pocket and handed it to her. 'Here,' he said, smiling, 'your mascara's run.'

'Oh, bloody hell. Who cares?' She wiped her eyes and nose and stared up at him. 'What are you going to do?'

'I honestly don't know,' he said. 'I can't think straight anymore.'

He put his arm around her, and they sat together for a few minutes, his cheek resting on her head, each lost in their own thoughts.

'It started about six months after we got married,' he said suddenly.

Daisy didn't speak, not wanting to interrupt him, but her

heart sank at the realisation that he'd been suffering this abuse for at least a decade.

'We'd been out to dinner with a colleague of mine and her husband. It was a pleasant evening. I honestly thought we'd all got on really well and was thinking we should invite this couple round to our house in return. When we got home, though, I realised Isobel had been putting on an act. She turned on me the minute the door closed, accusing me of flirting with my colleague and insisting I'd done it deliberately to humiliate her.'

A fresh tear rolled down Daisy's cheek as she listened to him speaking, his voice sounding odd and strangely emotion-less. She supposed he was being very careful to keep his feelings under control. He might not be able to finish speaking otherwise.

'It was just a few slaps that night,' he remembered. 'And, of course, in the morning she was deeply sorry. Couldn't apologise enough and promised it would never happen again. Needless to say, she didn't keep that promise.' He reached for his shirt. 'I'd better put this back on. What would Aunt Eugenie say if she caught us in my old bedroom, and me half naked!'

He managed a smile, and Daisy helped him back into his shirt, even doing up his buttons although he assured her he could manage perfectly well.

'Go on,' she said, when he'd finally tucked his shirt back into his trousers and had sat down on the bed again. 'If you're able to.'

He nodded. 'Now I've started I just want to tell you every-thing. Get it over and done with. I can't remember all the rows, obviously. They all blur into one in the end. I do remember, though, funnily enough, the first time she didn't apologise the next day. We'd been out for our second anniversary, and she'd taken exception to the attitude of one of the waiters at the restaurant. When we got home, she accused me of not standing up to him. Of not, as she put it, defending her. I honestly didn't see what there was to defend her from. He wasn't the best waiter in the world, but he wasn't particularly rude to Isobel. Anyway, she decided I'd let her down and accused me of being a complete wimp and—well, to cut a long story short—she lost her temper and lashed out. The next morning, she didn't mention it. It was as if nothing had happened. Usually, she'd be in floods of tears and couldn't tell me enough how sorry she was, but this time it was completely different. Like she didn't care. And it's been that way ever since.'

'So, what kicked it off this time? Clearly there was a reason.'

Noah shook his head. 'Something and nothing.'

She narrowed her eyes, unconvinced. 'What aren't you telling me? Oh, God! This wasn't about me, was it? Please tell me this wasn't my fault.'

'No, no honestly.' Noah put his hand on her shoulder, trying to reassure her. 'If you must know, it was something I did years ago.'

'Years ago? She did this because of something that happened years ago?' Daisy was trembling with anger but fought to stay calm. The last thing he needed was to see another woman losing her temper.

'Kat's pram,' he said at last. 'It was Isobel who damaged it and threw it in the river.'

Daisy's mouth fell open. She genuinely didn't know what to say to that.

Noah obviously realised that as he said, 'I know. It's a lot to take in. It was a shock to me, too, when I figured it out. I kept telling myself I must be wrong, but there was something about her that day when we were all outside the shop. I sensed something but I didn't want to believe it.'

'I don't understand. Why would Isobel attack Kat's pram that way? What's Kat ever done to her?'

With obvious reluctance, Noah said, 'She found out that it was me who bought the pram.'

A thousand thoughts ran through Daisy's mind at that moment as she tried to make sense of his confession.

'O-kay.'

'I'm not Hattie's father,' he said quickly.

'Obviously.'

He stared at her. 'What do you mean, obviously?'

Daisy shrugged. 'Well, if you were, we'd all know it by now, one way or the other. You just couldn't hide it, could you? If you had a child somewhere in the world, you'd have to be its father. You wouldn't be able to help yourself, whatever it cost you.'

He seemed lost for words, so she continued.

'Which means there was another reason you bought it for Kat. I'm guessing you knew she was struggling for money at the time, and prams are expensive. You, Kat, and Leon were good friends back in the day, and Kat was Leon's girlfriend, so you must have seen what she went through after he died. Knowing Leon couldn't be there for her, you stepped in and did what he couldn't. That sounds the most likely explanation to me.'

Noah swallowed and gripped her hand. 'That's more or less it,' he said slowly. 'Isobel, however, didn't see it that way. Unlike you, she immediately assumed Hattie was mine and that Kat and I had been lying to her all this time. It didn't matter what I said, she wouldn't listen. She completely lost it.'

That much was obvious.

'Those bruises...' Daisy wasn't sure how to put it, but it was bothering her too much to ignore. 'You didn't get those from her slapping you.'

'No,' he said heavily. 'It was mainly a p-pan this time. There have been various weapons of choice.'

'Then why stay?'

She really hadn't meant to blurt that out, but she couldn't help it. She felt so angry at Isobel and so very afraid for Noah. The way he'd casually mentioned weapons terrified the life out of her. What if, one day, it was a lethal weapon? What if, one day, Noah didn't get up from the floor? It didn't bear thinking about.

'Isobel's v-vulnerable,' Noah said, seeming not to recognise the irony of his words.

Daisy gave a bitter laugh. 'Vulnerable? She's a bloody monster!'

'She's not. Not really. She's not had an easy time of it.'

'And you have?'

'Her family life wasn't good,' he insisted. 'Her mother and father divorced when she was very young, and like I said, they used her as a weapon against each other after that. They would try to buy her affection and she had everything she could want materially, but she was sent off to St Egbert's away from her friends, and she'd be shuttled between her mother's place, her father's house, or other relatives' homes in the holidays, depending on who had time for her. It left her feeling very insecure.'

'Noah,' Daisy said earnestly, 'have you heard yourself? What did you just tell me this morning about your childhood? You were abandoned by your mum and dad and raised by your great aunt. And you went to St Egbert's too! Your mum didn't even contact you after your mid-teens. Did that strike you as an excuse to lash out at anyone? Why are you giving Isobel all these excuses then? Lots of people have bad childhoods, but it doesn't mean they have to turn into abusers.'

'I owe her,' he said stubbornly.

'You owe her? For what?' Daisy couldn't believe it. No matter how she tried to see things from Noah's point of view, she simply couldn't understand why he owed her a thing. He'd already put up with far, far more than he should have.

'You don't understand. You d-don't know everything.'

'Then tell me,' she said desperately. 'Help me understand!'

'I—I can't.' He swallowed. 'I'm sorry. You'll just have to trust me when I say Isobel needs me. If I left her she'd be devastated. She has huge abandonment issues, and most of this anger is born out of fear and pain. I can't just leave her to it.'

'You might have to,' Daisy said. 'You're putting yourself at risk by staying, don't you see that?'

'Maybe.'

'Noah, there's no maybe about it. You must walk away from this relationship. It's dangerous!'

When he didn't reply she said heavily, 'So if you won't leave her, where does that leave us? If you're so intent on clinging to this marriage, despite everything that's going on, what happens to me and you? What do you want from me?'

'I just...' He turned desperate eyes on her. 'I can't explain. I know this isn't fair, and I want to be with you, Daisy, I really do. I don't love Isobel, you have to believe me. But I can't just walk away and leave her.'

A nausea grew in the pit of Daisy's stomach. She remembered another time, many years ago, when she'd urged another married man to wake up and walk away from his marriage, to no avail.

Yes, she'd been in love with Eliot, but she hadn't just wanted him to leave for her sake. She'd been seriously worried about his state of mind, knowing how badly his wife was treating him. There'd been no physical violence in the Harlands' marriage, but Jemima Harland had tormented Eliot, lying to him and cheating on him, and ultimately betraying him in unimaginable ways.

No matter how much Daisy had begged him to walk away, he'd refused. There had been children involved, of course. Young children. Even so, Daisy was to this day of the opinion that things would have been better all round if Eliot had listened to her. As it was, the marriage had ended in tragedy, and it had taken Eliot a long, long time to come to terms with that.

Now here was another man caught in a loveless, abusive marriage, refusing to listen to her, to see sense.

How long was she supposed to stand by and let Noah put himself at risk? How long was she supposed to stand on the sidelines, being patient, hoping that one day he would see the mistake he was making and walk out on Isobel?

'You're right,' she said brokenly. 'It isn't fair. How can you expect me to stand by and say nothing, knowing your life could be at risk?'

'I know,' he said quietly. 'It's a lot to ask.'

'Then you shouldn't ask it of me! Noah, do you want to be with me or not?'

'Of course I do!'

'Then will you leave Isobel? If not for yourself, then for me?'

His eyes begged her to understand but she didn't. All she knew was that she'd seen another man she loved suffer and it had nearly killed her to watch. She couldn't go through all that again.

'I'd better go before Miss Lavender arrives home,' she said, getting to her feet.

'But—I'll drive you,' he said, but she shook her head.

'Honestly, the walk will do me good. I need to clear my head.'

He bowed his head. 'I understand.'

'No, Noah, I don't think you do,' she told him. She planted a kiss on the top of his head. 'The truth is, I can't bear to watch this happening knowing you're doing nothing to escape it. It's not fair of you to expect me to. You're breaking my bloody heart! Can't you see that?'

'Daisy, I'm so sorry.'

'Oh, you stupid man,' she said, tears rolling down her face. 'Don't you get it? I love you! I can't watch this. I just can't.'

She briefly registered the look of shock in his eyes before

she turned and ran. She needed to get out of here because she felt as if she were suffocating. Every part of her wanted to find Isobel Lavender and strike out at her. She wanted to punch her and punch her and keep punching her until that woman understood what it felt like to be Noah.

All the way home she seethed, imagining all the brutal ways she would attack her nemesis, shocking herself with how violent some of her thoughts had become. As she neared Market Square, though, her anger died to be replaced by sadness and overwhelming grief at the pain Noah was in, his stubborn refusal to walk away, and the futility of it all.

Just what did she do now?

EIGHTEEN

The annual sheep fair was one of the biggest events in Tuppenny Bridge, greatly looked forward to by the residents. During the last weekend of each September, the market square became a hive of activity, as pens were set up and sheep herded into place. Vans selling fast food were doing a roaring trade, and the air was full of the smell of fried onions and burgers, the sound of bleating sheep, and regular announcements over the tannoy.

Daisy had enjoyed herself at last year's fair, until the moment she'd spotted Eliot Harland. It was the sort of event she'd attended a lot when she was younger—first with her father and brother, and then with Eliot. She was actually rather fond of sheep, and looked forward to hanging out by the pens, casting her eye over the various breeds and trying to guess which animals would be successful in winning a prize.

She, Rowan, and Tess had agreed that they would take an hour each to spend at the fair, starting with Rowan. Daisy had said she would take her turn last, and as the day wore on she was so busy in the cafe, which had a constant stream of customers, she almost forgot about the time, until Tess nudged her and pointed out that if she didn't get a move on, the fair would be closed for the day.

Heading outside she was immediately back in that familiar world of sheep and farmers. She leaned over one of the pens, stroking a Swaledale ewe who was munching on hay and seemed unperturbed by the busy scene around her.

'Aren't you a beauty?' she murmured, remembering the many Swaledale sheep that had been at Crowscar and Wild-flower Farm. 'I hope you win a rosette, my lovely. You deserve it.'

'I've been looking for you.'

Daisy glanced up. Noah was standing at her side, staring down at the sheep.

'Have you? Well, you've found me.'

She looked furtively around her, wary of people spotting them together.

'Isobel's at work if that's what you're worried about,' he said. 'She wouldn't close Petalicious for anything, and she's not inter-ested in sheep, believe me.'

'Why doesn't that surprise me?' she said.

They stood in silence for a moment and Daisy pretended to fuss the ewe. 'How are you?' she asked him. 'How are the bruises?'

'I'm coping,' he said. 'More to the point, how are you?'

'Me?' She straightened, giving him a disbelieving look. 'I'm not the one who's been beaten up, am I?'

'You were upset,' he said gently. 'I'm sorry.'

'I don't want you to be sorry for me,' she told him. 'I want you to be sorry for yourself. This is breaking my heart, Noah, and I'm scared for you. Can't you see that?'

'I—I can,' he said. 'Daisy, did you mean what you said?'

She didn't have to ask what he meant. She knew all too well. She'd been going over it in her mind ever since, wondering if she'd done the right thing telling him how she felt. Even so, she knew she had. She wasn't about to start playing games with him.

'Yes,' she said. 'I love you. It's very inconvenient all round, isn't it?'

'Oh, Daisy...' He turned to fully face her, and she saw the conflict in his expression.

'Noah! There you are.'

He groaned under his breath as Miss Lavender approached, clearly not pleased to see the two of them together.

'It's okay,' she said. 'You'd better go.'

'I want to talk to you.' His eyes pleaded with her. 'I want to be with you.'

'I know, but we can't—'

She broke off as Miss Lavender pushed her way between them.

'Noah, Ross is looking for you. He wants you to mind the art stall for half an hour while he grabs something to eat. I said you wouldn't mind.'

She gave him a meaningful look.

'I was in the middle of a conversation, Aunt Eugenie,' Noah said pointedly.

'I'm aware of that,' she said. 'However, I'm quite sure Miss Jackson can spare you for half an hour. Family first, Noah. Remember that.'

She clearly wasn't budging. Noah shook his head, but Daisy decided enough was enough. The last thing he needed was more hassle.

'I'm busy anyway,' she said. 'I must be going.'

She left Noah and his great aunt to argue about his poor life choices and headed down Little Market Street, where there was a trailer parked up, on which shearers were giving a demonstration.

Daisy folded her arms, intent on watching the display. Her blood boiled at the way Miss Lavender had looked at her. If she only knew what was really going on she'd be begging Daisy to take him away from Isobel!

'Daisy?'

She jumped and spun round, her heart racing as she saw Eliot Harland standing behind her.

'It *is* you! I've been looking round for you all day, hoping to see you again. Oh, Daisy, it's that good to see you. How have you been?'

Daisy swallowed and looked around for a means of escape. He lightly touched her arm, his eyes full of sorrow.

'Aw, don't look like that. Please, Daisy, it's been so long. Can't we talk?'

'I don't think there's anything to say, is there?'

'Really?' His brow furrowed. 'After all this time? You can't spare an old friend half an hour for a catch up?'

Daisy slumped. What was she so afraid of anyway? Everything she and Eliot had gone through was years ago. She'd moved on. She had enough to think about in her life right now, and holding on to old grudges was pointless. Besides, he'd done nothing wrong. And he *was* an old friend when it came right down to it. She had to admit she'd missed him, and it was good to see him again.

'All right,' she said, mind made up. 'But not out here. Do you want to grab a cup of tea?'

'That'd be grand,' he said, his face lighting up with pleasure. 'Do you know anywhere we can go?'

Daisy grinned. 'As a matter of fact, I know just the place.'

As Eliot looked around him at the café, Daisy took the opportunity to study him. It had been more than half a decade since she'd last seen him up close, and she noticed he had a few more lines on his face but was as handsome as ever. Those dark curls had threads of silver running through them, but his deep brown eyes held a contentment that even his obvious nervousness couldn't mask. If anything, she thought he looked better than ever, but was surprised to realise at the same time that looking at him now didn't give her butterflies.

'And this is really your place?' he asked at last, turning back to face her.

'It is,' she said, glad she could say she'd achieved something at last. 'All mine. What do you think?'

'It's grand, Daisy,' he told her, sounding genuinely pleased for her. 'You always were a good cook. I reckon you've found your vocation at last, and good for you. I'm right pleased for you.'

'Thank you.'

'And you live around here?'

'I do. Just across the square. I rent a flat. It's not much but it's home, and it's my own space.' She gave him a wry smile. 'After living with our Tom and his girlfriend all that time I can't believe my luck, honest I can't.'

He wrinkled his nose in the way she remembered. 'Aye, I couldn't imagine you living under his roof for long. To be fair, I couldn't imagine you living in Leeds at all, nor any city come to that. It's not you, is it? I'm glad you found your way back to Skimmerdale, one way or the other.' As she nodded, he smiled and continued. 'It's that good to see you, Daisy. I've been worried about you, you know. And when I saw you last year, I really wanted to talk to you, make sure you were all right, but you took off like a fox with hounds on its scent.'

'I wasn't ready to face you,' she admitted.

'But why?' His eyes crinkled in confusion. 'Did you really still hate me that much?'

'Hate you?' Daisy stared at him in shock. 'I never hated you! Is that what you thought?'

'What else was I supposed to think? I let you down, Daisy, I know that now.'

She shook her head, laughing sadly at his mistake. 'Let me down? Why? Because you couldn't love me back the way I wanted you to?'

'Well...' His weatherbeaten face coloured in embarrassment and she realised he was still genuinely concerned about her feelings even after all this time.

'Oh, Eliot. None of that was your fault. You never told me you cared about me. You never gave me any reason to believe you loved me. I saw what I wanted to see, simple as that. I realise that now. If anything, it's *me* who let *you* down. I let my feelings get in the way of our friendship, and you were a good friend to me, all those years when Dad was being—well—Dad, and Tom had cleared off and left me to deal with him alone.'

'Still can't bloody believe he did that,' Eliot admitted. 'Not sure I'd ever forgive him for it if I were you.'

'It's water under the bridge now,' she said heavily. 'He had his reasons I suppose. He couldn't cope with Dad, you know that.'

'But he expected you to!'

'Yes, well...' Daisy sipped her tea. 'Let's not go into all that again.'

'No,' he said at last. 'Let's not. Any road, it's you who were a good friend to me. All the things you did for me after Jemima died. I can never repay you for that. What would I have done without you, eh? I know it must seem I didn't appreciate it at times, but I did, Daisy. I appreciated it all.'

'I know, Eliot, honest I do. It's okay. We're good.' She hesitated then asked, 'So how are things at Wildflower Farm? Are you and Eden...'

She saw the light in his eyes and didn't need him to answer.

Even so, he leaned forward, unable to disguise his happiness. 'We're really good,' he told her. 'We're running a sort of hostel now, you know. Like, bed and breakfast for hikers and the like, in one of the big barns. It's doing well, and Eden's doing cream teas for passers-by an' all. Well, you know how many people we get cutting through our land on them walks of theirs, especially in the summer when they want to see the wildflowers. And, would you believe it, we've got a pony trekking business started up. We don't run that, but we rent the stables and some land to a nice couple who do.'

'I'm glad. So you're doing better financially then?' She remembered how much he'd always worried about making the farm viable.

'We are.' He paused and added, 'We got married, you know. Did you hear?'

'No,' she said, 'but it doesn't surprise me. I'm glad it worked out for you, Eliot.'

'Thanks, love. Hey, I've got summat to show you.'

He fumbled inside his jacket pocket and pulled out his wallet. Daisy didn't have to wonder what he was looking for. No doubt he kept a photo inside that he wanted to show her. She wondered how it would feel to gaze down on a picture of the happy couple.

In the event though, she was wrong. It wasn't a picture of himself and Eden on their wedding day Eliot was looking for. He passed her a photograph and she gazed down at it, her eyes clouding with tears as she recognised some of the children she was looking at.

'Is that—oh my word, Eliot! Look how they've grown! Libby's a young woman!'

'Aye, they have, haven't they? Libby's eighteen now, and Ophelia's sixteen. And young George, he's ten.'

She smiled in wonder at the children she'd loved so much looking so grown up. Liberty and Ophelia weren't really children any more she realised, feeling a lump in her throat at the thought of how much she'd missed. Once she'd seen them every day. Now they were strangers.

Her gaze wandered to a little blonde girl in pink wellies, and a boy with dark curls and Eliot's scowl.

'Are these two...?'

'Mine and Eden's,' he confirmed. 'That's Rosie. She's five now. And that's Sam. He's nigh on three and a right handful.'

He grinned at her, and she saw the pride and happiness in his face and realised she was genuinely happy for him.

'I'm so pleased it worked out for you,' she told him. 'And I'm glad I was wrong about Eden. Clearly, you're very good together.'

'Aye we are. She's not what you thought at all, honest she's not. You'd love her, Daisy, if you got to know her properly. It'd be smashing if you'd visit one day, and I'm sure the girls would be over the moon to see you again.'

She handed the photo back to him. 'Maybe one day,' she told him.

He put the photo in his wallet and slipped it into his jacket pocket. 'Aye, well, I hope you do. It would be grand.'

'I should never have jumped to those conclusions about Eden,' she admitted. 'I still feel hot and ashamed when I remember some of the things I said.'

'Fair's fair,' he said, shaking his head, 'you weren't to know, were you? She had me right confused an' all, with the daft shenanigans that were going on thanks to the Carmichaels and their bloody weird ways. You were only looking out for me, and I appreciated that.'

He sipped the tea she'd made them and said, 'Not a bad brew that, Daisy. Not bad at all.'

'Wow!' She burst out laughing. 'I'll take that as a compliment, knowing how picky you are about your tea.'

'You know me well,' he agreed. 'But that's enough about me. I want to know about you.'

'As you can see,' she said, 'I'm very well settled now, with my flat and my own business. You don't need to worry about me.'

'But are you happy?' he asked earnestly. 'Is there anyone special in your life?'

'There are lots of special people in my life,' she told him. 'I have some amazing friends here.'

He eyed her knowingly. 'That's not what I meant.'

'I know!' She sighed. 'There is someone if you must know.'

'Aw, Daisy! That's—that's fantastic.' He beamed at her. 'Who is he? Tell me all about him.'

'Shhh!' Daisy cast a frantic look around the café, but no one was taking any notice, thankfully. She leaned closer to him. 'It's complicated.'

The smile slid from Eliot's face. 'Aw no. In what way?'

'What way do you think?' she said, feeling foolish.

He shook his head slightly. 'Not a married man? Aw, Daisy, no. After everything you went through before!'

'It's not the same thing,' she said quickly. 'For one thing, he feels the same way about me as I do about him. It's not in my head, Eliot. Not this time.'

'Then why is he still with his wife?' Eliot asked reasonably. 'Unless—are there bairns involved?'

'No. Nothing like that. Like I said, it's complicated,' she said sadly. Part of her wondered why she found it so easy to talk to him. They hadn't seen each other for years, after all, yet somehow it was like it had only been last week, or last month. She'd always found it easy to chat to Eliot, confiding in him when she was very young about her miserable time on the farm. It seemed natural to slip back into that mode somehow. He was a very easy man to talk to.

'Complicated, how?' He seemed confused, and no wonder. She was confused, too, and she had far more insight into the situation than he had.

'I can't explain it,' she admitted. 'You'll have to take my word for it. Thing is, I do really love him, Eliot, but...'

'But you're wondering if you should hang around waiting for him to be with you or if you should cut your losses and walk away.'

She didn't reply to his question but instead said, 'I'm so sorry for the way I nagged you. First about Jemima then about Eden. It was none of my business, was it? I was just so worried about you.'

'Daisy.' He put his hand over hers and gazed earnestly into her eyes. 'I never saw it as nagging. I saw it as concern from a friend who cared about me, and I was always grateful for that concern, even if I didn't always want to hear everything you said.'

'Really?' she asked doubtfully.

'Really. I know I didn't act when you warned me about Jemima, but the fact is I had to process it all in my own time. Deep down, I knew what you were saying was right, but I had to figure out what I was going to do for myself, you know? Sounds daft now, and by God, I've come to regret not acting sooner, but even so. I was allus very grateful for your support, I hope you know that. Fact is, the way you listened to me, let me pour out my worries and fears—Daisy, I'd have been lost without you. Honest, I would. It made all the difference, having someone to talk to. I'd have gone mad otherwise.'

'It was really that important to you?' she murmured.

'Daisy, love, when you're drowning you need some sort of life belt to cling to. You were mine.'

'But you took no notice of what I said,' she reminded him. 'You didn't leave Jemima and she broke your heart.'

'No, I didn't leave her, but it doesn't mean I wasn't taking in everything you said. You saved my sanity by letting me work it all out in my mind. God, I'm trying to imagine what it would have been like if I'd had no one to confide in. I can't even begin to think about it.'

Daisy thought about Noah, and all the years he'd suffered in silence, confiding in no one about what was really going on at home. How, she wondered bleakly, had he got through that?

Eliot drained his mug and glanced at his watch. 'Heck, I'd better be getting back to the sheep. Adey'll have my guts for garters.'

He got to his feet and Daisy stood, too.

'None of the family are with you?' she asked, half hopefully. 'Not the little ones maybe, but I thought maybe the older three...'

'No. Our Libby's at university,' he told her proudly, 'and Ophelia's got a weekend job as well as being at college. Oh, and George is spending the weekend with his grandma.'

'His grandma?' Daisy asked, puzzled.

'It's a long story,' Eliot told her, rolling his eyes. 'Maybe if you come up to Wildflower Farm, we can tell you all about it.'

She grinned. 'How would Eden feel about that?'

He put his hands on her shoulders. 'She'd be chuffed to bits,' he told her seriously. 'She did like you, you know, despite everything. She'll be really glad I've seen you and put my mind at rest, and you'd be very welcome at the farm, trust me.'

'Then maybe,' she told him, 'I'll drop by one day after all.'

'See that you do. And,' he added, his eyes suddenly serious, 'I hope you're able to bring that fella of yours with you. I hope it all works out for you, Daisy. I really do.'

'Thanks, Eliot.'

He kissed her lightly on the cheek and they said goodbye. Who knew how long for this time? Daisy thought, maybe not so long after all. It would be good to go up to Wildflower Farm again. As she watched him running down the stairs she sat back down and stared into the middle distance, reflecting how amazing yet how comforting it was to finally realise she was well and truly over Eliot Harland. He was a good man, and she would always care about him, but her feelings for him now were strictly platonic.

With Noah, though, it was very different. The whole time she'd been talking to Eliot her thoughts had continually strayed to the man she knew she loved and talking to someone who'd been through something similar to him, albeit without the physical violence, had made her realise that her continued support was vital.

Eliot had told her she'd kept him sane by listening to him and being there for him, and she realised that was all she could do for Noah right now. It was up to him to decide when to finally break away from Isobel. In the meantime, she would support him and be his shoulder to cry on. Maybe now he had someone to confide in, he would finally find the strength to leave his abusive wife and start again.

She could only pray it wouldn't take him long.

NINETEEN

To Zach's undoubted chagrin, many of the residents of Tuppenny Bridge only attended church for weddings, christenings, funerals, and at Christmas. Noah sometimes accompanied his aunt if she asked him to, but Isobel never went unless she'd provided the flowers for certain events and needed to decorate the church. This year, though, she'd announced that she'd like to be at the harvest festival service, and although it was undoubtedly one of the most popular church services of the year, her decision made Noah nervous.

She'd been surprisingly calm since her last outburst over the pram, and he'd been on tenterhooks ever since, wondering when the next attack would come. She hadn't said another word about Kat or Hattie, which unnerved him. He couldn't imagine for one moment that she'd accepted his story, which made him think her anger was still simmering away beneath the surface.

He couldn't help wondering if she was only going because she wanted to keep an eye on him. Maybe she suspected he would warn Kat that she'd found out their supposed secret. Maybe she was worried he would reveal it was Isobel who'd damaged the pram, although he could have done that at any time. He wasn't sure. The truth was, he wasn't sure about anything any longer. His mind was a mess of confusion. Even so, he knew he'd better be on his best behaviour today, because if he said or did the wrong thing he would pay for it later.

Fastening his tie in the mirror as Isobel luxuriated in a bubble bath in the next room, Noah stared at his reflection and wondered what the hell he was doing. His stomach was in knots about today, dreading what might happen, and his fear wasn't just for himself. What might Isobel do to Kat if she'd convinced herself that something was still going on between them? What if he accidentally glanced at Hattie? Yes, they had Jonah to protect them, but they shouldn't need protection. They'd done nothing wrong.

The only woman who'd done anything wrong was lying in a bath, listening to a celebrity beauty podcast as she soaked in ridiculously expensive bath lotion, without a care in the world.

He, meanwhile, was shaking inside at the thought of what was coming for him and when, and expecting the woman he loved to act as nothing more than his confidante. A counsellor.

Noah's eyes widened and he shook his head slightly. What the hell? Had he just said he loved Daisy? Not out loud, of course, but in his head. Yes, he had because it was true.

He loved her. He loved everything about her. He loved her expressive brown eyes, her silky, dark hair, those cute dimples that appeared every time she laughed or smiled, how soft her lips had felt against his as he'd kissed her...

He sank onto the bed, feeling dazed. He loved how happy Daisy was to go hiking through the Dales. How much she appreciated the beauty of the landscape and never took it for granted. How she didn't care if she was covered in mud, or if her mascara ran when she cried. He loved the way she'd shared her packed lunch with him without a second thought. How she made sure he had sun protection on. How she'd defended him when other people who'd known him far longer seemed willing to believe he'd harm his wife.

He loved her kindness, her humour, her compassion. He loved how strong she was, making a life for herself in a new place, starting a new business, leaving behind the bitterness and pain of her past to start again. He loved how she'd happily walked in the sand with him, wiggling her toes in the water and laughing as the waves splashed them. He loved how her eyes had lit up when he put the car radio on, and she'd loudly joined in singing along to 'Mr Blue Sky'.

Daisy, he realised suddenly, *was* his blue sky. And that woman in the bathroom, she was the rain clouds that could turn stormy at any moment.

He didn't want to stand in the rain any longer. He wanted to look up and see the sun shining in the blue sky.

'I have to leave Isobel,' he murmured, then his eyes darted around the room, his heart thumping, as if she'd sneaked into the bedroom and had heard him. He couldn't live like this any longer. He didn't deserve it. He'd more than paid the price for what he'd done to Isobel, and Daisy deserved far better than he was giving her right now.

But it was going to be hell. He wasn't stupid enough to think that his wife would just accept that their marriage was over. The thought of what she might do made him feel sick. What if she went for Daisy when he wasn't around to protect her? Would they ever be free of her?

There was so much to think about. Noah knew it would be easy to be put off before he'd even taken any action, but deep down he knew he'd reached the point of no return. He couldn't just sit back and allow things to drift on as they were. He had to get out. He now had someone to get out for, after all. He'd allowed himself to be punished for many years, but being with Daisy had made him see that enough was enough. For the first time in a long time, Noah wanted more for himself. He wanted a life with Daisy.

He wasn't going to allow even Isobel to stop him.

Last year, the harvest festival had fallen on the final day of the sheep fair, but this year it was a week later, which meant it was only local people who crowded into All Hallows that particular Sunday.

'What a spread!' Clive said, with evident enthusiasm. 'Zach's done a good job this year, getting so many donations.'

'Including Daisy's,' Bethany said, giving an admiring glance to the Victoria sponge Daisy was carrying with care.

'All this food!' Clive sounded as if he might start drooling at any moment. 'Making me hungry this. I must say,' he added, looking admiringly around All Hallows, 'the church looks stunning with all these autumnal flowers. Mind, I don't remember seeing so many loaves at the harvest festivals before.' He nodded at the produce table which was groaning under the weight of so much fruit, vegetables, and tinned foodstuffs, as well as a surprising amount of baked goods.

'Ava organised a bread making competition,' Daisy explained, laughing. 'She decided it was the best way to secure donations. I guess she understood the competitive spirit in this town. I wasn't allowed to enter, but I'm one of the judges, which is a great honour. I've heard even Rita and Birdie have entered.'

'Hmm, and what's the betting those are their entries,' Clive said, nodding at two enormous loaves that were standing side by side. 'I wonder how they taste?'

'More to the point, how will one sister react if the other wins?' Bethany pondered aloud, helping Daisy to set down her cake.

'Not our problem,' Clive said firmly. He winked at Daisy. 'Good luck with that.'

'Cheers.' Daisy grinned as they turned to make their way to their seats. Her smile dropped as she spotted Noah and Isobel sitting together on the second row, just behind Dion and Beatrix Barrington, Zach and Ava's children. Isobel was flicking through the service book, but Noah was watching Daisy, his expression unfathomable.

She didn't dare smile or even acknowledge him, but hoped her eyes sent him a message somehow, before she followed Clive and Bethany down the central aisle.

'I can't remember the last time I went to a harvest festival,' Bethany confessed, as they shuffled along the row and took their seats. 'I think I must have been at St Egbert's, which is a shame really because I always loved it.'

'Aye, it's a very popular service,' Clive agreed. 'Always draws a crowd, this one. Even when the sheep fair's over and done with.'

'I think Kat said they're hoping to announce how much they raised this year for the Tuppenny Bridge Fund,' Daisy said. 'Apparently, they haven't decided who to donate the money to yet. Last year it mostly went to Whispering Willows, did you know?'

Bethany grinned. 'Miss Lavender did mention it, once or twice. I'm not expecting anything from them this year, though. For one thing, it wouldn't be fair to accept a donation two years running, and for another, we're still in the process of becoming a registered charity, so I'd rather wait until then before I start fundraising in earnest.'

Clemmie, who'd been sitting in the row behind them with Ross and Dolly, leaned forward and asked, 'How's the building work coming on?'

Ross laughed. 'Not that we were eavesdropping or anything.'

'Eavesdrop away,' Clive said comfortably. 'As a matter of fact, it's all on schedule, which is a good thing. We're hoping to make lots of progress before winter sets in and slows everything right down.'

'And the planning permission for the veterinary unit has been granted,' Bethany said proudly. 'The Joseph Wilkinson Equine Unit will be up and running before we know it.'

Clive smiled and squeezed her hand. 'It will that.'

'Aw, I'm glad,' Dolly said. 'And like I've told Ross, if Eugenie can't decide what to do with the fund this year, there's a little bookshop that would happily take donations.' She laughed. 'I'll even throw in a signed copy of one of my books for her if that will help sway her.'

'I should think that would put her off for good,' Ross told her, his eyes twinkling.

'Cheeky bugger!' Dolly sighed. 'Ah well, it was worth a try.'

She craned her neck to take a good look round the church. 'Aw, look at the size of Kat's baby bump now! Just think, in a few weeks there'll be a new baby boy in town. Ooh, Sally's got a new frock. Very nice.' Her smile of approval faltered as she scanned the rows in front of them. 'Huh! I see Isobel's turned up. Not like her to grace us with her presence.'

'There must be something in it for her,' Ross said flatly. 'She wouldn't bother if there wasn't.'

'Probably showing off about the floral displays. She'll be back here in a couple of days for the memorial service, no doubt. I heard she's providing all the flowers for that too,' Dolly said.

'Well, fair's fair,' Clemmie chided. 'She was good friends with Leon, wasn't she? She has every right to be there.'

Daisy hardly dared look at Bethany, who had discreetly nudged her in the ribs.

'I meant to tell you,' Dolly said, leaning forward and tapping Daisy on the shoulder, 'whatever reason she had for wearing sunglasses in your café that day, it wasn't a black eye. I saw her in Maister's the day after that little rumour started, and her eyes were fine. So they're all barking up the wrong tree there.'

'What rumour?' Ross asked, startled. 'What do you mean, black eye?'

Dolly looked embarrassed. 'Oh, bloody hell! I forgot you were sitting there. Haven't you heard then?'

Ross's eyebrows knitted together. 'Heard what?' he asked suspiciously. He looked at Clemmie. 'What's she talking about?'

Clemmie shrugged. 'No idea. I've obviously missed something.'

Clive cleared his throat. 'There appears to have been some talk, Ross. All nonsense, I'm sure, but you know what this town's like.'

'What talk? Will someone please tell me what's going on?'

'Why didn't you tell me?' Clemmie asked Dolly.

'It's Noah and Isobel,' Bethany said hesitantly. 'There was some concern that, perhaps, Noah had been, er, hurting Isobel.'

'And that's why I didn't tell you,' Dolly said, nodding at Clemmie. 'You'd have told Ross, wouldn't you?'

'Hurting her?' Ross's tone was sharp. 'What do you mean by hurting her?'

Clemmie nudged him in a warning as his great aunt walked past them, arm in arm with Ava, on her way to her usual seat at the front of the nave.

Lowering his voice he repeated, 'What do you mean by hurting her? Noah wouldn't hurt a fly.'

'She had some bruises on her arms...' Dolly's voice trailed off as Ross whipped round to look at her.

'Are you joking?'

'It's all rubbish,' Daisy said immediately. 'Noah would never! I think people are starting to realise that.'

'*Starting* to realise it?' Ross sounded incredulous. 'You're not telling me there was any doubt?' When no one spoke, he sat back in the pew looking dazed. 'Bloody hell, what's wrong with people? Have any of you actually met Noah? Does he know about this?'

They were saved from answering as Zach's microphone crackled and the service began.

Daisy could barely concentrate, knowing that Noah and Isobel were sitting just a few rows in front of her. She had to force herself not to stare at the back of Noah's head, afraid that someone might notice if she paid him even a little attention.

This, she thought bleakly, was like having a steamy affair without any of the fun bits.

She wondered what Ross would say if he knew the truth about his brother's marriage. She was gratified that he'd been so incensed about the rumours and knew he would fly to Noah's defence if anyone dared say anything bad about him. She wished Noah had confided in him years ago. Maybe Ross would have been able to stop this somehow.

She tried to concentrate as Zach thanked everyone for their generous gifts of food, which would be given out to the elderly and needy in the parish. He told them about the wonderful entries they'd had for the bread making competition, and explained that the judges—Daisy, Miss Lavender (naturally), and Ava—would be sampling the entries at the back of the church after the service, where tea and biscuits would also be served.

There was a sermon and prayers, and they sang 'All Things Bright and Beautiful', 'Come Ye Thankful People, Come', and 'Morning Has Broken'. At any other time, Daisy would have been enchanted. She'd always loved harvest festival at primary school, and those were some of her favourite hymns. She was also looking forward to judging the bread competition and had felt flattered to be asked. She could hardly relax now, though, knowing Isobel was so close and worrying what Ross would say or do now he'd heard the rumours.

When the service finally ended, Zach reminded them all

that refreshments would be served, and that judging for the bread competition would be starting soon.

Daisy got to her feet and caught Ross's eye. He looked serious, as if the service had done nothing to take his mind off what he'd heard. She hoped he wouldn't say anything to Miss Lavender. It would be the last thing Noah would want.

'Daisy, are you ready?' Ava gave her a beaming smile and beckoned her to follow her to the back of the church, where several of Zach's devoted helpers were already brewing up tea and putting biscuits on plates.

Miss Lavender gave her a frosty look. 'A fellow judge, I hear.'

'I am,' Daisy said, her heart sinking. How had she forgotten that Miss Lavender didn't approve of her? Another tension to add to all the others. It was a wonder she could remember her own name right now.

Ross caught hold of her arm as his aunt headed off after Ava. 'I want to know about these rumours,' he murmured. 'Are you honestly telling me people believe them?'

'Why are you asking me?' she said, her eyes widening in alarm.

He glanced around then leaned close. 'My aunt told me about the conversation she had with Noah concerning you. She's very worried about your relationship with my brother. Should she be?'

Daisy was tempted to tell him to mind his own business and to pass the same message to his great aunt. But common sense prevailed, and she remembered that Ross was on Noah's side, and therefore not her enemy. Maybe it was time he was given the chance to prove it.

'She should be more worried about his other relationship,' she murmured.

Ross stared at her for a moment, clearly trying to work out what was going on.

'Daisy, you need to be with the other judges,' Bethany said, nodding over to where Ava and Miss Lavender were waiting.

Ross stepped aside and she walked past him, not daring to say anything else.

She spent the next twenty minutes immersing herself in the taste test and swapping notes with her fellow judges. They all tried to ignore the shameless attempts of the interested onlookers to sway their opinion.

'Those are so obviously Rita's and Birdie's,' Miss Lavender whispered. 'Honestly, trust those two to make loaves three times the size of anyone else's.'

'I hate to say it,' Ava told them in a low voice, 'but I didn't particularly like either of them. Too heavy and dense. It's a shame, but that's my opinion.'

'I agree,' Daisy said. 'Not very tasty at all, but maybe that's a good thing. Imagine what one of them would say if the other won! They'd be impossible. I do think that one, third from the left, is exceptionally good. I'd be pleased if one of mine turned out like that.'

'Yes, you're right.' Miss Lavender sounded almost grudging at having to agree with her. 'I think it's my favourite, too. Although I do think the one on the far left is quite tasty. I'm torn between them, to be honest.'

'And that one fourth from the right is good,' Ava added. 'Have you tried that one yet?'

They huddled in a corner, discussing their findings with as much solemnity as if they were negotiating world peace.

Eventually, after many impatient calls from the crowd, who were in severe danger of running out of biscuits, the winner was announced.

The one that was fourth from the right came third, the one on the far left was second, and the winner was the one third from left.

The cards announcing the decision were placed by the

plates and then the name tickets were turned over so that everyone could see who had won.

'Well, I never did!' Miss Lavender's shocked tones matched the surprise on Daisy's and Ava's faces at the result. 'Birdie Pennyfeather. You've won!'

'And Rita is second,' Daisy said, shaking her head. 'But I thought...'

They both turned over the tickets of the huge loaves that they'd been so sure belonged to the Pennyfeathers.

'Bluebell!' Ava burst out laughing. 'How come you've entered two loaves?'

'I wasn't sure if the first one was good enough,' Bluebell admitted. 'So I thought I'd submit two of them, just to be sure.'

'But the entry rules quite clearly state that there is only one entry per person,' Miss Lavender said crossly. 'We'd have had to disqualify you if you'd won.'

'Good job I didn't then, isn't it?' Bluebell said cheerily. 'Mind you, you might regret choosing Birdie's loaf over Rita's.'

Daisy could see Rita and Birdie were already exchanging words. It was clear Rita strongly disagreed with the judges' verdict.

Meanwhile, Jennifer was beaming with pride at having come third. As she'd never entered anything before, she considered it a huge achievement and most people couldn't have been happier for her, with Ben and Jamie looking fit to burst.

Noah and Isobel were standing with Clive and Bethany, and Daisy could hear her friend telling the Lavenders all about the building work that was going on at Whispering Willows. It was perfectly obvious that Isobel had no interest whatsoever, as she spent more time looking round at other people than at Bethany. Her eyes kept straying to where Kat was sitting, nursing a cup of tea on her bump, while Jonah and Summer kept Hattie and Tommy entertained.

Daisy's heart raced as Noah's gaze flickered over to her. She so much wanted to smile at him, to offer him some sign or signal that she was thinking of him and missing him, but she didn't dare.

'Ah.' The voice in her ear made her jump. 'I see Aunt Eugenie was right.'

'Ross, it's not...' She had no words to offer him. She could only pray he wouldn't make a scene.

'Wait outside,' he said urgently.

'I'm—I'm sorry?'

'Just make your way outside. Give me a couple of minutes, okay?'

Not entirely sure what to expect, Daisy extricated herself from the crowd and made her way out into the churchyard. It was a damp sort of day, typical of early October, and she realised sadly that summer was over. The grey skies had chased away the blue, and darker nights and shorter days lay ahead of them.

Out of the corner of her eye she noticed Jennifer making her way along the path, and guessed she was heading over to the Garden of Ashes to see Julian, her late husband, and Leon, their son. It would be Leon's memorial service in two days. Something else to add to Noah's sadness.

'Daisy?'

She jumped at the sound of her name and spun round, feeling a mixture of surprise, delight, and anxiety at seeing Noah standing there.

'What are you doing here?' she gasped. 'I thought Ross—'

'He told me to come out here and see you,' he said urgently. 'He's keeping Isobel occupied. He knows about us, doesn't he?'

'He only knows what your Aunt Eugenie told him,' she said. 'And really, there's not a lot to know, is there? It's not as if...' She bit her lip, not wanting to waste time when they probably had very little of it. 'How are you? Is everything okay?'

'She's quiet at the moment.' He glanced around then kissed

her gently on the lips. 'I haven't got long, but I wanted to tell you something. Daisy, I need you to know that I've been doing a lot of thinking, and I realised something today. The fact is, I love you. I love you so much, and I want to be with you, more than anything.'

'I love you, too,' she said, her eyes shining despite her worries. Hearing him say the words she'd longed to hear meant the world to her, even though, deep down, she'd already known that he loved her, even if it had taken him until today to admit it to himself. It was written in his face every time he looked at her. 'I've already told you that. But does it change anything?'

'Yes, it does.' He took a steadying breath then said, 'I'm leaving her, Daisy.'

'What?' She stared at him, hardly daring to believe he could possibly mean it. 'Are you sure?'

'I'm sure. I don't love her, and God knows, I've been punished enough. I can't make her happy, and she certainly doesn't make me happy. I can't live like this any longer. I just want to get away from her. I need to be with you. Build a new life with you. If—if you'll have me?'

'Oh, Noah!' Daisy threw her arms around him. 'Of course I'll have you. I love you. It's all going to be all right.'

'We'll have to be careful,' he warned her, holding her tightly, his eyes shining with hope and love. 'I don't know how she's going to take it, after all. But we'll face it somehow.'

'Don't tell her when you're alone with her,' she said, fear immediately replacing her joy. She let him go and stepped back. 'Please. Promise me you'll only tell her when someone's with you. If you want me to be there, I will be. Just say the word.'

'No, no! Definitely not. She might... No, it's best if you're not there.'

'Then who?'

'I'll ask Ross,' he said. 'I'll tell him what's been going on with you and me and ask him to be with me while I break the news.' He shook his head. 'He'll probably think it's weird when I say I need him, but I can't tell him the truth. It would break his heart. Even so, I can't do this without him. God, that sounds pathetic. You must think I'm so weak. What the hell do you see in me, Daisy?'

'You're not weak,' she said tearfully. 'If anything, you've been incredibly strong. She's a dangerous woman, and she knows you won't hit her back. When are you going to tell her?'

'I'm going to wait until after the memorial,' he said quietly. 'It's only another couple of days until that takes place. Once it's out of the way I'll do it. I promise you.'

They jumped apart as someone ran up beside them.

'I lost her,' Ross gasped. 'Aunt Eugenie would insist on talking to me and she must have sidled away from me. Has she been out here?'

'Isobel?' Noah sounded terrified, and no wonder.

Clemmie came out at that moment and put her arm around Ross's waist. 'What are you doing out here? You shot out of the door like you were on fire.' She looked from one to the other of them, clearly intrigued. 'Is everything okay?'

'Everything's fine,' Ross assured her. 'I don't suppose you've seen Isobel?'

'Yes, she's in there,' Clemmie said, jerking her thumb in the direction of the church door. 'She's talking to Zach—something about flowers for the memorial service.'

Noah leaned against the porch, looking pale but relieved.

'I'd better go,' Daisy said. 'If she finds me out here with you...'

'What the hell's going on?' Ross demanded. 'Don't try to tell me there's nothing wrong, because it's written all over your face.'

'Are you and Daisy...' Clemmie clearly didn't quite know how to finish the sentence.

Noah reached for Daisy's hand. 'Yes, we are. And I'm going

to tell Isobel after the memorial service.' He faced Ross, his expression determined. 'Please, don't try to talk me out of this. I know I'm a married man, and I have responsibilities, but—'

'Bloody hell!' Ross enfolded him in a huge hug. 'I couldn't be happier or more relieved! I thought you'd never see sense.' He turned to Daisy, who was quite stunned at this unexpected reaction, and hugged her. 'Thank you. Thanks for saving him from himself.'

She half laughed, but she was aware all the time that Isobel could come outside at any moment. 'I really need to go. Noah will explain everything.'

Well, not everything, although she couldn't help wishing he would.

'I'll see you at the memorial service,' Noah said gently.

She nodded and smiled. 'You will.'

'I love you,' he whispered, and she blew him a kiss then walked quickly away towards the church gates, little knowing what lay in store for them.

TWENTY

Daisy couldn't settle. All day she paced up and down the living room, flicked restlessly between channels on the television, made a big pot of chilli, vacuumed the carpets, stared out of the window, and sighed a lot.

It was raining. The market square looked damp and drab and grey, with even the orange and gold autumn decorations which adorned some of the shops failing to brighten the place up. Daisy's heart kept racing without warning, and she was beginning to wonder if there was something physically wrong with her.

Deep down, though, she knew that she was simply worried. She couldn't help it. Her stomach churned with nerves, and she felt too sick to even try the chilli, even though she'd concentrated hard on it, and it smelled delicious.

It would help if she could figure out why she felt so scared, but she couldn't pinpoint the cause.

'Maybe it's not anxiety,' she said out loud, as if the sound of her own voice would calm her down. 'Maybe it's excitement.' After all, she'd just been given the most amazing news. Noah had told her he loved her! And he was finally going to leave Isobel, which was even better news. Everything she'd hoped for was going to happen at last.

But she couldn't get past the fact that, first, Noah was going to have to tell Isobel that their marriage was over, and how Isobel would react to that Daisy didn't dare imagine.

'But he'll be with Ross,' she told herself. 'Ross will keep him safe. She wouldn't dare do anything in front of him.'

Besides, they had at least two days before they needed to think about it. Out of respect to Leon's memory Noah wouldn't say anything until the memorial service was out of the way. She knew that.

So why was her gut telling her that something was badly wrong?

She gazed at her phone, willing it to ping with a message from Noah. She couldn't ring him, obviously, and she didn't dare text him unless he texted her first, meaning it was safe for them to talk, but she longed to hear from him.

'He won't change his mind,' she said firmly. 'If that's what's worrying you.'

Was it? She didn't think it was. She just had a horrible feeling that things were about to go very wrong.

The rain had turned to that annoying drizzle that somehow managed to soak you through even though it didn't look very much at all. 'Wet rain,' her dad used to call it, which had always baffled her when she was little, but which she understood now.

Dusk fell. The sky was dark and heavy, and she thought maybe there'd be more rain later and that the churchyard would be muddy and squelchy for the memorial if it continued. Jennifer had invited her, even though Daisy didn't know the Callaghans very well at all and had no history in the town.

She wasn't sure any longer if she'd go, though. It seemed odd to be at the memorial for a person you'd never met, and besides, it might only add to Noah's anxiety, which was the last thing she wanted for him.

At the thought of him her stomach gave a sickening lurch, and she sank down into the armchair, gripped by a sudden panic she couldn't explain.

Without hesitating, she grabbed her phone and messaged Bethany, asking for Ross's number. If Bethany wanted to know why she needed it, she'd make up some excuse. Maybe she could say Ross had asked her to make a cake for the students at the art academy or something. It didn't matter. She needed to get in touch with him.

Bethany replied within ten minutes, although it felt much, much longer to Daisy. Thankfully, she didn't ask questions, and Daisy didn't have to lie or make up an excuse.

She quickly messaged Ross:

> Hi Ross, this is Daisy. Have you seen anything of Noah since the harvest festival this morning? I know this sounds stupid, but can you get in touch with him please? Just check that he's okay. I can't explain but I've got a bad feeling about him, and I just want to know he's all right.

She pressed send before she could change her mind then leaned back in the armchair, her pulse racing as she waited for a reply. The clock on her phone ticked over and she watched the seconds and minutes go by. She was just wondering whether she should call him when, finally, a message pinged into her inbox.

> Hi, Daisy. He and Isobel were at Lavender House earlier having Sunday lunch with Clemmie, Aunt Eugenie, and me. They left just before we did at around six. I've tried ringing him but there's no reply. What makes you think he's not okay?

Daisy gripped the phone in dread. Now what? Why hadn't Noah answered the phone to his brother, of all people?

Should she call Ross and explain? But what should she tell him? Noah might never forgive her if she told him what had been going on, but she couldn't shake this bad feeling, and what if something bad was happening to Noah and she'd done nothing to stop it?

She almost jumped out of her skin as, at that moment, Ross's name flashed up on screen and she realised he was calling her.

'Okay, you've really got me worried now. Come on, Daisy, what's going on? Don't try to fob me off. He's my brother, and if there's something I should know...'

Daisy closed her eyes. *I'm so sorry, Noah, but I don't know what else to do.*

'Ross, I want you to listen to me very carefully. There's something you need to know.'

Vaguely, as if in a dream, Noah heard voices.

'Well, I'm sorry to say it, but I'm sick of this awful weather already.'

He tried to sit up but didn't have the strength. Ava. He was almost sure it was Ava.

'I know it's autumn now, and one should expect all this murk and gloom, but I'm simply not ready for it. I wish it could be summer all the time. Can't you have a word with The Boss?'

There was the sound of laughter. 'I don't think the Almighty would listen to me about that, love. Besides, where would we be if you got your wish, eh? Sunshine's smashing, but we'd be in trouble without a bit of rain, don't you think?'

'Oh, I suppose so.' There was a resigned sigh.

Noah tried to open his eyes but realised he couldn't even manage that.

'I wonder if Rita and Birdie have stopped arguing yet?' Zach said.

Ava giggled. 'I doubt it, unless Eugenie has banged their heads together. Did you see Bluebell's loaves? Honestly, she kept that very quiet, didn't she? They were truly appalling, bless her.'

'God loves a trier.' Zach paused. 'Did you hear something?'

'No. Like what?'

'A moan or something.'

'A moan? Ooh, you mean like a ghost?'

'Don't be scaring me. I have to lock up on my own most nights.'

'Oh, bless you. Well, you've got me tonight, darling, but only because you've bribed me with dinner at The White Hart Inn. I'll protect you. Come on, let's lock up and get out of here.'

Noah felt a surge of panic and tried to sit up again. The pain shot through him, and he heard Zach say, 'There! You must have heard that.'

'I did!' Ava sounded deeply worried.

There was the sound of heels on the stone floor, then a cry. 'Zach! It's Noah. Oh my God, look at him!'

'Bloody hell!'

It struck Noah later that their language hadn't exactly been appropriate for the House of God.

'Noah, what happened?'

'He must have been mugged,' Ava said.

'Mugged? He's been attacked by a maniac, by the looks of him. Noah, can you sit up?'

Noah felt an arm go around him and groaned in pain.

'Best leave him lying down,' Ava advised. 'I'll call an ambulance.'

'And Ross,' Zach said.

'What about Eugenie?'

'No. It might be too much. Ross will know. Leave it to him.'

Noah felt his head being gently lifted and something soft placed beneath it. Then something else was laid over him, easing the chill that was seeping through to his bones.

'You're going to be all right, mate,' Zach soothed. 'Just hang on in there. Help's on its way.'

In the distance he could hear Ava talking to someone but couldn't make out what she was saying. Zach laid his hand on Noah's arm and began to murmur something. A prayer of some sort. For someone. Noah couldn't take it in. Maybe it was part of the harvest festival service. Or had that ended now?

He was very tired and decided he couldn't stay awake any longer. Yes, he had guests, but he simply didn't have the energy to talk to them right now. Maybe when he'd rested. He wanted to sleep and dream. Maybe, in his dreams, he'd find Daisy.

That would be nice.

When someone banged on the door Daisy almost flew down the stairs to answer it.

'Ross! What are you doing here? I thought you were going to—'

'I did!' Ross's expression was grim. 'I went to Peony Cottage and there's no one there. It was in darkness, and all locked up. I banged on that door for ages, and I went round the back, too. I tried looking through the windows, but the curtains were drawn, and I even looked through the letter box. There's nothing. No sound, no light, no sign of life.'

'Don't say that,' Daisy said with a shiver. 'You'd better come upstairs.'

She led him into her flat, where he refused her offer of a drink and sank into a chair, running a hand through his hair in obvious distress.

'So, what do we do now?' Daisy asked, her hands wringing together as she tried her best not to give way to panic.

'You're absolutely sure about this?' Ross said. 'I mean, I know Isobel's a bitch, and I've never liked her. Never understood what Noah saw in her to be honest. But even so... Are you absolutely positive that she's hurting him?'

'Ross, believe me, if you'd seen what I saw the other day you'd be in no doubt that Noah could be in big danger. She'd attacked him with a pan, but she's apparently hit him with loads of other things in the past. He was black and blue. I'm terrified.'

'Why the hell didn't he tell anyone?' Ross demanded roughly. 'Why didn't he tell *me*? I'd have stopped her nasty little game, believe me!'

'We can worry about all that later. Right now, we have to find out if he's okay. Where are they? You don't—you don't think she's taken him to the hospital?'

'Is it likely?' Ross stared at her, and Daisy guessed they'd both had the same thought.

'What if he's lying in that house, hurt? We should call the police. They can break in.'

'But if we're wrong...' Ross threw up his arms in despair. 'Why doesn't he answer his bloody phone?'

'I don't care if we are wrong now,' Daisy said, making up her mind. 'We need to make sure he's okay, and if that means Isobel finding out that Noah's confided in us, well, it's tough. I'll make damn sure she never gets anywhere near him again.'

'You're right.' Ross took out his phone. 'I'll call them. There's no point in—' He broke off as his phone began to ring. He glanced up at Daisy. 'It's Ava!'

'Ava?'

Daisy was about to tell him to dismiss the call as they had far more important things to do than make small talk with the vicar's wife, but Ross had already answered, and was now listening to whatever she was saying with a look of horror on his face. Daisy's blood seemed to turn to ice in her veins as she watched his eyes fill with tears.

'Have you called an ambulance?'

Daisy gasped and dropped onto the sofa, staring at Ross in dread. He glanced at her, and she saw immediately that her worst fears had come true.

'Yes, yes, we'll be right there. No, don't call Aunt Eugenie. Not until we know... Just leave it for now. Thanks, Ava.'

He ended the call and turned to Daisy, his body suddenly trembling as if he'd gone into shock.

'They've found Noah in the church. He—he's been attacked. They've phoned an ambulance.'

'How bad is he?' she whispered.

'Ava said it looks pretty bad,' he told her. 'But look, the main thing is they found him, and an ambulance is on its way. He'll be okay, Daisy. They'll fix him up, don't worry.'

She could tell from his voice that he was willing this to be true, but she could hardly reply as her throat was so full of tears. She grabbed her coat from the hall and said, 'Come on then. We need to get to the church, now!'

Half dazed, Ross followed her out of the flat and down the stairs. She slammed the front door shut after them and they ran to All Hallows.

The lamps in the church were on, and Daisy could see Zach and Ava sitting quietly in one of the pews. Ava got to her feet and hurried towards them.

'How is he?' Ross gasped.

'He's—he's pretty bad,' she admitted. 'There's a lot of blood and his face is...' She shook her head, as if to clear the tears in her eyes. 'He's unconscious at the moment. He keeps drifting in and out of awareness, I think. Zach's covered him with his jacket. Just be prepared. It's not a pretty sight.'

Ross and Daisy exchanged glances.

'Maybe you should wait here,' he said softly.

Daisy straightened. 'He needs me,' she said simply.

Ross nodded and they made their way to where Zach was

sitting. As they drew closer, they could see a form lying on the pew next to him. It might have been Noah, but it was hard to tell, especially as a jacket covered most of his clothes and they had only a swollen, battered face to go by. Noah's tawny coloured hair was matted with blood, and his left eye was swollen shut.

Daisy's hands flew to her mouth, and she heard Ross say, 'Is he awake?'

'I don't think so,' Zach said gently. 'He hasn't made any noise for a while. I've checked his pulse and he's breathing, and the wound on his head has stopped bleeding, thank goodness. I think he'll need stitches, though.'

'What the hell has she done?' Ross murmured.

'She?' Ava stepped forward, alarm on her face. 'You know who's done this?'

'His bloody so-called wife has done this,' Ross said bitterly. He crouched down and gently stroked the hair away from Noah's swollen face. 'Why didn't you tell me? Why didn't you let me help you?'

'Isobel?' Ava turned to Daisy, her expression incredulous. 'Are you sure?'

'Positive,' Daisy said, tears streaming down her face. 'Oh, God, look at him. Look at him!'

The church door opened, and two paramedics entered.

'Thank goodness,' Ava said, hurrying to meet them. 'I'm so sorry to call you out but this poor man is in desperate need of care and attention. He's the victim of an assault, and he's not conscious at the moment.'

Zach glanced up at Daisy. 'Isobel? Really?'

She nodded, unable to tear her gaze away from Noah.

'Dear God,' Zach said, getting to his feet. 'He was trying to tell me. Lord help me, I didn't understand.'

The paramedics arrived by Noah's side and Daisy, Zach, and a reluctant Ross stepped away to give them room to work.

They could hear the men asking Noah if he could hear them, but didn't seem to get a response, until after what seemed like forever, they heard him groan.

He's alive, Daisy thought, and right then it seemed like a miracle.

'I expect you'll be going to the hospital with him,' Zach said to Ross.

Ross glanced at Daisy. 'I think it's you he'll want with him,' he said gently. 'I'll follow on. But first...' He gave a heavy sigh. 'First I'd better go to Lavender House and break all this to Aunt Eugenie.'

'Would you like me to go with you?' Zach offered.

Ross hesitated, then nodded. 'That might be good. I'm sure you'll be able to comfort her, thanks.'

Ava said, 'Where is Isobel? Do you know?'

'Done a bunk by the looks of it,' Ross said, the anger returning to his voice. 'But don't worry. We'll find her, and she'll pay for this.'

'I simply can't believe it,' Ava admitted. 'It doesn't seem real. Thank goodness we came here to lock up the church, darling. Imagine if he'd been here all night. It doesn't bear thinking about.'

Daisy shivered. She honestly didn't think Noah would have survived the night if he hadn't been discovered.

They huddled together, the four of them, shocked and distressed as the paramedics looked after Noah. Finally, it was time to move him into the ambulance.

'I'm going with him, if that's okay,' Daisy told them, and they nodded.

'I'll be there as soon as I can with Aunt Eugenie,' Ross told her. 'Stay by his side, Daisy. Tell him we all love him.'

She nodded. 'Of course I will.'

She swallowed down tears as Ross hugged her tightly. 'He'll get through this,' he told her fiercely. 'You just watch him.'

She nodded and climbed into the back of the ambulance, where Noah lay, conscious but clearly not fully aware of what was happening. She saw the anguished looks on the faces of Zach, Ava, and Ross. Then the doors were slammed shut, and they were on their way to the hospital, leaving Tuppenny Bridge behind.

TWENTY-ONE

'I just can't believe it. I can't believe it.'

Daisy had never imagined Miss Lavender could ever look so utterly broken, but as she watched Noah's great aunt wipe away her tears, her heart broke for the old lady who was clearly devastated by what had occurred.

They were sitting by Noah's bedside—Ross and Miss Lavender on one side and Daisy and Zach on the other. Noah was sleeping peacefully, having been examined, his wounds attended to, and painkillers administered. It was early on Monday morning, and they'd been allowed to stay with him while he was settled into a private room at Miss Lavender's insistence. Daisy had managed to contact Rowan and Tess, who'd assured her they would manage the café just fine on their own, and that she needn't worry about a thing.

'Why didn't I see?' Miss Lavender wept. 'Why didn't I know what was going on?' She reached for Ross's hand. 'Why didn't he tell us?'

'I don't know, Auntie,' he soothed. 'The main thing to remember is that he's safe now, and he's being taken care of. And now we *do* know it will never happen again.'

'It certainly won't! That woman!' Miss Lavender shook her head, then her gaze fell on Daisy, her eyes full of shame. 'I warned him away from you. Told him to stick with Isobel. Be *loyal* to *her!*' Her voice cracked as fresh tears fell. 'If I hadn't said all that to him, perhaps he would have found the courage to leave her. Was this my fault?'

'No! No, Miss Lavender, you can't blame yourself,' Daisy said, wanting nothing more than to reassure this heartbroken old lady.

'If anyone's to blame it's me,' Zach said gruffly. 'He came to see me, back in mid-August. Told me things were bad between him and Isobel. He asked me if I thought all sins could be forgiven—even ones where people got hurt. I—I told him to put more effort into his marriage.' His eyes gleamed with unshed tears. 'I suggested counselling. Counselling! God forgive me.'

'You weren't to blame either,' Ross said flatly. 'There's only one person at fault here and that's Isobel, and with any luck she'll pay for it.'

'Oh,' Miss Lavender said, sounding for a moment like her old, determined self, 'she'll pay for it all right.'

They all fell silent, and Daisy turned to Noah. He had fallen asleep with his hand in hers. She gently squeezed his fingers, beyond grateful that the damage hadn't been worse.

An orbital fracture had caused the swelling of the eye. Noah had been given a scan and an assessment first thing that morning and they'd been told that the specialist would assess him again once the swelling had gone down, so they could better check the eye and its movement. He also had two fractured ribs, extensive bruising to his upper body, scratches all over his neck and face, and a deep cut to his head, which had been stitched.

'He has concussion, so we'll keep him in for forty-eight hours to monitor him,' the doctor had told them last night.

'We're keeping an eye on his blood pressure, too. It's rather high, although perhaps that's not surprising. Try not to worry.'

Easier said than done, thought Daisy. How Noah had managed to drag himself to the church was beyond belief. And why he'd made for All Hallows instead of her flat was another puzzle. It would have been just as near for him and much safer. What if Zach hadn't gone to lock up the church? What if he hadn't heard him?

'At least he's sleeping now,' Miss Lavender said quietly. 'Poor lamb didn't get much chance last night, what with all the tests and being moved around so much.'

'Do you think his eye will heal okay?' Ross asked, worriedly. 'It looks bloody awful.'

'It's hard to tell at this stage.' Zach gave Noah a compassionate look. 'They'll be checking his vision and if there are any problems they'll deal with them. I'm sure it will be fine.'

Daisy raised Noah's hand to her lips and gently kissed it.

'I'm so sorry for the way I judged you,' Miss Lavender said.

Daisy realised she was talking to her and shook her head. 'Please, don't worry about it. I totally understand.'

'I'm so glad he's had you to turn to, even if he couldn't confide in his own family,' Miss Lavender continued.

'I should have told the police,' Daisy said. 'I should never have listened to him when he said he'd deal with it. I thought I had to let him decide for himself when the time was right to leave her, but I should have realised. He was being abused, and people in that situation find it so hard to make rational choices. I should have overruled him. I'll never forgive myself.'

'Well, that makes three of us then,' Zach said sympathetically.

'Four,' Ross said. 'I know I said this is all down to Isobel, and in a way, it is, of course, but that doesn't stop me feeling bloody awful that my own brother didn't feel able to confide in me, or that I didn't spot the signs. I should have done.'

'It's not your fault—any of you.'

They all jumped upon hearing Noah's voice. Daisy leaned over and carefully kissed his forehead.

'Hey, you. Back with us then?'

'Looks like it. Can't get rid of me that easily.' He managed a smile and Daisy swallowed down a sob.

'The police will be here soon, my darling,' Miss Lavender said. 'They wanted to take a statement last night, but I wouldn't let them. But the sooner that woman's behind bars the better.'

Noah groaned. 'I don't want to talk to the police. I told you that last night. Who got them involved anyway?'

'They turned up just as you were being taken away in the ambulance,' Ross explained. 'I presume they were informed when Ava rang 999 and said there'd been a serious assault. They followed you to the hospital, but you weren't in any fit state to answer their questions. How do you feel now? Are you up to talking to them?'

'It's not about being fit to talk to them,' Noah said. 'I just don't want to. Can't we forget about this? I'm okay now. I'll be fit and well again in a couple of days.'

'I hope you're joking,' Ross said, clearly aghast at the idea that Noah didn't want to tell the police what had happened. 'That woman needs punishing.'

'She's already been punished,' Noah said heavily. He looked at Daisy. 'She knows about you and me. She heard what we were talking about outside the church.'

'That you were leaving her?' Daisy gasped. 'Is that why she did what she did?'

'That's—that's what started it.'

'Noah, why on earth didn't you tell us what was happening?' Miss Lavender pleaded. 'We could have done something. Darling boy, I would never have told you to stay with her if I'd known. I'm so sorry.'

'I heard what you were all saying just now,' Noah admitted.

'All of you, blaming yourselves. None of it was your fault. Any of you. This was all on me. I was the one who chose to stay with Isobel. I was the one who kept it all a secret. I was the one who drove her to behave in that way in the first place.'

'*What?* You can't possibly blame yourself!' Daisy cried. 'There's no excuse for what she did. Noah, you're the victim in all this, not her. You must tell the police what it's been like. What she's done to you all these years.'

'I can't,' he said quietly. 'I just can't do that to her. And I don't want to go through it all again. Can't we just put it behind us?'

'And leave her free to do it to someone else?' Ross asked, his gaze piercing through Noah, who seemed lost for words.

'She wouldn't,' Noah said at last. 'This was about me and my failure to make her happy. She wouldn't hurt anyone else, Ross.'

'Oh, Noah.' Zach shook his head sadly. 'Have you any idea how many victims of abuse say that? I'm sorry, I really am, but it's just not true. If she wasn't happy with you, she could have left but she didn't. Instead, she chose to stay and make your life hell, and she's managed to convince you that it's all your fault. If you let her get away with this, she'll find her next victim and put him through the same kind of hell. That's what these people do. Please believe me when I tell you I've come across this sort of thing far too many times before. You have to call her to account.'

Noah's fingers curled around the blanket, and Daisy saw how tightly he was gripping it.

'Who will believe me?' he asked at last. 'A man being assaulted by his wife? They'll think it's ridiculous. Isobel told me she would tell everyone it was self-defence, and that I'd been hitting her for years. You saw the bruises on her wrists that day, Daisy, after I'd tried to restrain her! You know what people thought. People who've known me for years, doubting me, thinking I was capable of that. I never did!' His voice, thick with anxiety, rose. 'I wouldn't. I never laid a finger on her other than to try to stop her. I just couldn't.'

'Shh, darling,' Miss Lavender soothed. 'We know. We know you would never!'

'No one will believe her,' Daisy said, choked. 'For God's sake, Noah, look at the state of you! That's not self-defence. And I've seen you bruised and battered before, remember, and I'll give evidence stating that if I have to.'

'But what will happen to her?' he pleaded. 'She couldn't go to prison. She'd never survive it.'

'And you nearly didn't survive what she did to you, remember?' Miss Lavender reached for his hand, prising his fingers from the blanket. 'Please, Noah. You can't let her get away with it. I can see she's done an exceptional job on making you believe this is your fault, but it's just not true. And the vicar is absolutely right. If you let her get away with this, she'll do it to someone else. That type always finds another victim. Please. For me. I can't...'

And then out of the blue, stoic, no-nonsense, common sense, tough as old boots Miss Lavender put her head on Noah's chest and sobbed her heart out.

Daisy could barely see for tears as a horrified Noah stroked his Aunt Eugenie's hair and tried to comfort her, while Ross and Zach seemed at a loss to know what to do or say.

'It's all right,' Noah said. 'It's okay. I'll do it, Auntie, I promise. I'll tell the police.'

'No!'

Miss Lavender sat up and mopped away her tears with her already sodden handkerchief. 'I won't have that! I will not let you do anything you don't want to do. You've been bullied and manipulated for long enough. I'm a silly old fool and I'm heartbroken for you, but that must have no bearing on your decision. You're an adult and you make your own decisions, Noah. And we will respect that decision.' She looked round at them all, a fierce glint in her eyes. 'Won't we?'

There was a moment's silence, then everyone mumbled variations on the same theme that, of course they would, and it was totally up to Noah, and they were on his side no matter what.

Noah looked dazed. 'I—I—'

The door was pushed open, and a nurse entered, followed by two police officers.

'Now then, Noah,' one of them said kindly. 'I'm Sergeant Jarman, and this is PC Brent. By heck, you've been in the wars, haven't you? How are you feeling? Are you ready to talk to us?'

Noah looked at Daisy, and she gave his hand a reassuring squeeze.

He gave a heavy sigh then said, 'Yes, I'm ready. I'll tell you everything.'

TWENTY-TWO

With Zach beside him, Ross guided his reluctant great aunt towards the door.

'Time to go home, I think, Aunt Eugenie,' he said, giving Noah a wink.

'And leave Noah here? Oh, I don't think so.' Miss Lavender was clearly itching to stay, but Ross was firm.

'Noah's in good hands, and we'll come back this afternoon for visiting hours. Come on. I'll treat you to a cup of tea and a sticky bun at Daisy's café if you're good. Let's leave Noah to deal with this, shall we?'

Miss Lavender gave Daisy an appealing look. 'You *will* look after him?'

Daisy nodded. 'I promise.' She smiled at Noah. 'Always.'

Evidently reassured, Miss Lavender allowed Zach and Ross to chivvy her out of the room and everyone immediately relaxed a little.

The police officers were kind and patient as Noah hesitantly told them what had happened the previous day.

'After the harvest festival we were invited to Aunt Eugenie's for Sunday lunch,' he explained. 'Me, Isobel, my brother, Ross, and his girlfriend, Clemmie. Everything seemed fine on the surface. Isobel was a little tense, but that's nothing unusual. She doesn't really like my family, you see, and she hates me having contact with them.'

'Is there any particular reason for that?' Sergeant Jarman asked.

'Not that I can think of,' Noah admitted. 'They've never done or said anything bad to her. In fact, they've gone out of their way to welcome her to the family. We've been together since we were teenagers, you see, so they've known her a long time. But the truth is, Isobel never liked them, and she seemed to resent any time I spent with them. She would get—difficult when I made plans to see them. And she seldom spent time with them herself. To be honest, I was amazed when she agreed to attend the Sunday lunch—or the harvest festival come to that.'

'And what time did you leave Lavender House?' asked the sergeant.

'About six o'clock,' Noah said, after a moment's thought. 'Some time around then anyway. We walked home and got back to Peony Cottage at about six thirty, so I should think that would be about right. Isobel was wearing heels so we couldn't walk very fast.'

'And how did your wife seem? Was there any indication that she was angry with you?'

'Not at first,' Noah said slowly.

His fingers plucked nervously at the blanket and the sergeant said soothingly, 'Take your time, Noah. No rush.'

Shakily, Noah told them how Isobel had sat watching the television while he'd made them both a cup of tea, and how they'd then sat on opposite armchairs, speaking very little.

'She asked me if we had any bread as she fancied some toast. I got up to make her some and she jumped up and followed me. As I tried to leave the room she pushed the door, trapping me against the jamb. I asked her what she was doing and then she...' He wrinkled his nose at the memory. 'She spat at me.'

Sergeant Jarman raised an eyebrow as Daisy covered her mouth with her hand in disgust.

'She spat at you?'

'Yes. In the face.'

'And did she give you a reason why she did that?'

'Oh yes.' Noah glanced at Daisy who reddened. 'She'd overheard Daisy and me talking outside the church. She knew I'd made up my mind to leave her.'

'You were going to leave your wife?'

'I was. I am. I have, I suppose.' Noah sounded as if he could hardly believe it himself.

'But she was abusing him before that,' Daisy burst out. 'It wasn't a one off.'

'Is that true?' asked the sergeant.

Noah sighed. 'Yes.'

'And do you have any evidence for that? Any witnesses?'

'Yes,' Daisy said. 'I saw the bruises. He was covered in them, from his waist up to his shoulder.'

'I see.'

'We're not having an affair!' Daisy said hastily. 'That is, I didn't see the bruises because... Well, he showed them to me because I could see he was in pain. We weren't...'

'No judgement from me,' Sergeant Jarman said. 'I'm here to gather facts, that's all. So, are you saying your wife attacked you on previous occasions, Noah?'

'I—I am,' Noah said sadly. 'She's been attacking me almost from the beginning of our marriage. That's why I knew I had to leave.'

'So, after she spat at you, what happened next?'

Noah swallowed. 'She told me what she'd heard. She was calling me names, telling me what a waste of space I was. The usual stuff. Then she started on Daisy. Calling her names, I mean. Saying the most terrible things about her, about both of us. I...'

He stopped and they all waited. Eventually, Sergeant Jarman said suspiciously, 'You what, Noah?'

'I told her a few home truths,' he admitted. 'I told her that Daisy meant everything to me, and that Isobel had made my life hell for long enough and I wanted out. And that, no matter what she did or said, I wasn't going to change my mind about that.'

'So, you didn't strike her? Push her? Touch her in any way?'

'Of course not!' Noah gasped. 'What sort of man do you think I am? I've never hurt her! I never would.'

'Even when she's shown no hesitation to hurt you?'

'I have never lifted a finger to Isobel,' Noah swore. 'I couldn't do it. If you don't believe me at least bear in mind that, at that time, it would be physically impossible. I was still pinned in the door frame at that point. If you find it hard to believe I wouldn't hurt her, at least look at the evidence.'

'Don't upset yourself, Noah. I'm just trying to establish whether your wife could reasonably claim she acted in self-defence,' Sergeant Jarman said.

'Really?' Daisy couldn't keep the sarcasm out of her voice. 'Have you seen the state of him? What kind of self-defence is that?'

'I have to ask these questions,' he explained patiently. 'I'm just trying to establish the facts here, that's all.'

Daisy nodded. 'I know. Sorry.'

'So how did Mrs Lavender react to your words?'

'Badly,' Noah said. He glanced down at his fingers, which were nervously pleating the blanket again. 'She released the door but then... She punched me on the side of my face. Before I could gather my thoughts, something struck me on the head. I sort of crumpled, and she struck me again and again.'

'Do you know what she was hitting you with?'

Noah nodded. 'Not at first, but then I saw the shoe in her hand and realised she was using the heel.'

'Sorry, where exactly in the house were you when this happened?'

'In the kitchen,' Noah said. 'There are two doors in our living room, as it runs the full depth of the house. One leads into the hall, the other into the kitchen. I'd gone through the kitchen door to make her toast.'

'So where did Mrs Lavender get the shoe?'

'She was wearing them,' Noah said, puzzled.

'Is it usual for her to wear shoes inside the house?'

Noah hesitated. 'No, as a matter of fact, it's not. She's usually very fussy about leaving shoes in the hall. I don't know why she was still wearing them.'

'I see. And these were shoes with heels?'

'Yes. Isobel never wears flats. She considers them ugly.'

Sergeant Jarman was writing quickly. After a moment or two he looked up.

'So, she repeatedly struck you on the head with the heel of her shoe?'

'Yes. I felt a bit dazed. I remember shaking my head and blood spattering over my hands. I managed to grab the shoe from her and turned to throw it across the room, but when I looked back at her something heavy hit me in the face. I couldn't tell what it was. The pain was agonising, and I covered my eyes. She pushed me and I fell over, and then I saw her reach for the meat tenderiser—'

'The meat tenderiser?' Sergeant Jarman asked sharply. 'But that's not what she hit you in the face with?'

'No. I saw her grab it after I'd already fallen to the floor. I just remember being hit, over and over again in my stomach and chest, while I lay on the floor. I tried to get up and she dropped the tenderiser and grabbed me by the throat. She was clawing at me, punching me in the face and scratching my neck. And all the while she was screaming abuse at me. Terrible things. Vile things.'

Daisy felt sick to her stomach. It was hard to believe that someone as cool and haughty as Isobel could behave in such a way. The picture Noah was painting with his descriptions was painfully realistic. She couldn't stop her imagination playing out the events in her head, and it hurt like hell. He must have been terrified.

A huge part of her wanted to walk out of the room. She needed some fresh air. To escape from what she was hearing. But Noah couldn't escape, could he? He had lived that dreadful experience, and he would probably relive it for the rest of his life. There was no way she was abandoning him now.

Instead, she forced herself to sit quietly and calmly, holding his hand while he finished making his statement.

'What made you go to the church, Noah?' Sergeant Jarman asked. 'Seems a funny place to head to.' He nodded at Daisy. 'Why not, for example, head to Miss Jackson's flat?'

'And what if Isobel had followed me there?' Noah tightened his grip on Daisy's hand. 'I was thinking clearly enough to know that I couldn't lead her to Daisy. Why the church? I honestly don't know,' he admitted. 'I don't even know where Isobel was at that point. I think she must have gone upstairs. I sort of staggered outside and I saw the steeple and I thought—I know it sounds stupid, but I thought, *sanctuary*. It was the only thing I could think at that moment. So, I headed there. Somewhere at the back of my mind I thought I'd be safe there.'

'I see.' The police officers exchanged looks, and Daisy saw the compassion in their eyes.

At last Sergeant Jarman got to his feet, thanking Noah for his time.

'What will happen now?' Daisy asked.

'Mrs Lavender isn't at home,' he told them. 'We've been to Peony Cottage, and it's all locked up. Have you any idea where we might find her? According to her assistant at the Petalicious flower shop, she was supposed to be at work this morning, but didn't turn up. Her assistant's called in her gran to help. She's in a bit of a state, actually, because there's some sort of service tomorrow at the church and they're supposed to be supplying the flowers.'

Leon's memorial! Daisy had forgotten all about it. Evidently Isobel had, too. Either that or she didn't care, which was more likely.

Noah gave them Isobel's mother's address in London, and her aunt's address in Harrogate.

'We'll send someone round to talk to her,' Sergeant Jarman promised.

'Talk to her? She needs arresting!' Daisy cried.

'Just let us do our job, Daisy,' he said gently. 'We take this sort of thing very seriously, believe me. I give you my word, this crime will be investigated thoroughly.'

'So—so you *are* treating it as a crime?' Noah asked.

Sergeant Jarman gave him a sympathetic smile. 'It *is* a crime, Noah. And if your wife has done this to you, she's a criminal. Simple as.'

When the two policemen had finally left, Noah let out a long sigh and leaned back on his pillows.

'I'm sorry you had to go through that,' Daisy said softly. 'It must have been so hard for you to relive it all.'

'I don't know how she'll cope if she goes to prison,' Noah said. 'I feel so guilty.'

'It's no use me telling you that you shouldn't, is it?' When he didn't reply she said, 'What didn't you tell them?'

Noah frowned. 'What do you mean?'

'When you were telling them about Isobel calling me names, you hesitated. You were going to say something else, but you didn't. I could see your brain ticking over. You're hiding something, aren't you?'

She saw the faint flush of pink on his cheekbones and knew she was right.

'What didn't you tell them, Noah?' she asked anxiously.

'Oh, Daisy.' He reached for a glass of water, wincing as he did so, and she hurriedly passed it to him. 'Thank you. I'll tell you, but it's not going to be pretty. And I warn you, I don't come out of this at all well.'

'What do you mean?'

He took a sip of water. 'Like I said, I told her a few home truths. And I just couldn't tell the police about that, because it doesn't just affect me. Isobel and I have been keeping secrets from each other for so long. I never thought they'd ever come out. But now...'

'Noah, whatever it is, you can tell me,' Daisy urged him. 'I'm on your side, I promise. I always will be.'

'I'm not going to hold you to that,' he said. 'But I'll tell you anyway. I need to unburden myself to someone. It's been a long, long time.'

TWENTY-THREE

The previous evening

Noah couldn't believe the insults Isobel was hurling about Daisy. It had been one thing listening to the things she had to say about him—he was, after all, used to hearing all that—but what she was saying about Daisy was unbelievable. He hadn't even realised she knew words like the ones that were pouring from her mouth in a torrent of rage.

'And if you think she'll stay with you, you can think again,' Isobel snarled. 'Even someone as desperate as that fat bitch won't hang around for long. Not once she realises how incredibly dull and stupid you are. How useless. You're rubbish at everything, aren't you, Noah?'

He closed his eyes, waiting for the inevitable stream of put downs and jibes.

'Useless! You only got that job because everyone in this town is scared stiff of your precious Aunt Eugenie. She's had to pull strings all your life to get you anywhere. I'll bet you anything she even bribed the people at the university to get you a degree. There's no way you'd get anything on your own merit because you're way too stupid.'

He opened his eyes again, staring at her face, contorted with rage. He wondered how he'd ever considered her beautiful. Right now, she was the ugliest person he'd ever seen.

It was as if she could read his thoughts and turned them back on him. 'Look at you! God, you're hideous. What did I ever see in you? P-pathetic. P-uny,' she said, mocking the stammer he'd struggled with for years—the stammer that had only been caused in the first place by her behaviour towards him. 'All those spots all over your face.' She jabbed at his freckles with her forefinger. 'Like a bloody kid. Who has freckles at your age? You're not a man at all. You never were. Stammering and stuttering like a big baby. Is there any wonder I can't stand you near me in bed? You're disgusting. You even fail there. I pity Daisy. She's going to be so disappointed. Although, the state of her, she's probably grateful for anything she can get. The only thing I could ever rely on you for was to let me down.'

Something snapped. Noah glared at her. 'Really? Well, I'm very sorry that I could never compete with your precious Leon!'

The shock in her face gave him a moment's satisfaction. She slumped against the door, her eyes wide.

'What did you say?'

'Did you really think I didn't know, Isobel?'

Oh, God! What had he said? All these years he'd kept what he knew to himself, but now the truth was finally out.

'You don't know what you're talking about,' she said faintly.

'I know exactly what I'm talking about. You and Leon—my *friend*, Leon—were having an affair. Behind my back. Behind Kat's back. And you say *I'm* the disgusting one!'

That was when she spat at him.

'Making up lies to justify your sordid affair with that tramp,' she said bitterly. 'How dare you say such horrible things about Leon! He was worth a hundred of you.'

'You clearly thought so,' he said.

'You're insane. Leon was with Kat. Everyone knew that.'

'He was, and they were happy. Like we were happy. Until you and Leon decided we weren't. Please don't deny it. You know as well as I do that the time for pretence is over. We've lied to each other for long enough, don't you think?'

She rammed the door harder into his chest. 'Stop saying such things! You're just trying to wriggle out of this. Don't think I don't know.'

The door slammed into him again.

'You want everyone to feel sympathy for you, don't you? You want people to be on your side when they find out about you and that cow from the café. Well, it won't work. No one would believe your lies. I'll make sure they all know what's really been going on.'

'Isobel...' He felt exhausted, too tired to argue any longer. 'Don't. This is getting us nowhere. I know about you and Leon. I've always known.'

The fight had gone out of him. He knew that, whatever he and Isobel had once had, it had gone for good. Maybe he'd been fooling himself. Maybe they'd never had what he'd thought they'd had. He'd been an idiot, believing what he wanted to believe. Needing her. Needing to belong to someone. A family of his own. Huh! Family. He and Isobel had hardly been that.

She let go of the door and folded her arms, trembling. 'When did you find out?'

Finally released, he slumped against the wall, rubbing his shoulder and collarbone where the door had pressed into him. 'I suspected for a while. When I got home from university you were different, and Leon was odd around me. Like he couldn't look me in the face. So, one night, I followed you.'

'You did *what*?'

'Yeah, I know. Not my finest hour. But not yours either, to be fair. I followed you to Larkspur Common. You parked up in the grounds of Grenley Hall. I left my car on the road and headed up there on foot, and I saw you in the car. I saw you...'

'You *watched!*'

'No,' he said, his lip curling at the thought. 'Do you really think I wanted to see that? As soon as I'd confirmed that you two were having an affair I got out of there as fast as I could.'

Isobel sank into the armchair and wrapped her arms around her body. 'I loved him,' she said flatly. 'He was everything to me. We had such a future planned. We were going to leave this place behind.' She gazed around the living room, her eyes suddenly full of tears. 'Get out of Tuppenny Bridge for good and just—just *live!*'

'I know,' he admitted.

'It was taken away from us,' she moaned. 'When he died that night, I died, too. Everything I'd hoped for, everything I'd dreamed of, gone. You can't imagine...'

'I'm so sorry,' he told her.

Tears rained down her cheeks. 'Oh, Leon. Why did it have to be you? I wish—I wish I'd been with him in the car that night. I wish I'd died with him.'

'Don't say that, Isobel,' he pleaded. 'You're still young. You can still be happy.'

She shook her head. 'I knew, that morning when we all found out, that I would never be happy again. But I thought... I thought at least with you I'd escape my mother. I thought I could mould you. If I couldn't be happy at least I could have some control. Happiness was for other people. And I was right.' She lifted her head to gaze at him. 'I was right, wasn't I? I've never been happy since that day.'

He wanted to tell her that couldn't possibly be true, but looking back on their life together he wasn't so sure.

'I tried to make you happy,' he told her quietly. 'I did every-thing I could to make it up to you. It was never enough.'

'You married me, knowing how I felt,' she said, dazed. 'For a moment she stared at him as if she was absorbing the reality of the situation. 'You never said a word. Why?'

'I never said a word to *you*,' he said heavily. 'But I had plenty to say to Leon.'

She wiped her eyes. 'You confronted him?'

'I did. We had one hell of a row. I reminded him that we were supposed to be friends. I told him—' He swallowed down tears at the memory. 'I told him that I loved you. That you were everything to me, and had he forgotten that he was supposed to be in love with Kat? He told me his relationship with Kat was just kid's stuff. That he'd grown out of her. Like she was some old jumper or something! He told me he was sorry to hurt me, but that he wasn't going to give you up. Not for anything or anyone.'

'You see?' She sat up straight, her voice eager. 'He loved me, too! Real love! Not the pathetic excuse for love you've offered me all these years. We had passion. We were soulmates.' She gave him a scornful look. 'As if you could ever have persuaded him to give me up!'

Every word she said was another wound. What had he done to her?

'You're right,' he said at last. 'It was a fruitless exercise, but I had to try. He wasn't budging though.'

'And what did you do then?' she asked, her eyes glittering with anger and tears. 'When he told you he wouldn't break up with me. What did you do?'

'I told him I hated him, that we were no longer friends, and that Kat was worth ten of him. Then I swore that I wouldn't let you go, and that I'd kill him if he tried to take you away from me.'

She gave him a disbelieving look. 'You hit him?'

'No. I didn't hit him. I walked away and left him.'

Her lips twisted in a sneer. 'Of course you did. What else would I expect? You wouldn't have it in you, would you?'

Noah's stomach seemed to have knotted, and he thought, for one awful minute, that he was going to be sick. 'As it turned out,' he said bleakly, 'I didn't have to hit him. That was the night. The night he was killed.'

Isobel rose slowly to her feet. 'What?'

'That night, after he and I had the row, he went to pick Ben up from the party, and he never came home.'

'And you never said a word,' she whispered, clearly dazed. 'I was heartbroken. Beside myself. You stood there, comforting me, pretending to be devastated—'

'Not pretending,' he said. 'I *was* devastated. You really think I wished that on him? He was my friend, and when I heard he'd died nothing else seemed to matter. I forgave him in that instant. And of course I comforted you. You needed me.'

'I needed *Leon*,' she said. Her face was pale, and her eyes suddenly seemed huge. 'I could have been happy, Noah. I could have been *happy*. Do you have any idea how I suffered? Trying to keep my grief to a suitable pitch while everyone around me fawned over Kat? Kat! She meant nothing to him, yet all anyone cared about was *her* feelings. It was like I didn't exist. And then you asked me to marry you! Knowing that! Why? Why would you do that?'

'Because I still loved you,' he said simply. 'And because you needed me.'

'No.' She shook her head and walked slowly towards him. 'It wasn't because of that, was it? It was guilt!' She stopped in front of him. 'You knew it was your fault! You knew that your stupid row with Leon, swearing to him that he'd never have me, had distracted him. That was why he crashed the car, wasn't it? Because he was thinking about that! Worrying that you'd stop us being together somehow. Oh!'

She clutched at her hair, desperation in her tone. 'The times I've gone over and over that night. What could have happened to make Leon crash the car. He would never have driven if he'd had a drink, so I knew it wasn't that. Had a cat run into the road or something? Had there been a mechanical failure that the investigators had missed? I went over and over it, tormenting myself with reasons for his accident. And all the time the answer was staring across the breakfast table at me every bloody day, lying beside me in my bed every night, droning on at me in that whiny, stuttering voice of yours. *You* did this! It was *your* fault.'

He didn't answer. He had no words. How could he deny it when she'd just voiced the very thing he'd feared all these years? The secret he'd carried with him all this time. That the argument he'd had with Leon had somehow caused the accident that night. He'd told Leon he would kill him if he tried to take Isobel from him, and somehow, he'd done just that, without ever meaning to. He would never forgive himself for that.

'You took him away from me,' she said. 'The man I loved more than anything in the world. You robbed me of the future that should have been mine.'

'I'm sorry,' he said, knowing two little words could never make up for everything he'd taken from her, any more than the years he'd spent with her, trying to make her happy had.

'You killed him,' she said, sounding dazed.

For a long moment she stood still, as if in a dream. Then he saw the realisation on her face like she'd finally awoken, the dullness gone to be replaced by that flash of anger he knew all too well. Her mouth twisted with rage, and then her fist landed on his face, and he was reeling.

Noah didn't have time to absorb the shock of that first punch. As he staggered into the kitchen Isobel moved like quicksilver to stand in front of him. Something hit him in the eye and the agony made him drop to his knees. He felt a sharp pain on the top of his head and, dazed, he put his hand up, feeling the wetness of blood on his fingers. As more blows rained down on him, he covered his eye, aware that something was badly wrong. It was already swelling dramatically, and he wasn't sure what he should be most worried about—that, or the blood that was running from the top of his head into his hair.

He'd told Isobel the truth. Now she was going to deal him her brand of justice.

Maybe, he thought, as he went sprawling on the floor and through blurry eyes saw her pick up the meat tenderiser, it was what he deserved after all.

TWENTY-FOUR

It was a sombre gathering at The Crafty Cook Café that evening. No one could quite believe what had happened. Daisy had kept the café open, though she'd sent Rowan and Tess, who'd both insisted on working that day, home. After Kat had locked the door to the craft shop and turned the sign to closed, the Bridgers had gathered upstairs, where Daisy served them all tea and coffee and they discussed the shocking events.

'I'll never forgive myself,' Sally said. 'To think, I doubted him! I thought it was him, hurting Isobel, and all that time... Oh! How am I ever going to look him in the eye again?'

'To be fair,' Kat said miserably, 'you hardly know him. I've known him for years and even I doubted him. She was so bloody convincing! And I was scared that I'd dismiss her hints out of hand and then find out she was genuinely being hurt by him. What do you do for the best?'

'That's the trouble, isn't it?' Bethany said sadly. 'No one knows what an abuser actually looks like. The most respectable people can turn out to be monsters behind closed doors and you have no way of knowing. That's why, when someone seems to be a victim, we have to keep an open mind, even when it seems unlikely.'

'But women who do what Isobel did, do all abused women a disservice,' Summer said angrily. 'Acting the victim when she was the perpetrator! It makes it so much harder to believe genuine victims.'

'I still can't get over the fact that someone like Isobel could hurt Noah,' Clive admitted. 'I mean, if it had been the other way round... Ach, I know he's only a slight fella, but even so, I'll bet he's a good deal stronger than she is. He could have fought back, no problem.' He held up his hands. 'I know, and I'm not saying he should have. I just—I just find it hard to understand how she got the better of him.'

'Because she'd beaten him down mentally,' Daisy said tearfully. She cradled her cup of coffee in her hands, thinking back to the statement Noah had given the police. 'She didn't just abuse him physically. She'd broken him. His self-esteem was on the floor. He had no confidence, no belief in himself. He thought he deserved this!' She choked down a sob. 'By the time she started to get really violent he thought he was asking for it. And, besides, the fact is he loved her.'

'I'm afraid that's true,' Zach said, shaking his head. 'I had a long talk with him last night. He genuinely did love her once, and he wanted their marriage to work. I do believe a lot of it had to do with the way his parents treated him when he was younger. Eugenie did a wonderful job of taking care of those boys, but I don't think Noah really got over his abandonment issues. He wanted to belong somewhere to someone more than anything, and he believed Isobel felt the same. I think he honestly thought that she shared his fears of being alone, but I think he was simply projecting that feeling onto her. He didn't want to call time on his marriage—not until it became impossible to continue.'

'And when Daisy came along and made him see what a real

relationship should look like,' Jonah said. He rubbed his face with his hands, clearly distraught. 'I should have known. Should have seen! Do you remember, Ben, back when we were decorating your cottage, and it was so hot we all took off our jumpers? All except Noah. He carried on working in that bloody jumper of his, even though he was clearly boiling.'

'I remember that!' Ben said, horrified. 'Do you think—'

'Of course I think,' Jonah said heavily. 'What else could it be? There was I, thinking it was because he felt he was too skinny next to me. Talk about ego! All the time the poor bugger was covering up bruises. Oh hell!' He thumped the table, making everyone jump. 'That poor man! Why didn't he tell me?'

'Jonah, you can't blame yourself,' Daisy said. 'Even his own brother didn't know. Ross is struggling to cope with the guilt, too, but it's honestly the last thing Noah would want.'

'And at least you didn't believe Isobel's performance,' Kat reminded him. 'When I told you what I suspected you had a right go at me, remember? You were adamant Noah would never do such a thing and you were right. Just shows you. I'm so ashamed that I ever doubted him. He was always such a gentle person.'

'I still don't understand why he didn't tell anyone,' Dolly said. 'Why keep it quiet?'

'Several reasons, and I think they were all jumbled up inside his head,' Daisy said. 'Firstly, because he didn't want to get Isobel into trouble. Even yesterday morning he was reluctant to tell the police what had happened in case she ended up in jail. He says she'll never cope. And secondly, because she'd threatened to tell everyone *he* was the one abusing *her*—a threat which she'd already laid the groundwork for, as we know.'

Kat and Sally looked at each other, their faces pink with shame.

'And, as I said earlier, because part of him felt he'd asked for it. That he deserved it.'

'And I suppose,' Clive said slowly, 'because of the embarrassment. Oh, I know there's no real shame in it, don't bite my head off! I just mean, it's hard enough for a woman to admit she's being assaulted by her man, but for a man to admit he's been assaulted by a woman...'

'And maybe he was scared he wouldn't be believed,' Dolly pondered. 'Lots of people think it's only women who get attacked by their partners. We've all heard the jokes, haven't we? People think the very idea is funny. Fact is, plenty of fellas get assaulted by the women in their lives. Yes,' she added as they all looked at her, 'I *have* been playing with Auntie Google again. I think men are capable of hitting harder and the injuries can be more devastating, but it doesn't mean some men aren't getting battered just like Noah. We need to start taking this a lot more seriously, don't you think?'

They all agreed that was definitely the case.

'How's Eugenie taking it?' Kat asked. 'I know Rita and Birdie are devastated, so how she is I can only imagine.'

'Badly,' Daisy admitted. 'She's at the hospital now, with Ross and Clemmie. That's why I'm here. I'll be going later, though.'

'I suggested to Eugenie that, perhaps, the Tuppenny Bridge Fund could go to a charity that deals with domestic violence,' Zach said. 'Either one that helps both male and female victims or, if not, two separate charities. What do you think? It certainly seemed to brighten her up.'

'I think that's a great idea,' Bluebell said. 'And I think we should all chip in for some flowers and a card, an' all. Let him know we're all thinking of him and that we love him.'

They all murmured their agreement.

'What do you think will happen to Isobel?' Kat asked. 'Have they even found her?'

'She's at her aunt's in Harrogate. She's been arrested,' Daisy said. 'They're questioning her now.'

'Rafferty said that, depending on what she's charged with, she could get anything up to a life sentence,' Sally told them.

'Good,' Dolly said bluntly.

'It's not likely, though,' Sally warned. 'In fact, she could get off with a caution. It all depends on what they decide to charge her with, if anything, how much evidence they've got, what Noah's statement said, all sorts of things really.'

'She won't get off with it,' Kat said fiercely. 'I'll make bloody sure of it.'

Jonah squeezed her shoulder. 'Hey, you need to calm down. It's not good for you or the baby if you get this stressed, and we've got another harrowing day ahead of us tomorrow, remember.'

Ben sighed as Summer put a comforting arm around him. 'Leon's memorial service.'

'Aye. Fifteen years,' Jonah said. 'Who'd have thought we'd all be where we are today back then? You just never know, do you?'

'Maybe it's a very good thing we don't,' Kat said sadly. 'How would we ever get through each day if we'd any inkling of what was to come?'

'Is your mum okay, Ben?' Clive asked.

'She's very shocked about Noah,' Ben replied. 'But to be honest, she says it doesn't surprise her. Isobel was always difficult to like, and Mum never fathomed why Noah stuck with her.'

Daisy wondered what Jennifer would think if she knew Leon had fallen in love with Isobel. She thought that was one shock too many and hoped that it wouldn't come out if the case went to court. Jennifer had had enough to deal with in her life.

'I suppose we'd better be getting home,' Kat said, pushing herself up from her chair with some difficulty. 'Rita and Birdie have got Tommy and Hattie, and I don't want to impose on them for too long. Are you all going to be at the service tomorrow?' she asked, looking around at them all.

They all said they were.

'Noah's really upset that he can't be there,' Daisy told Ben. 'He wanted to apologise to your mum, but they're not letting him out until Wednesday morning at the earliest.'

'Bloody hell! No one's expecting him to be there, least of all Mum,' Ben said. 'Tell him not to worry in the slightest. And tell him we're all thinking of him.'

'I will,' she promised. 'Right, well, I'd better get this lot tidied up for tomorrow and then get changed to go to the hospital.'

'I'll take you,' Zach said. 'I promised Noah I'd pop back this evening anyway.'

'Thanks so much,' Daisy said gratefully.

'And I'll see you all in the morning,' Zach added. 'Try not to worry, and try not to blame yourselves. I know it's easier said than done, believe me, but the truth is, this was Isobel's doing, no one else's. Now we must focus on helping Noah recover, both physically and mentally.'

'And thank God that he's found Daisy,' Bluebell added fondly, patting Daisy on the shoulder. 'You're a dark horse, missy, but I'm bloody glad you and Noah are together. He's going to need you.'

'The Lord,' said Zach, 'moves in mysterious ways.'

'You're not wrong there, vicar,' Dolly said with a wink. 'Someone ought to tip Him off about Google Maps.'

TWENTY-FIVE

8 OCTOBER

Zach ended the reading from Ecclesiastes and asked that his parishioners join him in singing one of Leon's favourite hymns. There was the sound of shuffling, and a few people cleared their throats as the organist struck the first notes of 'Amazing Grace'.

Amazing Grace.

Hadn't he lectured Noah only weeks earlier about grace? He remembered the conversation so clearly:

'I have to believe in the grace of God, or what's the point?'

'Even—even sins that are against another person? Even if you've *hurt* another person?'

'It doesn't matter what the sin is. The same applies. Christ has paid for our sins already.'

Oh, Noah. If I'd only known what you were trying to tell me...

But, of course, he hadn't known, and he knew deep down that he couldn't blame himself for not being psychic. It was ironic really, he thought. There was so much about the events of that night, fifteen years ago, that he *did* know. Noah's had been the missing bit of the puzzle. When he considered the matter, he supposed that he knew more about it than anyone else alive.

He gazed at his congregation as they sang, his heart filled with love and compassion for them all. They'd been through so much and had suffered deeply. He was glad that some of them had found it in their hearts to confide in him. Honoured that they had done so.

He thought about the inscription on Joseph's headstone. A quotation from the New Testament. Matthew 11:28

Come unto me all ye who labour and are heavy laden, and I will give you rest.

They had come to Zach, perhaps as some intermediary, and unburdened themselves to him one by one—some eagerly, others hesitantly, some weeping, some reluctantly as if afraid of betraying another's trust.

He had listened and counselled and hoped that he had given them rest. Peace of mind. He'd never have believed that fifteen years on, he would be doing the same again for the same reason.

Noah had seemed to find comfort by finally telling him about the row he'd had with Leon that night. As Zach had listened, so many things had started to make sense.

So, it had been *Isobel* that Leon was having an affair with. He'd assumed it was someone at the brewery, and thought Kat probably had, too. Noah's guilt over Isobel's loss was palpable. He felt responsible for Leon's death, and responsible for Isobel's grief. He'd tried to make it up to her ever since, and he'd paid the price for doing so.

And, of course, it made sense that he'd bought Kat the pram when she was expecting Hattie. He'd felt terrible for her, knowing that she'd been cheated on by the man she loved, and aware of her grief at his loss. When Kat finally seemed to have found happiness, Noah wanted to help her. The pram was the least he could do. And, although Noah hadn't said so,

Zach was fairly certain that it was Isobel who'd damaged the pram, once she'd found out Noah had bought it. Noah had admitted to him that Isobel was deeply suspicious of other women and had constantly accused him of being unfaithful, even though, until Daisy, he'd never considered cheating on her.

Projection, Zach thought. Good people believe the best in others. Those with darkness in their hearts believe the worst.

Of course, Noah had no idea that Kat had discovered the truth about Leon's infidelity, nor that she'd been left with far more than heartbreak when he died.

He'd found that out when the Pennyfeather sisters came to him a few weeks after the funeral. Looking back on it, he knew that Rita and Birdie had been nothing like their actual jolly selves back then. They'd been heartbroken.

'Kat's gone to stay with her father,' Birdie had told him. 'She doesn't even really get on with him, but she had to get away. Do you know, Zach—may I call you Zach? Do you know, things weren't as they should be between her and Leon? Kat told us the day after he died. We found her sobbing her heart out in the garden, and we tried to comfort her by telling her how much Leon had loved her and what a wonderful couple they were, and she turned on us, didn't she, Rita?'

Rita nodded. 'She did. We thought it was grief, but then she told us that she and Leon had fought that night before he died because...' She'd hesitated, glancing at Birdie, who'd given her a reassuring nod. 'Because she'd found out he was carrying on with some other girl.'

It had come as a surprise to Zach. Like everyone else, he'd assumed Leon and Kat were madly in love. It seemed their relationship had been one-sided, at least in recent times.

'Poor Kat,' he'd murmured. 'I'm so sorry to hear that.'

'The last time she ever saw him alive,' Birdie said, wiping away tears, 'she was rowing with him, in your churchyard of all places, Zach. That very night he drove off to collect Ben and—well, you know what happened next.'

'It's very sad,' Zach said, shaking his head.

'It's more than that, though,' Rita said. 'Kat thinks we don't know. She thinks we haven't worked it out, but we're not daft. We might be old, but we can read a calendar. We just don't know what to do, that's the truth. Do we tell her we've figured it out or do we let her believe we don't know?'

'Know what?' Zach had asked, thoroughly confused.

'You *will* keep this to yourself, vicar?'

'Of course. You have my word,' he'd promised.

Rita and Birdie had looked at each other. 'Kat's expecting,' Birdie said at last. 'She's having Leon's baby, and she hasn't told us. Instead, she's cleared off to Dorset to stay with her dad, and we can guess that means she won't be bringing the baby home with her. If she ever comes home that is.'

She'd stifled a sob. 'We can't help her if she won't tell us, can we? And we don't want to push her so we can't say anything. But our heart breaks for her, Zach. And the thing is, I feel for Jennifer, I really do. But I find myself hating Leon Callaghan, despite what happened to him, and I feel terrible for that, because when all's said and done, he was just a young lad with his whole future ahead of him.'

'Do you think we'll ever stop hating him?' Rita asked brokenly. 'And do you think Kat will ever heal?'

Zach had given them what comfort and reassurance he could, but his mind had been whirling. Because Rita's and Birdie's revelation about Kat had been just the latest in a long line since Leon's funeral.

Eugenie Lavender, distraught with worry about Ross and the heavy burden he was carrying, since calling the police on Ben and thereby unwittingly ensuring that Leon would head out in his car that night.

Jennifer, almost on the point of hysterical collapse, as she confessed where she'd been on the night Leon had died. Adamant that this was a punishment on her and begging him to help her find a way to forgive herself and live with what she believed she'd done.

Only last year, Zach had learned from Rafferty that Ben had been carrying the guilt of his brother's death all these years, because it had been him who Leon had driven to collect that night.

All this pain. He wished he could gather them all together and tell them how each one of them was feeling, and of how much grief and guilt they'd each been carrying all these years. But of course, he couldn't do that. What he'd been told, he'd been told in confidence.

Maybe, he thought hopefully, after today we can all draw a line under this tragedy and finally start to move on. No one in this church deserved to carry the pain any longer. They never had. They were good people, kind people. He was so happy to be part of the community at Tuppenny Bridge.

His gaze fell on Ava and his heart lurched. So happy and so lucky.

He saw Kat and Jonah singing, watched as they glanced at each other and smiled. Leon's girlfriend and best friend had moved on and built a new life for themselves. Next month, they would be welcoming a baby boy into their family. He looked forward to meeting this precious child.

Ben and Summer newly engaged. Ben had turned out a fine young man. Leon, he knew, would be proud of him. One day in the not-too-distant future, maybe Zach would marry them. Another happy ending.

Clive and Bethany, putting their guilt and sadness behind them. Finding their own family and a new start at Whispering Willows.

Jennifer. Zach watched her now, singing 'Amazing Grace', hymn sheet in hand, her eyes fixed on the stained-glass window behind him. He wondered what she was thinking. It had been a long fifteen years for Jennifer, but now she was stronger, with a new job and a new home. She'd remembered how to smile, and he couldn't be happier for her.

His gaze went to Eugenie and Ross Lavender, sitting side by side, their faces etched with worry and sadness.

He hoped, with all his heart, that they would forgive themselves and move on, because Noah would need their support, not their guilt.

He found Daisy standing at the back of the church. Her mouth was moving but he wasn't convinced she was actually singing. She looked miles away. No doubt she was mulling over the events of the last few days and wondering what would happen next. He was so glad she would be by Noah's side. In his opinion, she was the best thing that had ever happened to him.

He blinked and realised they were singing the last line of the hymn.

Was blind, but now I see.

As the last note of the organ died away Zach took a steadying breath and returned to the lectern. Time to reflect on Leon's life. To talk about the person he was.

He gazed down at the photograph of this young man. A flawed man. An imperfect man. Not the paragon of virtue too many people had built him up to be in their minds, but human, like all of them. A good person who made mistakes. A young person with so much unfulfilled potential. So much life unused.

They would remember him today as a beloved son, brother, best friend, and neighbour. They would honour his memory and say goodbye to him with love.

And then, God willing, they would face the new day with hope and peace in their hearts.

EPILOGUE

Six months later

'What do you think, Daisy?'

Noah gave her an enquiring look and she beamed at him.

'It's perfect! Better than I ever imagined. Oops!' She glanced at the estate agent. 'I shouldn't have said that, should I? Aren't I supposed to lie and pretend that it's just okay, but we can probably find something better?'

The estate agent laughed. 'I really appreciate that you didn't.'

Noah smiled affectionately at her. 'Daisy's not capable of playing games,' he said. 'What you see is what you get.'

'Then you're a very lucky man,' the estate agent said. 'So, am I to take it that you're interested?'

Daisy could hardly contain her excitement. 'What do you think?' she asked Noah.

'I think it's perfect, too,' he said softly. 'I think we'd be very happy here.'

'Then...' The estate agent looked from one to the other of them.

Noah nodded. 'We'd like to put in an offer. Subject to survey, naturally.'

'Naturally, although that won't be a problem. They don't build them like this anymore. Made to last, and well maintained by its previous owner.'

Driving into Market Square a little later, Noah said, 'I can't believe we've actually found somewhere. I was convinced we wouldn't. Do you mind that it's not in Tuppenny Bridge?'

'Not at all. We both work in Tuppenny Bridge, after all, so it's not like we won't be here most days, and West Colby's a lovely village.'

'It's not too isolated for you?'

'With Dolly just up the road? Hardly! And it *is* a lovely house, isn't it?'

'It is. I can't believe our luck. We have a lot to thank Dolly for.'

They'd been house hunting for three months but finding somewhere for sale in Tuppenny Bridge was proving impossible and they were beginning to despair of ever finding a new home. Then Dolly had tipped them off that her closest neighbour, Arthur Francis, was moving in with his daughter, Pam, and was selling Mulberry Cottage.

Today they'd gone to look around, hardly daring to hope that it would be the house of their dreams. The cottage needed updating, that was without doubt. It was old fashioned and probably needed a new kitchen and bathroom suite, as well as redecorating throughout, but it had, as Daisy said, the *feeling*.

They'd both felt the same, looking around. It had three good sized bedrooms and a large, if overgrown, garden.

'Perfect place to have a family,' the estate agent had said, and they'd smiled at each other, agreeing with him.

Letting themselves into the flat above Cutting it Fine, they paused on the threshold and kissed.

'One day,' Noah said, 'I'll carry you over the threshold of our beautiful new home, and you'll be Mrs Lavender.'

'I can't wait,' she told him, kissing him again.

They headed upstairs, their minds full of possibilities for the future. Daisy put the kettle on and dropped teabags into two mugs, while Noah rummaged in the cupboards for celebration biscuits.

It had been an amazing three months since he'd moved in with her. They couldn't believe how happy everyone was for them, and how easily they'd slotted into their new life.

Noah had endured an operation on his eye, since there had been bony fragments that needed removing. However, his vision was unimpaired, his blood pressure had finally returned to normal, and the panic attacks he'd had since the final attack were becoming a distant memory, as was the stammer, despite the trauma he'd been through.

Peony Cottage had gone up for sale just weeks ago and had sold almost immediately. As they'd realised themselves, it was hard to get property in Tuppenny Bridge, and there was high demand for it.

His divorce from Isobel would be through in the next couple of months, according to the solicitor. It had been surprisingly straightforward, with Isobel complying with every request and putting no obstacles in his path.

'I imagine it's her aunt, pushing her to be rid of me,' Noah had said. 'She'll want this whole sorry business over and done with as soon as possible.'

Petalicious was still open, though Kelly's gran had now been installed as the full-time manager of the place. Isobel would never return to work there, but it would continue to bring in an income for her, which, as Noah said, was something she would be glad of when she was released from prison.

There had been a great deal of anger that she'd only been sentenced to two years, thanks in part to the superb legal team her aunt had hired, but Daisy knew Noah was quite relieved. With good behaviour she'd be out in a year, and he felt that was as long as she could probably cope with. He didn't want her to suffer any longer, and Daisy knew he would feel happier when Isobel was out of jail and safely ensconced in her aunt's house in Harrogate.

At least she'd admitted what she'd done, which had meant Noah hadn't needed to go to court and relive what had happened. Daisy wasn't sure she could ever forgive Isobel for what she'd put him through, but she was grateful to her for that, at least, although she was pretty sure Isobel had only pleaded guilty on the advice of her legal team.

As they settled on the sofa, cups of tea in hand, they talked excitedly of the future, making plans for Mulberry Cottage—the way they'd decorate it, the new kitchen they'd select, the furniture they'd choose, the children they'd fill it with...

And as the daylight began to fade, they switched on the lamps, ate dinner, and toasted their happiness with glasses of wine.

'What shall we drink to?' Noah asked. 'There's so much I'm grateful for I don't know where to begin.'

'How about, to new beginnings?' Daisy suggested.

'Good idea,' Noah said softly. 'Or, to true love?' He paused, thinking. 'Or,' he said at last, 'to finding Mr Blue Sky, just when I thought it was going to rain forever.'

They smiled at each other, remembering that day in Camacker when they'd each gone to see the wildflowers, never dreaming that their lives were about to change so drastically.

'To Mr Blue Sky,' Daisy said, her eyes shining with love for him as she raised her glass and clinked it against Noah's. 'May he never hide away again.'

A LETTER FROM THE AUTHOR

Dear reader,

Thank you so much for reading *Hope Blooms in Tuppenny Bridge*. I hope you enjoyed Daisy and Noah's story. If you want to join other readers in hearing all about my new releases and bonus content, you can sign up here:

www.stormpublishing.co/sharon-booth

You can also subscribe to my own personal, chatty newsletter which I send out monthly:

www.sharonboothwriter.com/newsletter-sign-up

If you enjoyed this book and could spare a few moments to leave a review that would be hugely appreciated. Even a short review can make all the difference in encouraging a reader to discover my books for the first time. Thank you so much!

This story has been brewing in the back of my mind for a long time. In fact, it was originally going to be the storyline for my very first novel, *There Must Be an Angel*, way back in 2015!

At the time, as a newbie writer, I realised I didn't feel confident enough to tackle such a big issue, so Gabriel's story changed. However, the idea stayed with me, and I knew one day I'd subconsciously create characters who were going through this very situation and that they'd let me know, one way or the other.

When the idea for Tuppenny Bridge first formed, this storyline wasn't part of the initial arc, but as Noah and Isobel took form on the pages of book one, I had a funny feeling there was more to them than met the eye. By the time I wrote book two, *Second Chances in Tuppenny Bridge*, I knew exactly what was going on behind the front door of Peony Cottage, and realised their story had to be told, and that perhaps it was the final piece of the puzzle that made up that dreadful night in October, fifteen years ago, when a complicated young man lost his life.

I read a lot of articles about male victims of domestic violence and watched some shocking documentaries. I also found a couple of websites that you might like to check out for more information:

- www.mensaid.ie
- www.ncdv.org.uk/domestic-violence-abuse-against-men

Be warned that there are some harrowing stories and statistics. Some of the things I've read and watched over the last few months have been truly disturbing and heartbreaking.

I was very aware, while writing this book, that there might be some negative feedback from people who will protest that domestic violence against women is a much bigger problem. In terms of numbers that's true, and I have written about violence against women previously in *Fresh Starts at Folly Farm*, *There Must Be an Angel*, and *Once Upon a Long Ago*, as well as gaslighting and coercive control of women in *Christmas at Cuckoo Nest Cottage*, and *Christmas with Cary*.

However, that doesn't alter the fact that physical violence towards men *does* exist, and that these men suffer badly. My view is that all domestic abuse is wrong, whoever it's directed at, and the more information and understanding of this horrible issue there is, the better. I hope that, by reading Noah's story, people will accept that male victims need our support, understanding, and help, too.

As for Daisy—readers of my first Skimmerdale novel, *Summer Secrets at Wildflower Farm*, will be familiar with her. I had many messages asking me about her, and what happened to her after she left Crowscar to move to Leeds. Well, now you know!

Daisy wasn't shown at her best at Wildflower Farm, but I really liked her, and wanted to give her a happy ending of her own. I hope you'll agree that, although she's had to fight for him, she couldn't have found a better man to share her life with than Noah, and I predict the two of them will have a long and happy life, with the loving home and family they both wanted for so long. They certainly deserve it!

I have loved writing the Tuppenny Bridge series, and I'm so happy that the series arc is now complete, and Leon Callaghan is finally laid to rest. I'll miss my characters, but I'm glad they all got the happy endings that they worked so hard for and truly earned.

Thanks again for being part of this amazing journey with me and I hope you'll stay in touch—our adventures in Tuppenny Bridge may be over but I have lots more places to take you to, and many new characters to introduce you to!

Love, Sharon xx

KEEP IN TOUCH WITH THE AUTHOR

www.sharonboothwriter.com

facebook.com/sharonbooth.writer

x.com/sharonbwriter

instagram.com/sharonboothwriter

pinterest.com/sharonboothwriter

ACKNOWLEDGMENTS

It feels very sad and strange to be writing the acknowledgements for the final book in the Tuppenny Bridge series! Hard to believe that it was only in May 2023 that the first book was published, and here I am bidding farewell to my beautiful market town in the Yorkshire Dales.

So, my first and biggest thanks must go to the readers of this series. Some of you have followed the characters in Tuppenny Bridge from the very beginning.

Tuppenny Bridge first appeared briefly in the second book in my The Other Half series, *How the Other Half Lies*, and took centre stage in the final book, *How the Other Half Loves*. Many of you read those books and were delighted to be able to follow Summer, Sally, and Rafferty to Tuppenny Bridge. I thank those of you who have done that with all my heart.

To those readers who only discovered the town through *Summer in Tuppenny Bridge*, but have stuck with the series, a massive thank you. I'm so grateful that you took the Lavender Ladies and all my leading men and women to your hearts, and appreciate the lovely comments and messages about the series so much.

And if you are reading about Tuppenny Bridge for the first time in this book—well, congratulations! You get to go back and start from the very beginning, and there's a lot to catch up on. Happy reading!

I'd like to thank all the team at Storm Publishing, starting with Kathryn Taussig, who was the person who read my submission and gave me a contract in the first place. Many thanks, Kathryn, and also to "Big Boss Man", Oliver Rhodes. Being with a publisher was a new experience for me, as I had previously been an indie author. It's been so interesting seeing it all from another angle and I feel I've learned a lot.

The team at Storm have been lovely to work with. I was lucky enough, when Kathryn took on new responsibilities within the company, to get Naomi Knox as my new editor. Working with Naomi has genuinely been a pleasure from start to finish, and I'm so glad we were put together to finish this series. Thank you, Naomi, for being so kind, patient, and so flipping cheerful!

Thanks to the rest of the team at Storm who have helped me along the way: Elke, Anna, and Alex. To Debbie Clement for the beautiful covers, to Shirley Khan for the copyedits, and to Liz Hurst for the proofreading. If I've missed anyone out, I sincerely apologise.

Massive thanks to my best friend, Jessica Redland, who helped me to see my way forward on this writing path when I honestly felt I'd lost my way, and whose wise words and reassurance have given me the courage to let go of two things I needed to say goodbye to, as well as opening up new possibilities I hadn't even considered. You're always such a support to me, Jessica, and I can't tell you how much I appreciate your presence in my life.

A huge thank you to The Husband, long-suffering as he is! I can never thank him enough for all the cups of coffee throughout the working day, the incredible patience, the willing cheerfulness, the encouragement, the consolation, the endless support. I always say I wouldn't be able to do this without him, and he insists I would. Maybe he's right, but it would be a lot harder, believe me. For all he does and says I am eternally grateful.

And last, but never least, a big thank you to all my characters in Tuppenny Bridge. To Eugenie Lavender, Rita and Birdie Pennyfeather, Zach and Ava, Bluebell, Clover, and Buttercup, Dolly, Clemmie and Ross, Sally and Rafferty, Summer and Ben, Jennifer, Jamie, Kat and Jonah, Bethany, Clive, Joseph, Daisy and Noah, and all the others who have graced the pages of these five books. You've all been amazing, and I'll miss you so much!

Yes, I appreciate that must sound weird to some of you, but hey, what can I say? Writers are a funny bunch, and after spending so much time with our characters they become like friends.

Until the next time.

Love, Sharon xx

Printed in Great Britain
by Amazon

48587221R00158